ʃAPPHIRE DAWN - 2005

The world in crisis. An age when even a kiss can kill. The unthinkable becomes reality when research scientists accidently unleash the Blue Death. Common as the common cold, but fatal, this new respiratory form of AIDS threatens mankind's very existence. Homo sapiens sapiens may simply become a failed experiment in the evolution of life as the world falls into disarray. The single hope for man's future lies in just one woman who must be transformed by fire or see mankind perish.

ʃAPPHIRE DAWN gives a chilling look at what the near future may hold unless love and compassion inform our politics and how we choose to live together on the planet. ʃAPPHIRE DAWN reads with the force of prophesy as it delves into today's most crucial issues from the AIDS crisis to armed struggle in the Middle East and the last fight for Jerusalem. Will we realize our darkest fears or achieve enlightenment as we enter wary, into the new millennium? This extraordinary work of fiction may help us answer that difficult question.

ISBN 1-892323-20-6
Library of Congress Card Number 99-69805
An original Publication of Vivisphere Publishing.
Printed in the U.S.A.

VIVISPHERE PUBLISHING
a Division of NetPub Corporation
2 Neptune Road, Poughkeepsie, NY 12601

www.vivisphere.com

For

Josephine Jacobsen
Marjorie Guggenheim
Betty Lussier
Dorothy Harbison

Inspirations

"In this year and the following year there was a general death of people throughout the world. It began first in India, then it passed to Thirstiest, thence to the Saracens, Christians and Jews in the course of one year, from one Easter to the next..."

The Chronicle of Henry Kingston, A.D. 1348

SAPPHIRE
DAWN

For Alan
all best
Richard
6/27/00

BY RICHARD HARTEIS

Alaethos Anesti

Easter Sunday morning was the most brilliant day Connecticut had seen so far in what had been a very rainy spring. A fresh breeze blew in from Orient Point, the sky was an azure dome over the sound without a cloud in sight. The air was still chilly, but Michael decided to put the top down anyway as he drove along the river to Cramer Chemical. His 'candy apple '63 Vette was the only self-indulgence he afforded himself in the spartan life Michael Riley led as a scientist, and he kept the toy in mint condition. The red enamel was polished into a mirror, the engine tuned to smooth perfection.

Michael still felt a little washed out by a nasty cold that had dogged him all the previous week, but an exhilaration rose in him like the incremental power of the Corvette as he maneuvered deftly through the gears. He had made up his mind and there was no turning back now. A bit recklessly, he accelerated into the curves along the riverbank with mounting excitement. He'd made his decision, and now he flew along filled with high spirits, high resolve, rushing to the guard kiosk rising from a sea of yellow jonquils and daffodils at gate W9.

It wasn't unusual for a research scientist to return to his laboratory to work without interruption on a Sunday morning. But the weekend security guard who checked visitor's clearance took extra time to monitor Michael's retina and voice prints. The smiling face in his photo ID could have been that of Michael's little brother. "Each freckle is where an angel has kissed you," his mother used to tell him when he was a boy, but Dr. Michael Riley didn't look much older at age 36 than he did at age 16. "Kids," the guard muttered to himself and gave Michael a mock salute as the young scientist drove into the compound.

When he had gained entrance to the building and had safely locked the laboratory door behind him, Michael took the small plastic cryovial he had concealed in a voice-coded safe from freezer five. He sat at his desk studying the pink serum, holding it gingerly in the palm of his hand as it warmed to room temperature. For some reason he thought of the quaint Orthodox greeting his old Greek neighbor had insisted on upon rising Easter morning. Each year Michael exchanged the ritual greeting with him when the old man came across the lawn with his gift. The little mesh bag was tied up with a white ribbon and carried a brightly painted egg, the color of blood.

"Christ is risen."

"Indeed He is."

"The dead shall rise again."

"Indeed they shall."

Michael Riley had decided that he couldn't wait for the new century. He was sure his vaccine would work. The situation was critical. He had solved the problem of strain variation when he demonstrated that a genetically engineered loop of the HIV virus produced proteins that could elicit neutralizing antibodies in goats, rabbits and guinea pigs. He was certain he had inactivated the virus by altering the pol gene coding for reverse transcriptase as well as the rev and tat genes to lessen the versatility of the HIV life cycle. It would take additional years to complete primate studies for the vaccine and the world suffered a pandemic that threatened mankind's existence. He had no choice. Homo sapiens was rapidly devolving into an unsuccessful, withered branch on the great tree of evolution.

The crisis was not statistically overwhelming, only one little percent of the world's population was infected. Drought and famine were the rule in Africa, it was understandable somehow that Uganda and Zaire would be wiped out. Burma, Indonesia, and India were being decimated. The Philippines was a nation of orphans. But the tragedy remained distant in the imagination of the West. People had become bored with the disease just when public awareness might have done the most good.

By 1998, however, the millions of people infected with AIDS in Europe and America realized that the death rate for them would be an unqualified 100%. The disease had infiltrated into the heterosexual population and was no longer an illness one could discount among homosexuals and drug abusers. Trying to prevent AIDS by changing sexual habits had proven futile. What teenager ever gave credence to his own mortality, what drug addict cared, as the pain of withdrawal overwhelmed his resolve to stay clean.

Protease inhibitors and multiple drug therapies had proven to be a blind alley despite their initial exhilarating promise. Physicians still had nothing which might offer any real hope to patients and there were violent demonstrations for action at research institutions from the NIH campus in Bethesda to the Pasteur Institute in Paris.

When Michael Riley took science for his mistress, he had given up on religion, or at least put the large questions of existence on hold for a while. It was hard to believe in a god who permitted all the suffering he had seen as a medical student in the AIDS wards, suffering which forced him to turn to research in an attempt to find a cure for the disease. But he still felt the vestigial tide of conscience at work like a strong undertow in his soul. Michael knew it bordered on evil to plod along with primate studies when millions lived under the sentence of an excruciating death often preceded by terrible suffering, blindness, and dementia. In his dreams, the skeletal figures lay mute and cachectic in their sickbeds raising their stick-like arms to him for help. Despite the overturning of Dr. Kervorkian's conviction, the religious right still tied up the courts in their struggle against assisted suicide, and Michael was denied the right to help these tormented souls end their suffering.

"Unless it were an absolute, total emergency, I wouldn't move with a killed virus in uninfected people," Dr. Gallo had cautioned. But what in God's name did he think was going on in the world presently? The moat surrounding Gallo's ivory tower was filled with the victims of the disease. Michael thought of the plague engulfing North Africa in Camus's novel and Dr. Rieux's heroic struggle against the disease, the necessity for human compassion and sacrifice. Gallo's own colleague, Dr. Zagury, had served as a volunteer in their early immunization experiments, though he stopped short of actually

9

challenging himself with the virus. The vaccine simply couldn't wait any longer.

Michael Riley stood up from his desk chair, loosened his belt and let his trousers fall to the floor. He cleaned a small patch of white skin and copper leg hairs with an alcohol wipe and injected the serum deep into the muscles of his right thigh. He withdrew the syringe and flopped back into the desk chair to rest a second wondering just what Rubicon he had crossed.

He remembered how rigorous his teachers had been on safety precautions when handling the AIDS virus in the laboratory. "Once HIV gets a foot in the door and infects a single cell in your body, it's there for life. It might take five years, but when the virus reproduces it will probably get you," he heard Dr. Desrosiers saying again. But Michael was sure of his work. In this field you had to be. His classmates dubbed him "the roadrunner" in medical school for his type A personality, his energetic self-confidence.

The protocols for making a killed-virus vaccine were long established in the work of Jonas Salk, Putney and Girard. Restructuring the virus's RNA would render it harmless. The chances of something going wrong were statistically insignificant. There was too much at stake not to take the risk. Still, Michael felt a little silly sitting at his desk in his underwear musing on what he had just done like a modern day Dr. Jeckyll monitoring himself in his laboratory for the first signs of Mr. Hyde's dreadful onslaught.

Michael got himself dressed, incinerated the syringe and serum vial in the vacuum furnace, and began to dictate notes to the computer outlining the experiment he had just initiated.

"If I can induce sufficient immunity," he mused, "I'll have to challenge myself with the live virus, of course, to prove the vaccine's efficacy. It's the only way to know for certain. Potentially fatal, but there it is. I've got to have the confirmation. I won't risk it though unless antibody titers go through the roof."

Michael Riley was not even born when in the 1950's a manufacturing error disseminated doses of the Salk vaccine containing the live virus into the general population. As word of the vaccine-induced cases of polio spread, hysterical mothers refused to let their children be immunized and the vaccine program nearly failed. Had

Michael's mother been present that Easter morning in 1996 she might have given him the most basic advice any mother could offer: never take a vaccine if you already have some sort of sickness. For within the serum he administered that morning an HIV virus had managed to maintain its protein coat in the killing process and it entered Michael's blood stream alive and deadly.

The immune system did its job, of course. A passing macrophage engulfed the virus to destroy it, but instead became a reservoir for the pathogen. Like Madame Curie, Michael had inadvertently poisoned himself with his scientific experimentation. Unlike Madame Curie, however, Michael Riley did more than die before the experiment ran its course.

When the infected macrophage in his system tried to kill one of the adenoviruses causing Michael's cold, a budding HIV virion from the macrophage injected a single strand of nucleic acid into the cold virus. The mutant virus was infecting lung cells in no time, turning them into little factories for HIV and the destruction of the immune system. Michael took his cold with him to a number of scientific seminars in California, Florida, and Washington in the months before he was hospitalized with viral pneumonia. The autopsy after Michael Riley's suicide was initially inconclusive. It was only after body fluid samples were analyzed and the new virus they discovered was sequenced at Cramer Chemical that the unthinkable was proven in fact to be the case. HIV had mutated into a respiratory virus and was no longer transmittable only through semen or blood. Like its predecessors, HIV IV was impregnable, hiding inside the host cell to hatch more of the killer virus. Contracting AIDS had become as easy as catching the common cold. A kiss could be fatal. Around the world, so many people suffocated from the disease before they could be seen by a doctor, HIV IV became known as the Blue Death. And death dolled out his lethal treats as generously as a psychotic neighbor on Halloween night. Dr. Michael Riley had traveled across the American continent and ushered in the great pneumonic plague which greeted the beginning of the new millennium.

Siesta

Nadia studied a ladder of light extending down the white stucco wall and across the naked body of her lover, asleep beside her like a sweet Endymion. The brilliant light of the mid-day sun began to filter through the heavy wooden shutters, but she had no desire to stir from the dark fortress of their bedroom just yet. She stretched languidly and listened to the distant cries of children calling to each other from the little lake of a swimming pool at the center of the tourist oasis. All the months of hard work and deadlines were behind her now. At last she was beginning to stop that frantic engine which had driven her in her desperate search and was able to relish her triumph. Yes, a triumph, she thought. It was not too strong a word. A triumph for her as a woman of science, for her people and finally, even for humanity itself. In the past years she rarely allowed such smugness, but now a sense of relief and fatigue flowed through her which translated into a deep tenderness for the man who had shared her life all those difficult months. She watched his slow breathing and rested her hand gently in the little valley of his lower back.

Yves lay on his stomach, the rumpled sheet tossed aside. His legs were solid oak from years of road race training, rising into firm, full buttocks. His fair skin had tanned quickly into her own deep coloring except for the white triangle of flesh carved out by his swimsuit. She studied him with far greater fervor than in her student anatomy classes, attention informed now by love for the back muscles dimpling at the scapula and iliac crests, for his strong upper shoulders, and the strangely delicate hands.

Their holiday in Greece was in part a private pilgrimage for Yves, and each morning they began the day by running a segment of the course which led from Marathon to Athens. There simply wasn't enough time by 2004 to vaccinate the 200 million people in the world who were now infected with the AIDS virus and the Olympics Committee had finally canceled the Olympiad. The best an amateur marathoner could do was return to Greece and pay his private homage by running the ancient roads of the original course.

This morning before she dropped off at the villa and he continued on his longer run, she had the sudden desire to reach out to the dark crevices of his body where the silky running shorts clung to him. She wanted to stop right there along the road amid the olive groves to kiss the fine blond hair covering his body, kiss him all over, but then she remembered herself and pulled away from the fantasy.

From the beginning of their love affair, Yves had taken a breezy, egalitarian attitude toward sex, encouraging her to seek her own pleasure when they made love. That's how the game works, he explained, each takes his own selfish delight, and in pleasing themselves, please each other, two halves of a whole, balanced sides of a mathematical equation. He even pretended not to mind when David Schefflan, the public affairs officer they had met at the Ambassador's reception the previous night seemed to take more than a casual interest in her work. It had taken Yves years to learn that the quickest way to lose a woman was to try to control her. To demonstrate jealousy was like handing her a knife.

Nadia was charmed by David's easy smile, his openness, his intelligent questions about their discovery. She made it clear Yves would be taking her home at the end of the reception that night, but she couldn't resist a little mischief by inviting him to visit them at Marathon the following day. Sometimes she wished Yves weren't always so sure of himself where she was concerned. But her love for him was so transparent, he knew she would never seriously consider anyone else while they were lovers.

For Nadia, such self-indulgence would be a kind of sin. She never fully shed her Arab girlhood. Her sense of modesty and a woman's duty to a man were still as much a part of her as her deep green eyes and the chestnut hair spilling over her shoulders. She couldn't bring herself to sunbathe like the European women who sat topless in the their beach chairs, sipping cool drinks, gossiping idly, oblivious of the bathers around them. Yves teased her into trying it only once, but the waiters and umbrella boys came like bees swarming over honey and she quickly concealed herself in a cocoon of beach towels.

When she was a girl, the poor women from the medina would come to the edge of the sea, every inch of their bodies covered in black, and would strip naked without regard to the men who sat smoking cigarettes and drinking tea at the cafe. It was a simple necessity in a desert land without the luxury of running water. And so, the women remained invisible. One was modest depending on one's intentions. A woman displaying her legs in a miniskirt was obscene, five women bathing naked at the beach were invisible.

For a number of years Nadia worried that she would never mature into womanhood, even as she outgrew all her classmates at the lycee. But in the end she had developed into a tall, splendid beauty, just as her doctor father had predicted. The young men in her village called her "Jasmine." Rare, desirable, they pursued her ardently. And as with all extraordinary beauties, the more she withdrew into her medical studies, the more she tried to obscure her voluptuous figure and exquisite features the more her legend flourished.

She had hoped for the simple pleasures of the tourist on this Greek holiday, but instead she caused a mild sensation when she visited the ruins of a temple or walked into a taverna with Yves for a glass of Ouzo or Metaxa. The old women in the villages and clerks at the little hotels were certain she was an Italian film star. They seldom recognized her for the white-coated scientist staring shyly over her glasses from the covers of "Time," "Paris Match" and "Der Stern."

At the beginning of their vacation Yves was the proud French coq as he escorted her onto a crowded restaurant terrace and all heads turned to follow the beautiful strangers across the room, two mysterious shooting stars over the dark ocean. It was like the early days of their love affair before the director at Cramer Chemical began to interfere with their research, and the enormity of the situation consumed their life, before weekly global reports made it clear exactly how disastrous the new epidemic had grown, before their preoccupation with the crisis became all consuming, obsessive, and theirs became an automaton life of strategy sessions, conferences, and late hours in the laboratory all fueled by the mounting necessity to do something.

Finally, on this trip to Greece they had put that exhausting period of their life behind them and found each other once again. They no longer fell into a dead sleep at night before returning each morning to the hospital laboratory and their hopeless mission. They had learned to listen to each other once more and took the awkward first steps of making love again like children, or Adam and Eve newly evicted from the garden, slightly stunned by the enormity of their predicament. Physical intimacy primed the pump of their affection, restoring the easy flow of friendship between them.

But, of course, the serpent found its way into the brave new world of their restored love. Gradually, Yves grew furious at the swarthy young men undressing her in the street with their brazen eyes. He blamed her somehow for the energy it took to assert his claim on her in public. She would be just another beautiful woman on the avenues of Paris, but in Greece walking with her was like carrying a heavy wallet in a society of pick pockets. Both of them had forgotten that vacations rarely solve anything when two people are drifting out of love.

Nadia never made any special claim to her discovery. At all the press conferences before they fled to Greece, she tried to stress the team nature of their effort, especially his brilliant work in the chimpanzee and macaque studies and clinical trials among the death row convicts and volunteer nuns and priests he had enlisted for his trials. But as Yves had maneuvered the little Alfa along the deserted coastal roads overlooking the Mediterranean, he returned obsessively to the bald fact that she had discovered the blue epitope. Only she. Martin Cramer knew it and so soon would the entire world.

Against all conventional wisdom, she had persisted in her studies of RNA at the core of the virus and developed an aerosol vaccine from a curious gene segment that generated an explosion of high quality antibodies to fight off the virus. More importantly, a slight modification of the blue epitope used in her genetically engineered vaccine produced a unique shield response in the immune cells once they were sensitized, enabling them to prevent the virus from penetrating the cell membrane. Unlike the protease inhibitor found in saliva that helped defend leukocytes against HIV and seemed so promising early on in AIDS research, this aerosol vaccine altered the cell's DNA, producing a protein coat which acted like Teflon, covering the cell's CD4 receptors and keeping them from even attaching to the HIV virus in the first place. AIDS patients could be cured of the vicious parasite when the altered RNA was assimilated into infected cells. Without a host, the new viruses produced would self-destruct as they budded from the immune cell, and the vicious cycle of virus replication would come to an end, healing the patient's immune system. At last science had a vaccine that worked to prevent as well as cure the deadly disease. The world press was already speculating on a Nobel Prize for the glamorous young woman whose blue epitope had led her to the potent immunotherapeutic vaccine. Nadia's Arab origins made her irresistible given the turmoil that continued to plague the mid-east. She was a publicists dream, a living Joan of Arc rising like sunrise on a failed dream of peace. It didn't take much imagination to see his future in the shadow of her achievement. She would eclipse everything he had accomplished.

Despite his runners body, his constant battle with the bulging of middle age, Nadia noticed that Yves was beginning to grow just a little thick through the middle. Deep wrinkles punctuated his blue eyes as he squinted into the sun. She had teased him about the trace of gray among the blond hair as she applied suntan oil to his chest. It bemused and saddened her both, however, for his sake and her own, like a mother who realizes one day that her son is getting old.

She had sacrificed everything for her extraordinary career as a research physician and virologist, but it still wasn't too late to think about children. Sometimes she daydreamed like a child that she was bride at a Berber wedding, sitting like a queen on the nuptial throne. She knew Yves would never accept the traditional ceremony or divorce himself from his work. He insisted that they must come to each other of their own free will without legal or social pressure. "Freedom is the test of real love," he told her. But she was growing bone tired of her freedom and sometimes fantasized that he would sweep her away in his passion and make her his wife. She longed for the normal human joy of bearing her own child. They would have beautiful children, she thought, if Yves would only relent and give her a child.

She could never allow herself to become pregnant without telling him and she would not resort to a test tube to eliminate the father in the process of having a baby. She was no longer a practicing Muslim, but family life was a value from her past that she could not put aside just to indulge a biological yearning. A child would bind them to each other even more deeply than their work, would solve whatever jealousy he felt toward her for her discovery.

Nadia thought of all the forgotten children from her own village, dressed in rags, malnourished, but laughing as they chased each other in play over the ruined landscape. Soon enough they were sure to graduate to real war games, like other children struggling to outmaneuver the exterminators in the slums of Rio, or those still living like caged animals in the West Bank and Gaza years after the promise of liberation and a new life.

It was always the children, always the helpless that suffered most, predictable as the droughts of summer, she thought. How many had she seen die the year she returned to her village for her father's funeral. The disease affected mostly women now, polluting the well of human reproduction. There were armies of orphans living defeated lives in every corner of the earth.

She remembered their dark-eyed astonishment as the AIDS babies struggled to draw breath and withered into death. In her dreams the children encircled her like a sea of black-eyed wild flowers, imploring her silently. They were myriad tiny angels heralding the apocalypse.

Very few of Nadia's colleagues believed they had time to save humanity, and even Yves was skeptical. He saw little point in bringing a child into such a doomed world. Until now, she thought, listening to the children squeal to each other in delight at the swimming pool. Perhaps now they might risk creating a child, starting the world anew. A daughter or a son, it wouldn't matter. Now at last there was hope for the future. Their's would be the child of hope.

Nadia ran her hand over Yves' shoulders and curled the wisps of hair at the base of his neck into a dark gold ringlet. He sighed approval, coming out of his dream, but did not open his eyes. Nadia recited several lines of Arabic poetry in a low voice, sibilant and fluid as music. Like many of her countrymen, she often resorted to poetry when her heart was fullest and her own words failed her. One could hardly speak in Arabic without speaking poetry.

"That was nice," Yves said, turning to her with a sleepy smile. "What does it mean."

"It's Bedouin, very ancient. It says, 'I have love messages waiting to be delivered directly to your mouth.'"

"Well, you have my undivided attention," he said, taking her into his arms, covering her mouth with his own, searching her meaning with slow deliberation. Her dark hair fell over him like a silky tent obscuring the scant light of the room.

He savored the fullness of her, how perfectly they fit together. He took the palms of her hands into his own, arching his shoulders to embrace her. He made love to her with the entire expanse of his body, head to foot, like falling into a mirror. He'd never lost himself in a woman this way before. Beyond her intelligence, her gentle spirit and integrity, she was simply the most exquisite animal he had ever encountered. He would look into the gold-flecked green eyes, smiling, longing, questioning and consider again what a mystery another human being was, no matter the level of intimacy, no matter the sexual sharing. It would take more than a lifetime to know her.

Perhaps he ought to try to keep this woman forever, he thought, perhaps the child she had wanted was not such a bad idea after all, the image of making a child with her fanning his desire. He took her head into his hands like a precious chalice and thought he might only be seeing stars at first when the brilliant light exploded throughout the room. He moved slowly and tried to let his eyes adjust to the sudden light. But it was no hallucination. Standing black against the sun, the figure of a man guarded the doorway while others slipped silently into their room. When the dark figure shut the door and the light no longer dazzled, Yves was amazed to find that three men dressed in blue overalls had mysteriously appeared in the middle of his bedroom. Instead of rakes or clipping shears, however, they clutched stocky machine guns, and it was clear they had something else in mind than gardening.

Breakfast

Abdel Ayat studied the black architecture of a chestnut tree, stripped of its leaves, standing at the edge of the plaza outside his hotel. The tree spread its fingers into the gray sky and the thin winter drizzle filled the tiniest twigs with droplets of water, pinpoints of diamond light. The optical illusion held him like a child transfixed by a Christmas tree.

The mystery of water. Despite his travels to lush countries beyond the Arab world, the tedious years of study at the university to earn a degree in hydrology, water remained as alluring, held the same enchantment for him as though he were still a boy living in his arid village. He could smell water. The fragrance, the sense of its presence nearby came to him in his dreams sometimes like a slow well seeping up into an oasis, turning the desert into a verdant Eden with date palms, figs, orange trees, and hedges lined with hibiscus and bougainvillea. Sometimes the Prophet lay on a wondrous rug smoking a water pipe in the cool shade of a citrus tree. He smiled the smile of Paradise, inviting Abdel to take his rest in dar al-salam.

A hotel waiter circled about the table once again like a shark sizing up his prey, coaxing Abdel out of his reverie.

"Nyet, non, merci," Abdel said in exasperation. The waiter carried a pitcher of tepid coffee ostensibly to refill his cup, but when he thought no one was watching them, he produced several small jars filled with gray fish eggs hidden under his serving towel.

"Beluga, Mister," he whispered. "The best, very cheap. Russian beluga. How much? You say. How much?"

Abdel was tempted. Caviar was a luxury beyond the reach of a young administrator in the Authority Bureau for Agriculture. Sturgeon were virtually extinct since Russia stopped controlling fishing rights. He doubted the Bulgarian government would make much of a fuss if one of its invited guests dabbled in the black market just a bit. Visitors from Arab countries were to be courted, even if they came from the poorest countries. Ever since the first war in the Gulf it was becoming harder and harder for peripheral countries like Bulgaria to find sources of oil they could afford, especially since their old patron had self-destructed from the Bering straits to the Black Sea. Oil was the ultimate source of all power, economic, political, and military. Whoever controlled the world's oil supply had vanquished in the world's wars since the beginning of the modern age. A rising tide of Islamic fundamentalism was about to topple the corrupt dictatorships and monarchies that sat on the world's oil supply and Russia was crucially interested in befriending the revolutionary elements that stood in the wings.

Bulgaria was rewarded for its loyalty during the years when the Russian empire crumbled and the capitalist experiment ran its disastrous course. With the return of strong leadership in Moscow, Sofia had once again become the site of international conferences such as Peace for a Productive Planet. The first earth summit in Rio had degenerated into political grandstanding between rich nations and poor, north and south and set the tone for future conferences. At Sofia, third world countries being courted by Russia found a forum to rail against environmental disasters and incorporate these issues into their political agendas. They criticized the double-standard of justice for Israel and Arab countries on which the new world order was based. They denounced the continued defilement of their holiest shrines in Hebron and Jerusalem by Israeli security forces. They plotted their strategies in the civil war which had broken out among PLO factions after Arafat's assassination. They condemned the abysmal conditions of refugees living in the AIDS-infected camps across the mid-east and the lack of Western support in fighting the disease in the developing world.

Such meetings provided good cover for Bulgaria's highly developed intelligence service, the sole legacy left by the KGB and years of co-operative ventures with Mother Russia. With the death of Communism, the party quickly reincarnated itself as Socialism and after a few years of rehabilitation the old faces reappeared like forest mushrooms after a rain. Sofia became fashionable as a low-keyed, neutral capital at the crossroads of Europe where a businessman from the golden triangle could market his wares, or freedom fighters from various corners of the earth might order the tools of their trade from German, French, South African or Chinese merchants.

It was unlikely that he'd be bothered for an ounce of caviar, but Abdel didn't want to risk the slightest chance of having to explain himself to the local police and he waived the waiter away from his table. Abdel wanted to remain as ordinary as the ubiquitous mist which hung over the dull city. With his black hair, and dark eyes he could walk the streets as though he sprang from native gypsy stock or shared the pedigree so many Bulgarian men seemed to stem from, the famous local Count, Count Dracula. He had been able to move about the city incognito, and until he began to speak in his broken Russian, shop girls thought him only a very handsome boy deserving of a little special attention.

Abdel watched as occasionally a taxi circled the equestrian statue of General Dobrovolski in the center of the square and delivered a conferee to the hotel reception. He checked his watch and lit another cigarette. Major Kostov was usually very punctual and should have arrived by now. He kept his eye on the hotel lobby and watched the porters offer the same lethargic reception that greeted him when he had checked into the hotel. Few of the third world scientists and bureaucrats could offer the sort of gratuity that made a hotel bellboy come to life. These were not heads of state, merely third world technocrats convening at a small Black Sea country to talk about the dying planet.

For Abdel, that death began first in Nabulus, the village of his birth. The desert was taking back his village as quickly as the epidemic sweeping the earth. When it came to water, the Palestinians were beginning to see exactly what the Israeli's meant by "self rule." Farmers in his village were forbidden to drill beneath the limestone mountain into an aquifer which supplied Israel with a quarter of its water. His family was barely able to raise the few sheep foraging for something to eat in the barren landscape. The great dream of prosperity held out in Arafat's traitorous pact with Rabin had died along with its progenitors, a mirage lost in a sandstorm. The world faced a global economic recession and had little interest in helping his people out of their deprivation. The Palestinians, once again, found themselves at the bottom of the barrel. Even oil-rich Arab brothers used Israel's intransigence on Jerusalem as an excuse to renege on promises of financial aid, withholding any cooperation until this thorniest of questions was resolved. Religious principle once again conveniently camouflaged economic self interest. The West Bank remained as arid and impoverished as it had been in biblical times.

All his science, all his years of study could not stop the outbreak of cholera that had swept through the village two summers ago. With little running water and poor sanitation the disease spread quickly through the village. His mother and little brother had been among the first to die. All her sacrifices to send him to the university seemed pointless now.

Abdel had been one of millions watching that bright fall afternoon as the U.S. President nudged Rabin into the handshake with Arafat seen around the world. He felt the same exhilaration as thousands of his brothers in the occupied territories who believed they were finally watching the birth of a new Palestine. Abdel agreed to pay the price of peace and denounced the military solutions advocated by Hamas and Hezbollah. Yahya Ayyash had turned Israel into a sea of blood, but what had all the Engineer's suicide bombs accomplished in the end. The buses still ran on time in Jerusalem and a genuine Palestinian state was still only a dream.

When the seedling of hope withered under Barak's government and the world returned to its indifference toward his people, all the years of frustration had finally driven Abdel back into the ranks of the radical fundamentalists newly active in the West Bank and Gaza. Abdel had come to this conference to do more than demand water rights for his people. He had decided to take peace into his own hands for the sake of all Palestinians. He was about to offer himself to the cause, body, brain, heart and soul with a new strategy to save his people.

He felt a nervous rush of adrenaline when he saw Major Kostov appear at the entrance to the dining room. Now his mission would begin in earnest. He put out his cigarette and stood to greet her as she crossed the dining room.

It could have been the most normal of rendezvous. The woman took his hand and left slight traces of red lipstick on each cheek as she kissed him, a professor greeting her talented protégée, perhaps mother greeting son. But Abdel's waiter had seen this woman before and with the highly developed instincts of the smuggler, quickly disappeared into the kitchen.

Major Kostov made a mental note to have the waiter interrogated later. For the moment, the KGB had much more important fish to fry in the person of the dark young Arab offering her a chair at his table. She didn't wish to trouble the waters just at the moment. Besides she was intrigued by Abdel's good manners, the unexpected charm. She accepted his offer of a cigarette with a smile. His black hair had flecks of gray, but his cheeks were a dusky red above the dark line of his beard. His eyes shone with the energy and intelligence of a young otter as he struck a match to light her cigarette. The boy had possibilities, she thought.

Laboratory

Martin Cramer sat at the large marble island in the center of his office, a room reflecting the current minimalist decor espoused by the company interior decorator. Dappled light from clouds passing overhead played through three walls of glass. A single stylized caduceus adorned the fourth wall, black onyx on gray concrete, world symbol for Cramer Chemical. A tall banyan strung with violet orchids flourished inside an electronic greenhouse, the only visible concession to the biological world which gave rise to the Cramer enterprise.

"A shaving mirror, please," Martin commanded, and a computer terminal rose silently from the marble desk in front of him. The screen turned the color of liquid mercury before resolving into the video image of a slightly wilted matinee idol.

Martin studied himself in preparation for the meeting. He adjusted the red silk tie, subtly interwoven with the Cramer symbol. His rugged face had gone a bit fleshy, but the gray temples and earnest, slightly questioning gaze projected the desired authority. He had years of experience with board members. A little weathered, but it was still the handsome face that looked out from the opening pages of the annual report each year, reassuring stockholders. He knew how to project affable good will, competence. The board of directors always came away with the feeling that they had been carefully listened to. There were very few problems he couldn't talk his way out of and Martin was satisfied that today would be no different.

He was annoyed that Robert had called in sick again this morning, however. His assistant could coax a smile out of the most strident matron on the board of directors and today that talent would have come in handy. Martin thought him too much a pretty boy, but there wasn't a secretary at Cramer who wouldn't bend over backward for Robert, and he got on well with the surly prima donnas in the research departments just as well. Robert was pleasant, efficient, and politically correct. In the age of AIDS, having a gay assistant demonstrated Martin's sensitivity and compassion. Martin silently congratulated himself for bringing the little fag into the head office after Michael Riley's death. Martin could keep an eye on Robert's behavior, monitor the boy's grief and find out just what Michael Riley had told his lover about his work before he died.

Martin had managed to conceal the results of the investigation into Dr. Riley's suicide ten years ago. But if the press ever discovered that Michael Riley was the typhoid Mary responsible for disseminating the mutant AIDS virus which now threatened the world, Cramer Chemical might just as well fold its tent or start selling pencils. Epidemiologists at Cramer speculated that Riley first carried the new virus to the west coast on a lecture tour he'd given shortly before his death, just as the handsome young airline steward, Gatton Degas, Patient Zero had spread the original AIDS virus from Fire Island to the pool parties of L.A. in the 1970's.

But fortunately for Cramer Chemical, no one back then investigated the possibility that Dr. Riley had created the very virus responsible for his own illness as well as the death of millions since. With a publicist's genius for turning tragedy into triumph, Martin had sold his vision of Michael Riley to the media. Michael became the first victim of the virus's monstrous natural ability to adapt and mutate. Instead of being a foolhardy researcher stupid enough to risk his own life by violating procedure and endangering his parent corporation, Riley was now an anointed martyr in the war against AIDS. Cramer Chemical had endowed a Chair in Microbiology at Harvard in Riley's name, as well as a number of scholarships at universities across the country. They had even named the new virtual hyper-reality laboratory in his honor. The only thing that concerned Martin now was the staggering corporate liability that loomed over him if the world should ever discover Cramer's culpability. It would make Thalidomide, the Dalkon Shield and poisoned Tylenol scandals seem trifling by comparison. The gigantic industrial corporation his great grandfather had founded would collapse in ruin.

Against that contingency, Martin had managed to reallocate a considerable share of last year's profits into a joint-venture with Akan Pharmaceutical in Lausanne and arranged for private access to the Swiss bank account dedicated to that project. The Japanese hadn't exactly taken him into their inner circle, but Cramer didn't need to be part of the enormous pharmaceutical monopoly in order to secure a mutually attractive limited partnership. The Japanese could perform all the necessary government and military bribes which kept the information flowing and warned them of any threats to their operation. When needed, they could also bribe the security agencies hired by large competitors to protect industrial secrets. They could fix prices and undersell a targeted product to lock in market share. They could circumvent all the American anti-trust laws that usually restricted Cramer Chemical when it tried to monopolize a new discovery, even when the discovery had been funded by Government research grants. They had perfected the art of the dang, secret agreements established to keep out competition. And price fixing was standard operating procedure for Japanese CEO's, of course.

As a limited partner and a westerner, Martin didn't have to sell his soul to the Japanese corporation the way all Japanese executives were expected to do. He didn't care if they deemed him lower than Japan's outcast untouchable, the *burakumin*. Their racism was universal: anyone unlucky enough to be born outside Japan was simply a barbarian.

Still, one had to deal with the barbarians if only for business reasons. Cramer Chemical had produced plenty of innovation in the field that the Japanese were anxious to buy. In the long run Martin would be sacrificing years of research and the patents it generated at Cramer Chemical, but in the short run he would make a fortune. And the way things were going, it looked like it was time to play his best hand.

So far, Martin had contained the potential explosion that would ensue if the world discovered the truth about Michael Riley's experiment and subsequent death. Martin had been able to achieve this damage control with help of his research chief, Dr. Yves Bourret. Bourret had been easy enough to persuade, fortunately. Martin had convinced the Frenchman that nothing was to be gained by ruining the reputation of a dead man. More to the point, if Cramer failed, Dr. Bourret's new vaccine wouldn't stand a chance of reaching the market. And Martin had been careful to guarantee a healthy bonus for the French researcher if and when the vaccine was finally approved for use.

For the moment each of them benefited from such cooperation, but Martin Cramer was beginning to feel uneasy with this unlikely bedfellow. He knew from experience that it wouldn't be long before Bourret's conditions crossed the line from imperious suggestion to the quicksand of polite blackmail.

It was Bourret and especially Dr. Mansur that the committee wanted to meet when rumor of their discovery began to circulate among the board members. The President of Cramer Chemical wasn't meant to be a tour guide, but the cocky Frenchman had become too much of an unknown quantity and Martin couldn't risk including him in the dog and pony show Martin had prepared for the board just yet. A little vacation and public relations trip to their European operations would keep the two scientists on ice for a while until he got a better sense of how things were going to play out.

"Margaret, let's see what our guests are up to, shall we?"

"Yes sir," a pleasant voice answered from the computer terminal. He swiveled in his chair to face the wall behind him. As the Cramer symbol rose into the ceiling the entire wall transformed itself into a video screen monitoring the convoy of stretch limousines carrying the board members to the gate of Cramer Chemical.

Martin decided that when the visiting committee had been sufficiently coddled, he'd address himself to Dr. Yves Bourret, review the options, make some hard decisions. Bourret had suddenly become a rather large frog in Martin's exclusive pond and something had to be done about it.

Housekeeping

When his eyes adjusted to the light and Yves recognized the danger they were in, he had the bad judgment to leap up from bed and was rewarded with a smashing blow to his face. He fell back onto the bed, stunned and bleeding from a gash over his right eye. Nadia instinctively drew him to her, covering his head.

"Don't, don't please," she cried to the man who seemed to be the leader of their assailants. The scarves they had pulled over their faces when they burst into the room hid their identity as well as any sense of their intentions. In spite of her fear, Nadia remembered to try to note details to give to police after the intruders had finished the robbery.

The gunman in command was smaller than his two accomplices, but the gardener's uniform couldn't camouflage the stocky, powerful body underneath. His dark eyes were familiar somehow, but could have been those of any boy they had seen on the beach all week. He moved like a small panther and gave silent orders to the other two to secure the villa. They carefully checked all the rooms, entrances, and closets while he kept his weapon and his eyes fixed on them.

"The money is in the drawer over there" she began, but was pinned by two of the intruders who immediately sealed her mouth and Yves' with strong adhesive tape. Her claustrophobia gave rise to a scream, which carried little more than a muffled whimper.

"Quiet." the leader said, directing his machine gun at Yves' head. "Dress."

She felt him take in her nakedness, and hurried to obey his command. When she had put on sandals and a white sundress, she helped Yves get on his clothes. Then she took a clean towel the gunman handed her to bandage Yves' wound. When she had ripped the towel into strips and applied a pressure bandage to his forehead, she and Yves were lashed to straight-back dining chairs. She watched while the men searched the drawers and closets. She began to feel sick when she saw them begin to pack all their belongings into suitcases and started to clean up the villa the way one might when checking out of a hotel.

Yves and Nadia sat blindfolded, silent, listening the sounds of afternoon fading. The maids no longer called to each other as they padded back and forth between the bungalows with fresh towels heaped on their service carts. The children had all been coaxed away from the swimming pool as twilight fell. The peace and quiet of the villa helped mollify her terror slightly. At first when they had gagged her she began to breath rapidly like a drowning swimmer whose panic only makes his predicament worse. She realized that they only needed to pinch her nostrils closed and she would suffocate without even the consolation of screaming. She thought she might faint from hyperventilation. When she felt someone begin to massage her shoulders and whisper for her to "stay calm," she obeyed like a helpless child.

She tried to think of what to do. If they waited much longer David Schefflan would arrive for cocktails. But they might capture him too or harm him before he had the chance to alert anyone. The gunmen looked like they would use their weapons if David burst in unexpectedly. What could she do? She listened for the approach of his car trying to think of a way to warn him.

Nadia lost track of the hours before she finally felt the coarse hands lift the blindfold from her eyes and carefully remove the tape from her face. She couldn't see for a minute in the darkened room but sensed that he was standing behind her. As he loosened the ropes from her wrists, he ordered her to sit at the desk and begin writing a note for the housekeeper.

"Say it is an emergency, you must leave early," he instructed.

The pain and stiffness in her wrists resolved a bit as she began to write.

"Nani dear, thank you for all your help during our visit. We have been called back to the states unexpectedly. I'll leave the key in the box. I meant to buy you a little present, but now I'm afraid you will have to do even that for me as well. I'm sorry. Good bye."

He took the note from her and studied it carefully before putting some drachmas on the desk along with the note.

"If you're taking us somewhere, may I please use the bathroom first," she asked. He motioned her inside. There was no window and all the cabinet drawers had been emptied of anything she might use to help escape. She returned to the room sooner than anyone had expected. Their kidnapper turned around and quickly drew up his scarf but not before she got a look at his face.

"You," she cried with a shock of recognition. "What are you doing, what do you want with us?"

She made a move toward him but was caught once again, bound and gagged. She heard a car door slam in the alleyway behind the villa, but it was not David Schefflan coming to their rescue. Her captors lifted Nadia and Yves into the back of a truck. The coarse hood pulled over her head made it impossible to see Venus just rising like a tiny diamond over a crescent moon which hung on the black curtain of night.

Infestation

Martin studied the slow parade of stretch limousines as it snaked into the compound of Cramer Chemical. Flat black windows stared out from the cement bunker like the eyes of the dead keeping watch. Once inside the fortress-like exterior the procession stopped at a glass kiosk and was directed to the administration building by a young policewoman. A silver caduceus formed epaulets on each shoulder of her uniform. She tossed her pretty blond head and gave them a cheery salute as they passed into the compound. Concealed inside the warehouse facing her modest station, a well-armed security force was at her disposal, but the arriving visitors had been thoroughly scrutinized by camera and long distance microphones patched into Martin's office before they had even arrived at the guardhouse. On rare occasion, unwary visitors were imprudent enough to discuss business strategy as they drove to the head office and the sophisticated eavesdropping equipment had paid for itself many times over. Invariably, Martin at least had some idea of what to expect from his guests by the time he greeted them in the lobby. This morning he was annoyed to hear the delegation wringing their hands over the Riley question once again. He listened intently to try to discern just how the rumors had begun.

Once inside the concrete envelope of the outer structures, the cars wound their way through the labyrinthine central gardens, a living model in ornamental boxwood of the double helix structure of DNA. Five white stretch limos came to a stop in front of the god Hermes, rising naked and heroic from a fountain of crystal arching over the lobby entrance. In his arms he held the mortar and pestle, symbol of medicine and anesthesia, unique provinces of the god.

"Because of his slight of hand, and his magical powers, Hermes is also the god of thieves and pickpockets," Martin explained once the visitors had assembled in the lobby. "But this is an aspect of the god's behavior we tend to keep in the family here at Cramer Chemical." After a small silence, one of the Japanese board members laughed enabling the rest of the group to follow suit appreciatively.

Martin continued his pleasant banter with his visitors, monitoring their responses for some clue to their actual frame of mind. It was difficult, as usual. The Japanese always avoided any direct confrontation when they had a problem; the response was always indirect. The first indication of their displeasure might be a massive sell-off of company stock or a pink slip for an unwary CEO. Even their silences held meaning for the careful observer.

They had a talent for concealing their intentions went beyond the public mask every good Japanese business man developed early on to protect his private thinking. In the traditional *sempai-kohai* relationship it was even becoming difficult to tell who was the senior boss, who the junior protégée. As in certain African countries, one was rarely sure who actually held the power in a given exchange. Martin remembered the time once, in Mali, when he had discovered too late that the chauffeur in front of whom he had outlined his marketing plan while they were on their way to the ministry was actually the tribal prince with whom he had come to do business.

Martin always felt he had stepped in a nest of red ants when he was required to deal with the Japanese consortium dominating the Board of Directors at Cramer. In the beginning they seemed a mere nuisance, but invariably the Japanese members of the board kept at a subject with the single-minded group intelligence of swarming ants out to ruin a summer picnic. It was more than strength in numbers. Despite their position as a world power, Martin had come to realize the Japan was fundamentally a rural culture in which the individual could not survive if he were foolhardy enough to anger the group.

The rumors of an NIH investigation into Michael Riley's early vaccine work had brought the Japanese pouring into Cramer Chemical as sure as if Martin had spread his blanket on top their mound and spilled a jar of honey. Martin forced himself to follow Japanese etiquette. Calm, even voice. No large gestures or rapid movements of the arms. Control, always control, regardless of the ants crawling up your thighs.

"It's going to be a long morning," Martin thought to himself, the automatic door sliding open and shut, open and shut as they each politely protested that the other should be the first to enter the building. He finally bumped into Mr. Nakamura with an embarrassed laugh and the rest of the committee filed in after like a line of ducklings.

"I'm afraid some urgent business will keep Dr. Bourret from joining us today," Martin began. "I'm no match for his expertise, of course. This is his life's work,- and that of his colleague, Dr. Mansur," he hastened to add when he noticed that one of the trim gray suits the group wore, differed by virtue of a tailored skirt instead of pants. "But I'll try to answer any questions you might have the best I can," he said, smiling expansively to Mrs. Nakamura.

Martin led them through the cafeteria, a large cavern capable of feeding 1000 employees under its huge glass dome. In a smaller private dining room he invited them to an international breakfast including a waffle and omelet bar and various sorts of meats and breads. But there was also fish, rice, yogurt, and a gray sort of porridge which African visitors were always surprised and pleased to find on the menu.

Martin started with the bad news first, the record quarterly losses and troublesome lawsuit over a failed blood pressure medication whose teratogenic side effects were only now becoming evident, five years after the FDA had given its approval. But he laced his report with teasing allusions to the triumphant story they had all come to hear. Third stage trials seemed conclusive. Dr. Bourret and Dr. Mansur had developed a curative as well as preventative vaccine that might finally end the plague of blue death engulfing the world. Already Cramer stock had risen several thousand points on the Nikkei market and feature stories in the national media had sent a surge in Wall Street.

In the lobby to the library archives, Martin walked up to an ancient white heron gracing a 16th century Japanese silk screen and said "video please." The panel slid silently into the wall, the skylight clouded over and the television monitor lit up with the face of a pleasant Japanese narrator who politely touted the innovations that had made Cramer one of the world's most powerful pharmaceutical firms.

The film documented the development of a new class of antibiotics based on the maganins Zasloff had discovered in the poison glands of West African frogs. An anti-fungal agent discovered recently in the Brazilian rain forests showed great promise in treating certain resilient forms of pneumonia in AIDS patients. Their biggest star, however, was a new class of nasal antihistamines that the marketing department had dubbed Fresh Air. It virtually eliminated the ENT symptoms connected with the allergy season. Little green inhalators of Fresh Air were sold over as the counter medication in every drug store in the country after a considerable lobbying effort by Cramer Chemical with the FDA including a few judicious "contributions" to the president's re-election committee.

The library was always one of the most popular stops on the standard tour of Cramer Chemical and Martin decided to start the tour there.

"Of course, it's not as big as a university research center," Martin said as they filed in, "but then, it doesn't have to be." Simple black work stations lined the walls like race horse gates at the track. The ubiquitous Cramer caduceus hung suspended from the center of the glass ceiling like a crucifix in the nave of a contemporary church. The lobby was filled with over-stuffed leather furniture, but little else in the room made it recognizable as a library.

Martin took a gold compact disk from the file of those most frequently used and inserted it into the computer.

"With Medline, for example, I can instantly access a synopsis of every article on a given subject written in the past six months. Let's see. Suppose I wanted to get recent studies of resistance to Hypericin-C in prolonged treatment of HIV infected patients."

Martin's fingers raced over the keys calling up information. He hadn't lost his touch despite years of toil in the front offices. The computer screen split into windows correlating data into multi-colored graphs.

"You see there's really no need to keep the actual books here in the library anymore with this system," he said, "though we do keep several hundred of the principle journals, the hard copy, there on the shelves for older scientists who like to have the feel of the document in their hands. The stacks were camouflaged by a wall of glass filled with tropical fish.

"I'm something of a dinosaur myself in that regard," he said with a self-deprecatory smile. "With the oral research booths, however, we've obviated the need for manual searches altogether."

Martin entered one of the glass cabins and his visitors poked their heads in after.

"How many journal entries in the past month for Retrovir do you list," he asked.

"Four hundred and twenty eight, Dr. Cramer," a pleasant voice responded and the screen lit up with the listings. "Cue please."

"Could I have a female librarian please," Martin directed.

"Yes sir," the computer said, feminine now, a tone modulating just at the edge of sultriness. Mr. Nakamura giggled, and was pinched into silence by his wife.

The visitors were as delighted as children in a toy store when Martin led them into a room filled with glass stomachs all churning away. Occasionally, robot arms swung over the stomachs adding acids, pepsins, other solutions to simulate human digestion.

"Once we've designed a new time release capsule, for example, we need to test out its efficacy," Martin explained. "These robots work twenty four hours a day, just like real stomachs, and save us thousands of man hours were the work to be done by hand. They help us test many different components of successful delivery of a medication from the shape of the pill to the thickness of micro layers needed to space delivery over time.

"What is 'Wanda,' and 'Prince Charming'," Mr. Nakamura asked.

"Oh, the technicians have given them names," Martin said. "I guess the robots don't like being just a number either. Wouldn't want them to go on strike on us, now would we?"

He held the door for Mrs. Nakamura, each bowing slightly to the other as they left the laboratory. Martin felt himself warming to his task as he approached the security counter at the end of the corridor and looked into the retina scanner that would identify him and grant him access to this most top secret chamber in the Cramer labyrinth.

Missing

The Michael Riley Virtual Hyper Reality Laboratory and Test Center, the newly opened shrine Cramer had erected to the young scientist's memory, Martin saved for last. He was ready for anything his visitors might try to spring on him, but few visitors kept their presence of mind in the dazzling new facility. The laboratory went far beyond anything Sutherland could have imagined when he pioneered virtual reality in the early 1960's. The new technology enabled one to control experience, actually create a synthetic reality for the brain, and not merely view animated simulations. The implications of VHR went beyond mere questions of ethical propriety.

Martin led the visitors into the laboratory as though they were pilgrims entering a darkened Cathedral. He invited them to take a seat and lower the plastic helmet that hung over each over stuffed armchair like dryers in a fancy hair salon. Camera sensors mounted in each helmet monitored their eye movements and projected visual images to the individual retinas of each visitor which corresponded to the actual dimensions of the laboratory space where they were seated.

Incorporating the latest imaging capabilities, VAR technology had allowed neurologists to use the ophthalmic nerve to serve as a window to the brain. Beyond visual fidelity, however, the system enabled computer access to portions controlling other related senses such as touch and smell to complement the images "seen" by the brain through the eye.

"Of course, it's the brain that actually "sees" when it registers the electrochemical stimulation on nerve endings that we call vision," Martin explained. "But we have been able to take the process a great deal further. Watch how we are able to fool the brain's sense of proprioception, for example."

Martin warmed to his task like a talk show host inciting his radio audience to rebel over a new tax on the elderly. He made some fine adjustments at the computer controls to demonstrate the sensual override capability of the laboratory. Soon he had the board members floating terrified near the ceiling while their bodies remained comfortably seated in their easy chairs.

"The entertainment potential of this technology is enormous. Marketing projections indicate we have already reached the ten dollars per minute level for public distribution," he said, letting the board members glide gently back to their seats.

"Let's see. Apply this texture to the polygons, we're in real time here..." Martin spoke to himself, working the laboratory like a child with a new train on Christmas morning. "Virtual hyper reality has applications which are far more important than the entertainment industry, of course. It will be useful in several fields of medicine. Neurologist can now actually explore the brain from within. VAR has already revolutionized the treatment of CVA's, stromas, and genetic anomalies. Psychiatry has benefited most perhaps. More complex neurological centers such as the emotional and moral gyroscopes found in the limbic system of the brain remain impervious to the computer's tricks, but research continues. One day we might actually end the criminal behavior in sociopaths or finally offer some hope for schizophrenics locked in the prison of their madness. Science might finally be able to correct their misconceptions of reality and enable them to check their broken circuitry from without. Unlike electro-convulsive therapy, this technology will help order the mind, rearrange the furniture, do a little housekeeping as it were."

Martin did not point out the implications of such technology in his brave new world. In the wrong hands virtual hyper reality when applied to the psyche might produce anything from a unique new tool for torture to the ultimate slave state and the end of the human spirit itself. It would be some time before the government would permit the sort of human experiments he envisioned, but he was working on the problem.

"At this point, I'd like to make a very special introduction," Martin said. "We are indeed proud of the work done by the video archivists and ophthalmic projectionists who have made his appearance possible."

A figure standing at the center of a cone of light greeted them in a soft, resonant voice: "Ladies and gentlemen, welcome to the revolutionary universe of molecular biology."

Ibo Nakamura gave a startled cry, for in an instant, out of nowhere, Dr. Michael Riley stood before them in the flesh, the flesh as it had been in the months before the young scientist began to waste away with disease. Michael smiled the same disarming smile that Mr. Nakamurara remembered from almost a decade ago when Dr. Riley conducted the first tour of Cramer Chemical for the Board of Directors. This was no ghostly holograph, however, and the elderly businessman turned clammy when the young man approached to shake hands. Nakamura felt he might faint.

It was like shaking hands with the living dead, however, since Michael could only project programmed responses to cues fed to him from the computer control. And he had a limited range of physical movements within the space of the laboratory like the mechanical dinosaurs at in a theme park.

"By now you have all seen the wonderful machines that help us sequence the genetic structure of the simplest organisms right up to the human genome itself. With molecular scissors we are able to cut out those genes which we identify as coding for the expression of defects or add genes to correct such problems. But identifying such troublemakers is hardly an easy task. I invite you consider the genetic complexity of even a simple retrovirus like HIV IV which is causing such devastation in the world presently."

Michael Riley pointed to the ceiling like God touching the hand of Adam and unraveled the complex string of molecules like rolling out a ball of yarn. A dizzying spiral of three-dimensional spheres shot forth and encircled the walls of the laboratory. They burst into the room like thousands of doves released for the opening of a peace conference. The board members were walled in by a rainbow of molecules that threatened to smother them.

"Though the genetic blueprint for the virus is a hundred thousand times smaller than that of a human cell, one still has ten thousand nucleotides to study before unlocking the virion's pathogenicity. Let us take a segment and look a little closer," Michael said, reaching out to stop the flow. The bright molecules disappeared except for a mass the size of a hundred tennis balls hanging suspended in front him.

"We are actually able to measure the energy required to break the molecular bonds found in nature by simulations such as you see here. It was in this very laboratory, that Dr. Nadia Mansur discovered the segment of the virus's genetic map she has labeled the blue epitope and which may be the greatest contribution to world health that Cramer Chemical has yet achieved. The segment first caught her attention by the strange distribution of guanine molecules represented in these Cerulean spheres. By modifying the molecule at this juncture...." Michael Riley stopped frozen in his gesture as he reached for the molecule in front of him.

"Sorry about that ladies and gentlemen," Martin said, working the computer keyboard. In reverse motion, like a film being rewound, Michael Riley retreated to the beginning of his sentence.

"By modifying the molecule at this juncture...." and again he was frozen like a store mannequin.

Martin tried once again to continue the presentation but a computer voice announced, "Access denied. Security code 938, key, Dr. Yves Bourret, program continues at 17.3 digits."

"Well, we seem to have an even better security system than I had realized," Martin joked with his visitors. "I'm sure you find that reassuring given the importance of this discovery." But Martin was anything but reassured. The knot in his stomach tightened when he realized how Bourret had outmaneuvered him, and he made a vow to take care of the meddlesome scientist once and for all. As Martin reached into his pocket for a Cramer mint antacid, Michael Riley disappeared into thin air.

Yellow Rose

Once past the airport on the road heading east to Sounion, David Schefflan was finally able to breathe a little easier. The inconspicuous sedan he had checked out from the embassy car pool had all the amenities: two way radio, extra horsepower to carry the weight of bullet proof glass, and an even-numbered license plate which gave him permission to drive in the city alternate days of the week. Unfortunately, five minutes into rush hour, the air conditioning began wheezing and finally gave up the ghost. David was now too late to take the car back for another.

The best air conditioning system in the world didn't stand much of a chance anyway, he thought as he made his way through the ubiquitous brown smog. The ancient hills ringing Athens turned the city into a great soup bowl of pollution, killing more and more children and elderly each year and eating away at the Acropolis and other great monuments that had survived for thousands of years until now. But as the stolid Chrysler climbed through the mountains toward Marathon and the coast, pine forests began to clean the air and the heat dissipated somewhat with breezes off the Aegean.

David's persistence had paid off. Amazingly, the Ambassador's guest of honor had invited him to Marathon at the reception last night, though he still wasn't sure why exactly. The Frenchman who brought her to the party treated her like an old favorite armchair, familiar and comfortable and definitely his private property. She stood dutiful and radiant at his elbow, unable to get in a word as the guests questioned them on the progress of their work.

Was she simply trying to make the Frenchman jealous? David wondered if he really stood a chance with her or if he were just a pawn in some slight lover's quarrel.

He had looked forward to meeting this woman ever since he first read her dossier in Tunis six months ago before being transferred to the embassy in Athens. It was ironic, he thought, that the woman in the photograph he studied might as easily be a Sabra beauty as Palestinian. The face was more likely to adorn the cover a fashion magazine than the copy of *Newsweek* beside him that featured her work. "Hope At Last?" the headline asked in bold golden letters like a halo suspended over her head on the cover photograph. The luminous hair drawn into a prim knot high on her long-stemmed neck, the stunning eyes, the ripe mouth. In a different world he might be keeping her under surveillance for personal reasons rather than reasons of state.

All of the facts outlined in her file still didn't quite explain how she had managed to escape the cycle of poverty and bitterness that usually consumed these people and kept them from achieving much. She was one of the lucky ones with liberal parents willing to give her a good education. She had worked hard to develop her talents. But he was surprised that she hadn't been drawn into the sort of political activity that had eventually killed her father. How did she resist joining the *Intifadah* when her father was blown up in that Mossad car attack. Had she entered her life as a scientist like a nun fleeing the real world for the comfort of the cloister? Did she really think she could escape that world?

Intelligence reports already gave indications that a splinter organization of Hamas was attempting to draft her into its ranks. Her father's martyrdom had given her the status of a princess in exile. She was a public figure that needed to be watched closely. Now that she had captured the world's imagination by her accomplishments, she could easily become a political leader like her father. She might become a powerful force to unite the PLO leadership which the Israelis had worked so hard to fragment after Arafat's death.

"Mind if I steal one of these, Marjorie," David had called breezily to the Ambassador's wife last night as he plucked one of the long-stemmed yellow roses from a brilliant bouquet in the foyer. Marjorie Hunt had trained the embassy gardener to grow the roses in her huge greenhouse. She liked to use her home state's flower whenever she played hostess at a special event at the residence. They always evoked compliments from her guests. She had, in fact, created a fashion for the brilliant yellow blossoms and they were now featured predominantly each spring at the Varkisa flower exhibition and florists shops throughout Athens.

"I've got a beautiful lady in my sights and I'll need all the help I can get." He grinned at her.

"I doubt that, you old smooth talker," she said in her Texas drawl. He was by far the best looking of the junior officers at the embassy. A bit small perhaps, but small packages can be deceiving she thought, following the well-defined torso and sculptured backside out onto the penthouse terrace. His most important attribute, of course, was his bachelorhood. There was always a dearth of suitable single men in these foreign posts, especially this good-looking, and apparently heterosexual to boot. His easy smile and deep blue eyes were so much gilding on the lily for a hostess constantly in need of a single dinner partner to round out a table.

"I want a full report sweetie, you hear," she called out after him.

All night long he had kept his sights on Nadia who stood silently beside the Frenchman holding forth nonstop. David saw his chance when Bourret turned his attention to the Greek actress Fotini Theodorou who had come into the room with her entourage and Nadia slipped away onto the terrace by herself. None of the other dinner guests had been lured out from the air conditioning, despite the floodlit Acropolis blazing against the midnight sky or the city lights flowing like a sea of diamonds down to the Mediterranean.

"It's a miracle, isn't it," he asked as she stood captivated by the precision, and elegance of the Parthenon. "Perfect sanctuary for the Virgin Goddess."

"I never tire of it," she said, turning to him. "Such purity and harmony. I feel complete somehow, just looking at it."

"I see that," he said. He thought how simply beautiful she was. Her white evening gown was brocaded with a pattern of tiny pearls and sequins mirroring the points of light shining in the stars and the city lights below. The dress accented the deep tan of her bare shoulders.

A single blue tear of sapphire hung suspended by a gold chain at her breasts. Nadia cast down her eyes, conscious of his attention.

"My name's David Schfflan," he said, handing her the rose.

"Hello," she said. She was reluctant to accept his gift.

"Oh, it's all right. I'm with the embassy. Government issue," he said. "I've been trying to meet you all night in that crunch, but I feel I already know you. The *Paris Match* feature on you last month turned you into Joan of Arc."

"There was a lot of hyperbole in that article, I'm afraid," she said, taking the flower from his hand, returning his smile. "The marketing director at Cramer Chemical is ecstatic about such journalistic pieces, but I hate all the publicity."

"It's still a pretty a spectacular achievement. You can't blame the world for wanting to know more. Have you really developed a shield response at the CD4 receptor sites?

"You seem to have followed our progress very closely," she said, pleased. But Martin Cramer's paranoia over industrial espionage had proved to be no fantasy on several occasions in the past months, and Nadia had learned to be on guard when she met someone who seemed to exhibit more than the casual interest of the layman. "What else do you know about me," she said, skirting his questions.

"Oh, I've read the whole remarkable biography," he said, recounting the litany of her success from the first scholarship at the American University in Beirut, doctoral studies at the University of Paris and finally her post doctoral work at Harvard and her breakthrough discovery of the mysterious HIV III virus, a variant appearing in the late 90's that caused AIDS but resisted detection and treatment. The diagnostic tests she developed early in her career had saved the world's blood supply and kept research focused on a cure for the disease.

"I've read about your youth on the West Bank too, and your family. I read of your father's death, the terrorist attack that killed him."

Her face drained of color. Had he gone too far?

"I don't wish to discuss my father's death. I really don't think you could understand..."

"My parents died in the violence of the mid-east too," he said, trying to justify himself.

"I'm sorry. I didn't know."

"They were killed in Pan Am Flight 103. Do you remember the Libyan bombing over Lockerbie? They were returning from a visit to my grandparents in Israel and stopped in Germany to visit our cousins."

"Israel?"

"My grandfather was a holocaust survivor," David said with pride. "He and my grandmother came to Haifa from Poland just after the war. But my parents hated the life they led in Israel. They wasted their youth in a country at war, no security, no tranquillity—a land of bitterness and fear. I guess they never really had a youth. That is, until they decided to emigrate to pursue the American dream. Peace, freedom, a better life for their children. Me and my sister. Only I never got to live that life with them. That dream was blown to bits by Ahmed Jebril in the skies over Scotland. I lost them all."

"I'm sorry," she said, surprising him by touching his hand.

He didn't often tell this story to strangers. His years in the Foreign Service had trained him not to be inappropriately personal. Everyone, after all, had his own story to tell. But sometimes when he least expected it, the orphaned child came after him and insisted on the enormity of their death. To lose a parent after a long and full life was understandable somehow, but not in the prime of their life. And his sister. She would never know the joy that life can sometimes give. He knew the orphaned child in him might turn up any time until the day he died, demanding attention, holding a small bruised heart in his hands like a broken toy.

David was grateful for the tenderness she had shown him that night, and when Yves Bourret had come bursting out onto the terrace like a nasty little pit bull, David accepted her surprising invitation with genuine pleasure. He could see the boring Frenchman was not very enthusiastic about the idea and David enjoyed poking him in the eye, as it were, by agreeing to visit.

When he arrived at Marathon and found villa number three in the resort complex, David walked to the front door, thinking perhaps he had made a mistake. All the lights were out and he couldn't discern any movement in the house. Perhaps they didn't hear his knock, perhaps they were cooling off in a swimming pool at the back of the villa? David followed a flagstone path that seemed to lead through the garden to the rear.

One of the French doors leading to the terrace was unlocked and he let himself into living room calling "hello" as he entered. The villa appeared empty and he was sure he must have the wrong house until he saw the note on the table with the drachmas.

She would certainly have canceled the invitation if they had been called back to the U.S., he thought. Something didn't seem right. No vacationer left a house so tidy, especially if they were in a hurry. The house was immaculate, but for one odd exception. In the small bathroom off the hall he discovered the rose he had given her last night shredded into a pile of yellow petals on the vanity table.

David called the reception and was informed that the American couple had not checked out to anyone's knowledge. When he questioned the maid, his suspicions were confirmed.

"Thank you, mister, but there must be mistake," the maid had told him. "Yesterday Dr. Nadia gave me a beautiful silk scarf for a present," she said after she had pocketed the drachmas. "But maybe this is her extra gift."

Then David didn't waste any time contacting the embassy. After some effort, he reached the political officer on duty and relayed his suspicions. The attaché would alert the director of intelligence to a possible abduction and assess the implications of such a kidnapping before contacting the local police. When he determined that he'd learned all that he could at Marathon, David Schefflan then called the American Embassy and gave a diluted version of the same information that he had just conveyed to his contact at the Israeli Embassy. It would look suspicious if he didn't contact his own embassy, and he didn't want to jeopardize his position. It had taken him years to make his way up the ladder in the US Foreign Service and his value as an agent for the Israeli secret service, Mossad was far too valuable to jeopardize by any mistakes now.

Night Sweats

Michael Riley sat penitent in his wheel chair. The large brown eyes filled with tears and spilled silently down his cheeks. Despite the wasting of his body, his face was still that of the boy Robert had first come to love, though Michael's carrot mustache was flecked with gray now, and his beautiful eyelashes had grown long and translucent and curled up at the ends as a result of the medication.

"Why couldn't you hold off for once, god damn it," Robert shouted. "I just cleaned you up, and now I'm going to have to change you all over again. I can't stand it. I can't stand it anymore."

"I didn't mean to Robert. I'm sorry. I'm so sorry." Michael bent his head.

"I can't stand it," Robert called out again, thrashing about, waking himself from the nightmare with the sound of his own shouting. He sat up in his bed unsure for a minute where he was. It was a dream, of course, but it could have been any one of the frustrating breakdowns in their friendship in the last months before his death when Robert served as Michael's nurse. Just a dream. But the image of Michael crying was so real. He remembered his sick friend's pain and embarrassment so acutely, he regretted his impatience so deeply that Robert sat in his bed and let the emotion carry him into a flood of his own real tears.

This month it would be nine years since Michael's death, but the young scientist seemed to emerge from the shadows at will, waiting patiently at the edge of Robert's consciousness, waking or sleeping. The person Robert loved more than anyone in his whole life was gone forever and he had never managed to accept that lonely and devastating reality.

For some time Robert took an eerie sort of consolation in meeting his lover in the virtual hyper reality lab that Cramer Chemical had recently installed. At some level he realized it wasn't healthy for him to slip into the laboratory to recreate the sexual intimacy they had shared in life. At first Robert was willing to accept anything that helped ease the pain, but finally the sessions he programmed with Michael were little more than a sort of high-tech masturbation. Sometimes he even came away feeling like a spent necrophiliac. The laboratory was becoming an obsession and so Robert had vowed not to return to there, even if Dr. Cramer insisted that he accompany visitors on tours.

There was a lot Martin Cramer was going to have to get used to, Robert thought. When Robert first took the job as assistant to the Director, he believed Dr. Cramer to be one of the finest people he had ever met. Talented, successful, tolerant, and compassionate. But after a few months watching him operate up close, Robert saw how thoroughly he had been taken in.

Martin Cramer could eviscerate an enemy before he even felt the knife, could stab him in the back without letting the smile ever fade from his lips. He encouraged Robert to think of himself as Martin's protégée, the son Martin never had, with whom he would share his vast experience and talent as a businessman. But what Martin Cramer called business, Robert discovered, most people considered fraud or blackmail. His duplicity became clear with a vengeance last month when Robert came across Michael's video memo.

Dr. Cramer had asked him to pull the visual record of a meeting that took place nine years ago and Robert, in a slip of concentration, had inadvertently typed Michael Riley's name in the search request. Robert was stupefied at first, but then vaguely remembered the meeting with Dr. Cramer he had taken Michael to in the last months of his life.

"Hi Robert. How are you doing, buddy?" Robert sat in front of the screen in a stunned silence, his heart racing.

"I've asked Dr. Cramer to let me have this private moment with you. I don't know when you'll get this message. You already know how much I love you. I can't ask you to forgive me, but I have to try to explain."

Michael's wheelchair sat in front of the orchid garden at the far end of Dr. Cramer's office. He looked so alone and Robert could hardly bear to watch him.

"I'll ask him to give you this message after I, after I'm gone."
He looked like a marathon runner devoid of any physical resources
coming to the final mile of his race on willpower and courage alone.

"I accept my death, Robert. Remember that Hindu saint
Krandall was always going on about, 'Care deeply about life but be
able to walk away from any part of it or life itself at any moment.'
Well, I've never loved my life more than I love it now. But I accept
my passing.

Last night as I watched you trimming and potting the new
Japanese maple bonsai I was filled with such love for you I thought
I might float away like the cloud of white blossoms on the plum
tree. I was so in the heart of my life, so fully alive I actually felt the
blue light of dusk fall on my face as I watched you nurture those tiny
trees in the failing light. I understood how terrible and wonderful
life can be, like watching a crocodile surface on the radiant Ganges.
It was a transformation for me Robert. Seeing you tend to the trees
from the kitchen window, such a simple gesture, a final image in the
dusk of my life to carry me into eternity."

Michael's head bobbed involuntarily like a heavy sunflower on
its stalk sending spasms of pain down the length of his cervical nerves.

"It is time Robert. I'm exhausted by all this illness and the way
I am ruining your life. You didn't deserve to have to go through all
this with me. I am so sorry Robert."

And the great crock opened his jaws slowly, a long line of slimy
teeth lifting into a knowing smile as Michael's courage at last failed
him.

"Oh Robert, I'm so lost. You see, there's an even bigger horror
for me than death. I'm convinced now that I'm responsible for
creating this virus, for killing all these people. I've set a time bomb in
the house of mankind's future. This mutation is so virulent, the
dissemination so volatile. Millions and millions are going to die
because of my work. It's inescapable." He propped up his head with
his elbow resting on the arm of the wheel chair, but was unable to
relieve the fire burning at the base of his skull.

"You see, when I first developed the AIDS vaccine I inserted a
sequence of base pairs into the viral DNA which served no other
purpose except to mark the virus strain I was using for my experiment.

I assigned combinations of adenine (A), cytosine (c), thymine (T) and guanosine (G) for each letter of the alphabet and actually spelled out "Robert and Michael" into the POL gene of the structure of the virus DNA. I wanted the world to see our achievement someday, Robert. It was silly, guess. I was proud of the work. I wanted to carve our initials into history. Robert and Michael were here. It's all there in my note books.

Today we completed the viral sequencing of 87 AIDS patients from around the world and the results are undeniable. My private marker was demonstrated in every case. You see, I didn't get the disease by challenging my immune system with the virus after the vaccination. The vaccine itself produced the mutation into HIV IV.

Dr. Cramer has convinced me that this information will ruin Cramer Chemical. When I think of all the people who are dying now, the guilt I feel is almost more than I can bear. Oh Robert, can you imagine it? What have I done?

And what have I done to you? You are such a dear friend, such a beautiful guy. I know how hard it has been taking care of me. You have worked so hard. It can't be easy for you to watch this deterioration. And God, Robert. If I gave this disease to you, there wouldn't be a torture in hell bitter enough for me. I love you more than I can say, Robert, and I can't continue to put you through this suffering. I know you will understand. I want you to try to be happy when I die, will you promise me that?

The suicide clause in my life insurance is long past so you shouldn't have too many financial problems. Dr. Cramer has promised to look after you for me. He's even told me he'll offer you a position in his office if you like.

Please don't blame me Robert. I did the best I could. I'll love you as long as my spirit survives. Perhaps I'll be a better friend in the next life. Good bye dear Robert." The Cramer Caduceus filled the screen above the record of transmission data.

If only Martin Cramer had given him the message as Michael had said. It would have made Michael's suicide understandable somehow, ended a chapter in Robert's life and enabled him to move on. Cramer had denied him the chance of such reconciliation, and Robert was determined to make the bastard pay for his evil.

Martin Cramer seemed to acquiesce in the meeting Robert had demanded with his boss, but in the pharmaceutical industry it was said that when you sat down to talk with Martin Cramer you had better count your fingers before you left the room.

Robert didn't trust the easy victory, the slick reassurances. He knew Cramer was only stalling and the deadly virus poisoning his blood left a very little window of opportunity for action.

It had begun almost imperceptibly at first, the sense that the room was too hot, that his shirt sticking to his skin. Robert ran his hand over the soaked bed sheets and realized again that they had nothing to do with nightmare. The night sweats were routine now and he knew the virus was replicating furiously. Unlike its predecessors, the new AIDS virus was a far more virulent microbe. The gene regulating expression of the disease had mutated catastrophically, greatly decreasing the latency period for the disease. The onset of AIDS was now a matter of months, not years, once a person had been infected. Robert knew he was doomed, but he planned to settle a few accounts if he was about to join his friend in the brotherhood of Blue Death.

Though exhausted, he got into the shower and began to get ready for his trip. The 6:45 train would get him to Washington by late afternoon. But it wouldn't matter if he were a little late. When he first called the Office of Research Integrity at the National Institute of Health, the Director had wanted him to come immediately. More than any scientific wrong doing, the government office was crucially interested in hearing what the young whistle blower might tell them that might help end the new plague Michael Riley had introduced to the world.

Mossad

David Schefflan sat at the quiet end of the Koloniki where the tables along the sidewalk were sparsely populated. A few matrons, dolled up in rouge and mascara like children playing make believe ladies at a tea party, and two ancient homosexuals eyeing the young men passing by were the only other customers. Further down, crowded cafes lined the street corner where a modern sculpture of winged victory in combat boots holding a mandolin marked the favorite meeting spot for hoards of chain-smoking students and American tourists. The fashionable square was particularly alive in the spring, all of young Athens swooping in on motorbikes like swallows diving for insects at twilight. Not even a global AIDS epidemic could dampen the Greek's love of the promenade, though facemasks were often worn by cyclists and pedestrians alike. Some students flaunted the epidemic by wearing skull masks like so many grim reapers flying through the square on Vespas and mopeds.

David Schefflan often came here after work and sometimes found a Greek poulet of his own to join him for a drink or dinner. It was rare for the popular young American not to run into a friend along the strip of cafes, and Schefflan knew it was risky to bring the report he carried in his briefcase to the busy social center of Athens. But he hadn't had a moment to himself since the Ambassador had assigned him to the negotiating team and sitting alone with his back to the wall drinking an ouzo might in fact be a fairly safe place to review the material he had brought with him. Good camouflage perhaps.

It was logical that the Public Affairs Officer on the scene would be brought into the kidnapping, of course. They would need a capable pressman to deal with the media, balancing the public's right to know with the danger of providing a podium on which the terrorists could legitimize their actions. David's experience as a journalist would enable him to give the hostages a face, especially since the green eyes of one of those faces had lately begun to haunt him so.

David would be able to keep a check on the more competitive reporters who were always after a scoop. But most important, Mossad would have an inside view of how the crisis was developing and what dangers Israel faced should the west decide to make any concessions to the Arab scum.

He wasn't always so intent on defending the homeland of Israel, of course. When he was an undergraduate at Georgetown's Foreign Service school, he never thought of Israel as the homeland. He was aware of the intellectual and cultural heritage Judaism provided him, and he was not adverse to showing his ID card to the Jewish Mafia if those connections could give him a head start as he made his way in the world. But David entered college as a skeptic, nurtured by all the Philip Roth novels he had turned to in high school to help him make sense of what it meant to be a Jew in America. He espoused a kind of personal Zionism, where one was responsible for his own survival. He had no need for the State of Israel or a Holocaust Museum to show him how to live his life. He was not a survivor of Auschwitz. He felt no melancholy for the destruction of the temple or the exile from Spain. Culturally, yes, he was a Jew. He claimed Freud and Einstein, Rash and Maimonides as his cousins, but he was not devout. He didn't require religion for self-validation. He didn't feel the need to seek visions in the Negev wilderness, or contemplate God's being in the hills of Galilee. The coastal plain of ancient Philistia did not stir his heart. He was not swayed by Jewish history or orthodox economic philosophies and politics. He did not think capital was evil. He was not particularly inspired by the dumpy little Israeli politicians with their thick Yiddish accents, carping at the United Nations.

David was rather the model of assimilation, a Nietzschean superman newly sprung up on American soil. His dark good looks were refined over the adolescent years with expensive orthodontics, contact lenses, and some elective plastic surgery in the process of correcting a deviated septum. Whether it was a genetic fluke or just good nutrition—his father couldn't decide—but by the time David was a freshman at college, the boy was already a head taller than any male of memory in the Schefflan family tree. Or any uncle or grand sire on his mother's side, for that matter. His height augured tennis, of course, not basketball, and his parents enlisted the local pro for private lessons the minute David showed an aptitude.

Though his mother remained calm and dignified the day he left home for prep school, once the driver had pulled slowly down the lane and he could no longer see her wave goodbye, the grief she felt at the loss of her dark haired angel provoked a flood of private tears. Only her love for him enabled the sacrifice. At the Gunnery David would get a fine education and make the sort of friendships that would sustain him his entire life. It was one of the schools the powerful old boys attended when they were still young boys on their way to the top.

Those prep school years had flown by quicker than a May fly's courtship, and by the time David began cruising the Georgetown campus in the Mustang convertible his grandmother had bought him for graduation from the Gunnery, he pretty much had his pick of young coeds to satisfy a hormonal system that had gone into overdrive.

David didn't hide his religion, but he always managed to disappear when the guys in the dorm got into one of those discussions lasting late into the night after someone's grandfather died, or they tried to decipher Whitehead and Wittgenstein for Philosophy 103, or the time abortion became anything but academic for an unfortunate classmate who'd gotten himself in a paternal way. If David professed any belief it seemed to come closest to the conventional agnosticism with which most college freshmen hedged their bets as they first began to encounter life's complexities.

When his roommate invited him home for the Easter Break it became clear to everyone that David was Jewish and needed rather to be home for the family's Seder at Passover. Every year since he made his debut in public speaking at the family table, his was the job of asking the family patriarch the four ceremonial questions.

"Why is this night different from all other nights of the year?" "Why tonight do we only eat matzoh?"

For thousands of years Jews had celebrated the flight from Egypt, but David wasn't convinced that Moses had done such a great job leading his people. What freedom was to be found in the State of Israel when anarchy ruled the land, the freedom to shoot a terrorist before he fire-bombed your house? Just as well that Moses never made it to Jerusalem.

"It would have been sufficient," they sang in the *Dayeinu*, "If God had taken us out of Egypt, but not split the Red Sea, it would have been sufficient." But from David's point of view God had indeed sent a sea of blood washing over Israel and David wasn't about to get swept up in that tide. He'd take his chances in cultural wastelands of the good old USA.

Early in his sophomore year, David's roommate transferred to the business school and found an apartment of his own a little closer to his classes there. It was logical that they should part company, it would have been neurotic to ascribe the move to anti-Semitism on his roommate's part. But David sensed that a slight uneasiness had entered into their friendship from the date of that failed spring break invitation. It was like looking into the face of someone who you had known for years, suddenly realizing that one of the friend's eyes was green and the other blue. A small thing, but as easy to overlook as Adam and Eve's nakedness in the garden once they'd had a bite of the apple of knowledge. The more you tried to focus on both eyes and pretend you saw nothing out of the ordinary, the more your discomfort blazed up in your face, until it became like trying to hide a forest fire from the oddly pigmented irises trying to understand the curious awkwardness which had just burst into flame in front of them.

David wasn't naive about anti-Semitism. You couldn't grow up in America without it hitting you smack in the face at some point early on. He was six years old playing in the school yard when he first heard the word "Kike" and had to ask his teacher what "like" meant. He learned to take care of himself when gangs of little Italian thugs auditioned for the Mafia by beating up on Jew boys in his neighborhood. Once, before his family moved away from Brooklyn they caught him and beat the meaning of the word into him properly after class in the school yard. He'd been insulted on plenty of playing fields since.

Still, he wasn't intimidated by the non-specific hatred that the word *Jew* automatically generated in some people like an odorless, lethal gas seeping into the room. David knew what he wanted and wasn't going to be deterred by this particular occupational hazard on his way to success. He was so gifted, so talented that he didn't mind playing the game with a handicap. On occasion, he could even use such irrational hatred to his advantage.

David never really understood the Zionist fervor that animated his uncles' arguments sitting around the family table during the holidays. Ultimately, a Jew's rights were protected by law in America, unlike the institutionalized anti-Semitism so many of his ancestors had fled in Europe and Russia. On paper, the democratic ideal celebrated ethnic diversity, religious freedom, and separation of church and state. When that ideal broke down in hate crimes or illegal discrimination, Jews could appeal to the courts. That's all David cared about, a level playing field. It didn't matter what sort of epithets he might hear on that playing field along the way. Besides, he rarely had any trouble charming his way into whatever social circle he set his sights on. He was a good dresser, a good dancer, and told better Jewish jokes than any *goy* at the country club.

The change in his roommate that spring during freshman year still baffled him, but he decided to ignore his misgivings, to rise above such insecurity when it threatened to sidetrack him from his goals. By the end of his sophomore year, his good will and emotional discipline was rewarded with the most profound friendship that he had yet experienced in his young adult life. And because it was an earned friendship and not just the genetic luck of the draw, it transcended even the love he felt for his own family.

Years later, sitting at a cafe in Athens David studied several young men at the next table, oblivious to the world passing by, lost in politics, taking light only from each others eyes. He remembered the three extraordinary friends for whom, during those magic years at college, he'd have given his very life. And he remembered how finally those friends had led him into the ranks of the Mossad.

They were so inseparable, their classmates friends called them the Four Musketeers. If they hadn't been quite so successful with the women on campus, the rumor mills might have made even more of their relationship. The degree to which they shared college life was intense, even by fraternity brothers standards. But theirs was a private fraternity, with an exclusive membership of four.

David ran into the first of the brothers, literally, during an intramural soccer match. It was a fierce, inadvertent body check which sent Paul Kingsley sprawling on the field. David was terrified that he might have killed the fellow, the freckled face grew red as his carrot hair, then purple with the effort of trying to get his breath back. When he was finally able to speak, Paul looked up at his petrified teammate, smiled and said, "Nice block."

Paul's roommate Clarke was the son of the senior Senator from the state of New Mexico, John Wagner. Clarke was the smallest Musketeer, like his father, short and stocky, but he was strong and a sure bet to make varsity crew by his junior year if he could keep up with the rigorous training schedule. Having a Senator father who chaired the powerful Senate Finance Committee wouldn't hurt Clarke's bid for the varsity squad either. Georgetown men learned to respect the importance of social status early on in the informal education process of athletics. Like cubs in a wolf pack, they learned in play who would dominate and where they stood in the hierarchy of the pack. From the minute they entered their freshman dorms, the four musketeers emanated the aura of pack leaders, each in his own way.

Clarke's best friend at Andover was Philip Hull and they had gone on to Georgetown together after prep school. Their fathers had served together in WW II, making the friendship between their sons a second generation affair. It was common knowledge inside the Beltway that Senator Wagner was pressing the President to appoint Philip's father to replace an ailing Justice O'Connor on the Supreme Court.

The four classmates did everything together. They signed up for the same core classes and had their own private study group. They ate together, cheered the Hoyas on to victory together. If they managed to convince their parents, they planned to move out of the dorms and rent a house so they'd soon be living together as well. The musketeers had their own table at the Tombs where they settled all the world's burning questions over brew and burgers. There was only one law at the round table when they met, *"sempre veritas."* They vowed to tell the truth, no matter how difficult or painful that might be. Their friendship was a little island in a sea of sham and superficiality that seemed to widen the longer they took in the vista at Georgetown. They could be a genuine sounding board for each other and didn't need to shoot the messenger when one of them felt impelled to give some bad news. They cut through the hypocrisy with the idealism and self-assurance typical of college sophomores and were appropriately skeptical about what they were learning in their classes.

Yet when it came to their own fraternity, and the break up their friendship after graduation, they saw reality through the rose colored glasses of a romantic adolescent reading the *Tale of Two Cities* or *Treasure Island* for the first time.

It went without saying that they would one day assume important leadership roles in society. Clarke and Philip seemed destined for domestic political careers, David and Paul leaned to Foreign Service. Unlike some classmates, they were all sure they would live beyond age thirty, but they were struck with the melancholy of aging that strikes so acutely when one is in the fullest bloom of youth. They were refined enough to see how beautiful they were, physically and in the quality of their devotion to each other at that exact moment in their young lives. And they were smart enough to discern the corruption of the rose underlying their pleasure in life.

In self-defense, they determined to spend two years together after graduation, savoring their friendship, sharing exotic adventures before they settled down to law or graduate school, marriage and the responsibilities of the real world which awaited them. Paul's recent good luck inspired the plan when he inherited his uncle's ninety-foot yacht, named the *Whiplash* for all the cases his lawyer uncle had settled out of court to pay for the vessel. Paul was always his favorite nephew and on a whim he had written the boy into his will before one too many martinis and a spill overboard in the Bahamas the previous year turned him into fish food.

The four comrades planned to sail the ship over the seven seas before acquiescing to the demands of the real world. One night after exams and a large bottle of Jack Daniels, they decided to seal the plan with a blood oath. David felt silly, elated, proud, even physically excited, with his sliced index finger entwined with those of his friends bleeding into a small pool of bright blood at the center of his desk.

They had had the bad judgment to outline their plan at Senator Wagner's dinner table, however, the week the four of them convened at Clarke's home in New Mexico for a hiking trip.

"Assuming you had the sailing skill to make such a trip," the Senator asked over cognac and cigars in the library, "how would you plan to go about financing this expedition?"

They looked out into the desert, a pitch black ocean flowing beneath the senator's stucco fortress in the mountains outside Santa Fe. His grandfather had built the family castle, rising like Bishop Lamay's cathedral, long before all the nutty artists and star gazers had taken over the town and turned it into a New Age Mecca.

"Well, we can hire on as crew for a year," David ventured. "We can earn money and get the experience we need at the same time. The *Whiplash* is there waiting for us. Paul and Clarke are already good sailors, but maybe we could hire a captain and haul cargo to make it a paying operation as we go."

David looked around at the others, pleased with this last spontaneous notion.

"You're dreaming, son." The senator chuckled for emphasis. "The yearly maintenance alone on a ship that size would pay for your tuition next year and then some. Besides our old friend Dean Howells won't be at Harvard Law School forever Clarke. We don't want him to retire on us while you're off hauling mangos from Tahiti to Greenland, now do we? No, I'm afraid Clarke won't be joining you on the trip."

The senator might have been less amused with a little less *Corvoisier*, David might have found him more amusing with a little more perhaps. No one had called him son since the third grade. He felt his face flush with anger and embarrassment as though he'd just wet himself in front of his friends and ruined the Senator's velvet couch.

"Maybe Clarke isn't interested in law school right at the moment," David said. "It's his life after all." He could feel his heart beating at his temples. "Maybe he'd like to make his own decisions about his future."

Few grown men dared to contradict John Wagner this blatantly in the United States Senate, let alone his own home. But John Wagner hadn't gotten this far in life by always saying in public what he had a mind to say.

"When it's time I'm sure Clarke will do the right thing," the senator said calmly. "The people of New Mexico are waiting for another member of the Wagner family to take a seat in Congress, and Clarke's not about to disappoint them any more than he is me. But you're right David. It is his life. So I'll amble out of here now and let you boys plan your itinerary."

It all happened so fast. The patriarch rose amiably, dignity in tact, leaving David holding the bag for his rude remark.

"Don't drink the bar dry now, you hear."

David watched incredulously as the old man put the palms of his hands on Clarke and Paul's heads in blessing like a born-again preacher about to shake some sense into a couple of thick skulls as he cried "heal, heal in the name of Jesus." The patronizing gesture revolted David. If the old fart tried to handle him that way, he'd knock him down.

David hoped that he might show off one of the musketeers to his family and friends in Connecticut during the winter break, but it seemed all three had to sit around the Christmas tree with their own families to reassure mothers in the midst of the empty nest syndrome. And if they were loving sons during the vacation, Santa might just give them permission to move off campus next semester.

Several weeks after the Christmas break Paul came to David's dorm unexpectedly.

"Hey Davie, got a minute," he said sticking his head into the room.

"Yeah sure, Paul. What's happening."

"Listen, David. About the Christmas vacation. I mean, I'm sorry I couldn't ..."

"That's okay. You'll just have to come next year. My mom makes the ultimate turkey, and you get matzoh ball soup to boot."

"Well, that's what I wanted to talk about David. You see, I didn't go home for Christmas."

"You didn't?"

"Actually, I spent the holiday with Clarke."

"I thought..."

"Senator Wagner decided to take this fact finding boondoggle to East Africa to check out endangered species in the some of the game parks in Kenya and Tanzania and he asked me and Clarke along for the ride."

"Right."

"Well, actually, he asked Philip too."

"Philip? You mean the three of you were in Africa together without..."

"I feel really shitty about it, David. You see, I guess Senator Wagner was pretty upset when you called him out in Santa Fe that time and he told Clarke that if you came along the trip was off for us."

"Why didn't you say something?"

"Well, no one wanted to hurt your feelings."

"Or give up a trip to Africa."

"It was the chance of a lifetime. No one thought you'd find out."

"All for one and one for all. Jesus. All the old bastard had to do was take you for a spin through the jungle to have you eating out of his hand. I thought you were my friends. I thought we weren't going to put up with all the bullshit. I thought we were better than that."

"I said I feel bad about it. I couldn't keep it a secret from you. Besides, it didn't turn out to be all that great a trip anyway. Turns out Clarke's old man has a broom up his butt about Jews, for some reason. Believe me it wasn't much fun. He kept going on about how pushy you were that night in Santa Fe, how we were ruining our future if we took off a couple of years after graduation. I finally told him off myself. I couldn't believe it, him being a senator and all."

David took in his words, refusing to respond, drumming a pencil on the desktop.

"Listen," Paul said, "Why do you think I came here. I didn't want to have to make up a bunch of lies about what I did over Christmas."

"You mean like Phillip and Clarke."

"Yeah, I guess so."

"Well, thanks for telling me."

"This doesn't have to change anything." Paul attempted to put out his hand but David just sat like a stone.

"I'm going to want some time to think this through."

"Yeah, sure."

"Just close the door, will you. I gotta get ready for this history quiz. I'll catch you in the cafeteria later."

When Paul left the room, David put his forehead down on the desk for a minute. He was very tired of studying, felt a stinging in his eyes. Now he had some of his own history to contemplate. He imagined his three friends roaring around the game parks without him, chasing down rhinos and elephants in Land Rovers, camping in the park lodges, rummaging through the markets of Nairobi, sailing a dowel off Mombasa. He remembered how much he wanted one of them to come visit Westport for Christmas, how bored he'd been during the vacation. When he had called the Hulls to wish Philip a happy holiday, his mother just said Philip wasn't available. Their conspiracy was stunning. Philip's mother would actually lie for him? He realized he was just an extra wheel on the little wagon of their friendship as he stared down at the spot on his desk where only last year his brothers had let their blood flow together and promised lasting friendship.

When he had reached puberty, David gradually relinquished that loving intimacy a little boy feels for a father as a new sense of privacy grew in him. But occasionally, when something very personal went wrong that he couldn't sort out on his own, David returned, ego in hand, to ask for a little help from his dad. The weekend after Paul's visit, he found himself sitting with his father in the kitchen at Westport trying to make sense of what had happened to his life.

"It's not the end of the world, David," his father said. "Here, have a bite."

His wife had gone to the hairdresser and he had quickly fried up the forbidden egg sandwich topped with Swiss, his favorite, with which he indulged himself on rare and guilty occasion.

"Your friends just made a lousy decision. They're young. It happens all the time when you're young. But it doesn't mean they don't like you anymore. They told you they were sorry, didn't they?"

"Yeah, after the fact."

"I know your feelings are hurt. But give it some time. Things take time. You don't want to cut off your nose to spite you face, do you?"

Howie Schefflan had made a very comfortable living on Wall Street, largely on his talent for batting the breeze. "Your dad could live on the chit chat of his chit chat," a family friend once told David. He was a regular guy and people liked him, trusted him. But David was an English major now and the Wall Street rap, as he called it with a superior air, irritated him.

"You don't understand. The four of us were different. We promised we'd never lie to each other. It was, it was a sacred trust. What they did was totally calculated. Old man Wagner just bought them off plain and simple, the way he buys off his opposition in the Senate. We said we'd never prostitute ourselves to the system that way. We were going to live our lives with integrity. We were supposed to spend our junior year in France next year, we were going to sail..."

"David I respect your idealism here, but sometimes you have to compromise, to survive. I mean, I don't go where I'm not wanted. If these boys don't want to be your friend, then the hell with them. You're a great kid and you don't have to take a back seat to anybody. But they have apologized. Don't you think you're being a little severe on them? People are human. If you burn all your bridges you're going to wind up a very lonely guy."

"I can't go on my junior year abroad with them next year, not the way things are now."

"Look David, why don't you give it a little breathing space. I know it's an awkward situation for you, but you can't let it destroy your self- confidence. I have an idea. What do you think of this?

Why don't you go visit Uncle Joe in Tel Aviv this summer. He's wanted you to come ever since your Bar Mitzvah. I know you don't buy his politics, but it won't hurt you to see first hand what the Israelis have accomplished over there. You might even approve. If you plan to be in Foreign Service you've got to make up your mind about Israel sometime. And Uncle Joe will give you plenty of practice at being a diplomat. When you come back, maybe you'll see things a little differently. If you still don't want to go to Europe with your friends, then that's the end of it. At least you'll have thought it through. What do you say?"

So, David went off to Israel, and as his father warned him, from the minute the El Al jet landed at Ben Gurion Airport his uncle held forth non-stop on the miracle that God was working in the homeland of the Jews. At first David played devil's advocate, pointing out that while the original settlers might have transformed the desert, by now all the construction going up was being built by Arab workers, that every dirty job in the country from sewage disposal to ditch digging was done by Palestinians, jobs no self-respecting Israeli would even consider. The two cultures depended on each other, the one for work, the other for cheap labor to a degree that would never permit Israel to return to the heroic early days when Israel was founded. The occupation had imprisoned them both.

After a couple of weeks with his cousin Aharon on Kibbutz Gallel near the buffer zone in the north, David was singing a slightly different tune. The young families who had moved to this colony with their children lived under perpetual threat of terrorist attack from radical groups who refused to recognize the peace accord. But the settlers faced that threat with defiance, pride. The world would see here that Jews would no longer wither in the face of intimidation. "Never again," was the motto by which they lived. The Holocaust was an act of inhumanity beyond forgiveness or compensation, but their courage and hard work counted for something. It was like a prayer in the physical world for the millions of ghosts who deposited their ashes in the mud of Dachau and Auschwitz before rising to Abraham's bosom.

David learned how to shoot a gun, and though he considered handguns one of the root causes of violence back in urban America—last year he had even joined a protest against the NRA at their headquarters in Washington—he couldn't deny the exhilaration he felt, the sense of power each morning when he tucked the automatic pistol into his jeans and headed for the mess hall. As in any frontier town in the old west, guns were a necessary evil, he reasoned. Attack could come across any border and despite stiff military reprisals, a demented Arab might pick up a butcher knife and make a suicidal attack on a passerby. Political arguments here were a question of life and death, not empty palaver spewed out over chicken and peas at campaign fund raisers. There was nothing hypothetical about the bomb that killed two schoolteachers in Lod the week he arrived in country or the bus attacks that occasionally terrorized the citizens of Tel Aviv or Jerusalem. Taking control of one's physical safety in an environment where one could easily die if he weren't careful produced the first slight movement in what became a transforming paradigm shift in David's life. By the end of his summer in Israel, all the rules had changed.

David had never met young Jews like the friends who were carving out a new life in Kibbutz Gallel, strong, optimistic, self-assured. For them giving up land was a rebellion against Moses. There was no gray middle ground in a world where one struggled for one's very survival. You learned to trust your instincts. In the fields, the first week, an almond-eyed Sabra girl watched him all day and came to him that night in his monk-like cell. They barely spoke. There were no games, no seduction, no guilt. She wanted him, he wanted her. Simple as breathing.

Each day David came back exhausted from the vegetable harvest which had just begun in the village when he first arrived in country. It was back-breaking work, harder than anything he'd ever experienced before in his life. But the camaraderie of it dissolved the studied sophistication he had cultivated at Georgetown. He sang the work songs along with his new friends in Hebrew, his heart filled with the simple joy of hard work, a common purpose. He was a Jew and that was the end of it. His destiny was tied to that of his people. There was more meaning to life than sustaining his little ego. There was no need to prove himself, or earn anyone's respect anymore than one justified membership in the life of a family. Friends were fine, but when he went to Israel, David became a member of his own tribe once again.

Snorkeling in the coral grottoes of Eilat that summer, he'd come face to face with a Moray eel one day, the poisonous teeth frozen in a deadly smile. His spear missed the serpent, and the creature slid back into its cave and did not pursue him. But David had stood his ground. He was proud of himself, proud of his courage. He'd spent his whole life learning the art of compromise, accommodation, learning how a Jew swam in a sea of non-Jews. But that summer David heard the first sweet notes of the dolphin's song swimming in the aquamarine waters off the Negev's southern coast.

Like a 19th century English gentleman making the grand tour of Italy and Greece to savor heritage of western civilization, David set out to discover the Jewish homeland and his newfound identity. He visited the mountain fortress of Masada where a nine hundred and fifty Jews committed suicide rather than submit to the Roman legions besieging them. In Jerusalem he stood among Jews from all over the world in silent reverence before the Wailing Wall, teaching himself how to pray. He listened for God's response in his heart, as though these ancient rocks could transmit God's plan will for him, reveal to him what he must do with his young life. He wandered the Orthodox section of the city, Mea She'arim, watching the people get ready for the Sabbath, despite the stone throwing Arabs trying to turn Israel into the monster Goliath in their bid for world support of a "Palestine" encompassing Jerusalem.

Israel had paid an exorbitant price in Jewish blood to recover their ancient capital. The Arabs could sooner part the Dead Sea than divide this very foundation of Judaism which went back to biblical times. "When Arabs pray, they pray to Mecca. When Jews pray, they pray to Jerusalem," Uncle Joseph was fond of saying. The status of Jerusalem was non-negotiable. It would be the undivided capital of Israel for eternity.

"Remember the Psalms, David," Uncle Joe said. "If I forget thee, O Jerusalem, let my right hand forget her cunning. If I do not remember thee, let my tongue cleave to the roof of my mouth."

That summer David found his voice. In Herzliyah, north of Tel Aviv Uncle Joseph had shown David an out of the way monument on the grounds of the Center for Special Studies. Gigantic angular blocks of sandstone formed a labyrinth of five alcoves, each representing a period in Israel's history. On the walls were inscribed the names of 360 fallen comrades from all three branches of the intelligence community, Mossad, Aman and Shin Beth. There was Jacobi Bokai, the first to die in 1949, executed in Jordan, members of the team that captured Eichmann in Latin America, an Israeli diplomat, Yakov Bar Simantov, murdered outside his home in Paris. How many more had died whose heroism in defending the nation must remain forever secret.

"Operation Pay Back, the raid on Entebbe, the liberation of the Al Aqusa hostages. None of these would have succeeded without their courage, " Uncle Joseph insisted. "Who do you think got the uranium for our nuclear weapons? You think the world would simply hand it over or agree to sell it to Jews? Who do you think finally brought justice to the assassins who butchered our Olympic athletes in Munich? Would the German government or the world court have acted so efficiently? You remember your Old Testament, David,' Uncle Joseph asked. "And Moses sent them to spy out the Land of Canaan... and see the land, what it is; and the people that dwelleth therein, whether they be strong or weak, few or many." From the beginning of our history, we have been surrounded by enemies, but I sometimes think the greatest enemy is right in our midst. Some liberals in the Knesset would even sacrifice Jerusalem in the name of peace and security."

When David came back to Georgetown that fall his classmates observed a change in David more spectacular than brilliant fall foliage which had replaced the dull summer jungle lining the banks of the Potomac. David was on fire. Ethnic diversity had come into fashion on other politically correct campuses, but the Georgetown elite found it irritatingly anti-social that he would insist on his Jewishness by wearing a yarmulke to lectures, the library, even basketball games. It provoked an immediate if subtle ostracism, as though he had changed his skin color overnight. The more he persisted in celebrating his heritage, whether in political science class, or Anti Defamation League demonstrations against hate crimes and neo-Nazi activities in Germany, the deeper his isolation became. He would sit at the student center alone studying the Talmud, repeating the verses out loud sometimes just to hear Hebrew spoken in the middle of the wasp nest. It was not a fashionable "lifestyle" in the 1980's when *Self* magazine was extolling the Donald's comeback and featured articles on how to assure a comfortable retirement by age thirty.

Paul, Clarke and Philip had not been able to convince him to come along to France for their junior year abroad, and the few close friends he had on campus decided David was having some kind of identity crisis or nervous breakdown. It was as though he had called them all together and burned his membership card in that exclusive country club to which they had so magnanimously granted him admittance. David began to see his university as a microcosm for the larger anti-Semitism woven into the fabric of American society. No matter how august the hall, the Senate cloakroom, the Century Association, the Foreign Service Club, he always risked walking in on the tail end of a Jewish joke. These were the facts of life.

He might pass the Foreign Service exam and be given an entry-level position, but promotions would come grudgingly. The State Department was just another extension of the club. There were exceptions, of course, but someone like Henry Kissinger needed to be twice the man as any of his competitors to reach the top spot. The ground rules became embarrassingly clear to Madeline Albright when the *Washington Post* revealed her ancestry to the world and she became a Jew overnight.

David realized he was going to have a tough time if he refused to assimilate. A political career was out of the question unless he represented an urban district with a large Jewish constituency. He was terribly lonely thrashing it all out by himself, and his seclusion only fueled his paranoia.

Then in his senior year, David's world exploded, pushing him into the decision that would enable him to survive the disaster and change his life forever.

He had gone up to New York to surprise his parents and meet their plane on its return from Israel. Uncle Joe had suffered from angina for years, but his passing still seemed unimaginable. He was the favorite uncle, and the first real person ever to die in David's adult life. The death filled him with grief, but also a terrifying sense of his own mortality. It seemed that the little white pills and his uncle's passion for Israel would keep the man alive forever. David could have tried for permission to retake the semester exams and attend the funeral, but Uncle Joe wouldn't have wanted that. Like most Jews, Uncle Joseph's reverence for education was paramount.

There were direct flights but David's mother and father decided to connect through Germany so they could make part of the trip with cousin Yael who was returning to Munich after the funeral. David had given himself plenty of time to get to JFK, and so he couldn't believe it when he saw Pan AM Flight 103 listed as *canceled*. When he got to the information desk, all was pandemonium.

It is an ancient impulse. In Bulgaria there is a necropolis 6000 years old where the graves contain only swords and shields for soldiers lost abroad. A mother must see the stillborn infant to enable the grieving process, a memorial must be held for the sailor lost at sea before his widow can live her life again, the husk of an Alzheimer's victim must blow away before the loss can be truly imagined. And so, a year after the murder of his parents, David found himself standing once again at the Wailing Wall trying to make sense of their death and his life.

"I understand you are beyond our knowledge, your purposes are beyond our understanding. But I'm going mad with this anger. I can't get their image out of my mind, God. The fear and pain they must have felt when the plane exploded into flame. My dear mother, burning, falling through the sky. Oh mother, mother. No.

Why God, why did you have to let them die such a death. Why did you deny them an old age together. I am so lonely God, I can't bear it. A year has gone already, and the pain for me is like they died only yesterday."

He had used up all his tears months ago. David only stood in silence watching the devout Jews praying from the Torah. This was all that was left for him. His Judaism was the only thing that connected the meaningless dots of his life now. He remembered all the family celebrations, the tour of Israel with Uncle Joe, his first Seder. He remembered singing the final song of the Seder, the *Had Gaya*. He and his cousins loved this song best, a silly song really, like the song of the old lady who swallowed a fly, will perhaps die. But in the *Had Gaya* a stick beats the dog, fire burns the stick, water quenches fire, an ox drinks the water, a butcher kills the ox, the Angel of Death takes the butcher, and finally God himself comes and slays the Angel of Death. Uncle Joe never lost the chance to explain the riddle.

"For this is a song of warning, you see," he heard his uncle repeat, "how those who would harass or subjugate the Jewish people will be destroyed by others, until, in the end, God will vanquish the Angel of Death and redeem the whole world."

David surprised himself by weeping at the memory of his uncle and happier days when his family was alive. But he wept too for joy now. For in the memory of his uncle's words, at last David saw the purpose God had designed for him.

David would act as the Angel of Death for the enemies of Judaism, those who would bring fire and destruction to the skies. He would avenge his parents' death and be the strong right arm of the nation of Israel.

Before returning to graduate school in the United States, he made some discrete inquires at the Institute for Intelligence and Special Services. It would be many more years of deep cover before he proved himself and actually met the Patriarch, as the head of Mossad was called. But David always marked that day, listening to God's voice in the brilliant October sunlight of Jerusalem, as a rebirth and the beginning of his life as a man.

David had admired Yitzhak Rabin when he first took office. The commander of the '67 war was strong and clever. He would consolidate Israel's gains and crush the *Intifadah*. A hundred thousand acres had been developed by settlers. Three thousand terrorists hideouts had been demolished. When Hezbollah continued to terrorize settlers in the north with Catechu rockets he had thundered into Lebanon with operation *Settling of Accounts*. He didn't ask permission, or make apologies.

Then with the surrealism of nightmare Rabin stood in front of the whole world shaking hands with a butcher who affected the role of respected political leader. With a foothold in Judea and Samaria, the PLO now had a legal base from which to launch terrorism on Israel and throughout the world. No tourist was safe, no settler.

David mourned Rabin's assassination, but only that an Israeli leader had been torn apart by bullets. He saw no hope in Rabin's martyrdom. "Saying peace, peace," Rabin's death proclaimed there is no peace. His vision would lead only the loss of Jerusalem and continued terror for the settlers in Judea and Samaria. Perpetual vigilance was the only answer, crushing the Hydra's head wherever it rose to strike at the heart of Israel. And now an even larger threat.

Islamic Rebirth had come out from under a rock and announced its intention to hold the world hostage to the AIDS epidemic, a dangerous tactic that might actually work.

David studied the carefully drawn up manifesto that had come through the Greek mails to the American embassy in Athens. The laboratory had found it clean of any useful clues, unfortunately. Whoever sent it was professional, carefully piecing the document together from tabloid newspaper typeset. Rubber gloves certainly, no trace of fingerprints. But what it had to say was even more disconcerting that how it had been put together. David read the melange of history, philosophy, Koranic scripture, and nationalist rhetoric with growing alarm. Their manifesto was clearly more than the ravings of a disgruntled cell from Hamas or Hezbollah.

Communiqué

"In the name of God, the merciful, the compassionate. No voice can rise above the voice of the Palestinian people, the spirit of the martyrs who have entered Paradise, knowing the peace of God's embrace and the certain future of their people on earth. We pledge to you, O symbol of martyrs and teachers of generations that we will be true to our vow and will continue to struggle and to fight until we realize all our people's aims and aspirations. The blood of martyrs will never be in vain. Either we court martyrdom or we will raise the banner for which you devoted your life over holy Jerusalem, the capital of our independent Palestinian state. It will be the same pledge and vow until we realize victory or court martyrdom on the path of freedom and independence.

Today we announce to the world that there is to be a new beginning for the people of Palestine, a rebirth of Islam in our historic homeland we will continue to purge ourselves of the false leaders like Arafat who have squandered the blood of our people for personal wealth and political power. What sacrifices have these leeches made, living in luxury out of harm's way all the years of our struggle while we were dying in the streets and our youth fought the Zionist armies with nothing but stones and bravery. What have we accomplished in the long decade since the PLO National Council concluded their treacherous agreements. Do the Israelis look us in the eyes and see a Palestinian people with its own history and aspirations? What was to have been the dawn of a Palestinian state has become instead its demise. Have we seen the restitution of lands stolen from generations of Palestinian farmers in Gaza, have we seen reparations for the destruction of our homes and our lives? The Zionists continue to "create facts" by expanding the settlements they have planted in our midst, islands of wealth and privilege sustained by the sweat and blood of Palestinian workers. Every year their illegal settlements grow like a cancer in heart of Jerusalem built on land stolen from the Palestinian people. By what right did the United Nations establish the Jewish homeland in 1947 in the very beginning? Was the Arab majority effectively consulted? What authority did resolution 181 hold, save the authority of power to force its will? Did Western guilt for the slaughter of Jews in Europe entitle the Allies to steal our lands and declare the state of Israel? The *Balfour Declaration* was simply a gross violation of the principle of self-determination. From the beginning the Palestinian majority had the right to defend itself against the rebellious Jewish minority who were trying to create a state of their own. The Zionists have always failed to understand a simple fact. They are ruling a foreign nation and that nation will no longer tolerate such subjugation.

Three generations later, have we achieved justice or security under the new autonomy? Do not the police remain as brutal as before, even if our own Arab brothers now fill their ranks? Do we control the waters flowing through our own land, or determine how the territories will be developed? Do we have embassies or free trade? Do we rule our own borders like any sovereign nation. Do we have the right of free passage to worship in the sacred city of Jerusalem? We long for thee, O fair Jerusalem, like water unto the parched earth of our homeland. For years the world ignored the slow economic slide of our people in Gaza and the West Bank, the withering of our very soul. The broken promises mean nothing to nations trying to escape the plague God has sent as a punishment for their injustices toward us.

It is time again for the voice of the Palestinian people to be heard. Our suffering, our cries for justice have gone unanswered because until now we had nothing the west needed. We had no oil, no influence, not even a shared cultural or religious identity that might have prompted some fraternal move to help us. We are a small people entangled in a huge global drama not of our own making, and until now, beyond our control.

It is time to stop temporizing and end half-measures. It is time for the West to see what it is like to be at the mercy of forces it can not control, to taste the bitter medicine on which we have fed for generations.

We insist on the right as affirmed by even your own United Nations resolutions to resist foreign occupation, colonialism, and racial discrimination as well as the right to struggle for independence. We will no longer tolerate the half measures taken over the years in a charade of peace and progress toward a homeland offered by the west and Zionist overlords. We demand full implementation of the *Palestinian National Council Political Communiqué* delivered before the treachery of Yasir Arafat (who had been Brother Abu Ammar) deepened the state of drift and degradation into which the Palestinian people have fallen."

It was clear to David as he began their list of demands that if this group succeeded it might just provide the sort of political and moral leadership that the PLO had failed to achieve, might even mend the broken vessel of Palestinian aspirations that Mossad had worked so hard to smash into shards.

Voyage

When the new arrivals finally settled into their seats and the train lumbered out of Penn Station, Robert relaxed his guard on his luggage and let the rhythm of the train lull him to the edge of day dream. He toyed with the idea of struggling up to the cafe car but he knew the lines would be long this soon after leaving the station, and he frequently had trouble keeping his food down since Dr. Shwartz had started him on AZN.

Despite researchers' initial optimism, whole classes of new AIDS medications such as BIRG 586, TIBO, the L drugs and protease inhibitors had failed to overcome the virus's staggering ability for mutation, and AZN, a recent cousin of AZT found to be effective in slowing down process of replication in the virus, was still the only drug able to arrest the course of the disease, even temporarily.

Cramer Chemical had set the world afire with the news of a vaccine cure developed by Mansur and Bourret, but even if the pubic relations hype were true, Robert doubted there would be time enough for it to offer him any hope.

He felt in his left breast pocket for the gold pill box he had engraved with the single word "always" and given to his friend in the months just before Michael died. It was another of the ironies that seemed routinely to work their way into Robert's life these days. Would he ever be able to stop ruminating on these ironies, stop torturing himself with what might have been. If only he'd had the chance to talk with his lover before Michael emptied the bottle of phenobarbital and taken his eternal sleep.

Yesterday Robert had filled the golden keepsake with his own prescription of AZN that Whit Bingham dispensed for him at the employee pharmacy. The gold piece passed through his fingers like a worry stone or lucky coin and Robert had worn down the inscription until it was barely legible. But he knew his luck would not hold forever, that one day soon he must pass on the amulet to some other unfortunate friend trying with magic to forestall a death that science could not stay.

AZN was even more exorbitantly expensive than the precursor AZT, though it cost Cramer only a fraction of the selling price to produce. As a good will gesture to employees, and to vindicate such price gouging, Martin Cramer had established a personnel policy offering it to employees free of charge. Robert would have preferred that everyone with AIDS receive the medication free of charge, but he was in no financial position to reject the public relations gimmick Cramer was offering. Despite the lawyer's efforts, Michael's life insurance company had managed to default on Robert's beneficiary payment because the death was a suicide. Michael had been wrong in his reading of the policy. Michael had never been very good about the nuts of bolts of domestic life, in fact. They joked about his being too young to be the absent-minded professor, but making ends meet since Michael's death was hardly a laughing matter now. He could just afford the co-payments at the HMO specializing in AIDS that he had been assigned to. Robert tried to be conscientious at first, but the sicker he got the less it seemed to matter. Would the oncologist tell him anything he didn't all ready know about the little purple bruises that were beginning to appear on his chest. He knew it was too late for him to hope for a cure, and at times the overwhelming nausea and exhaustion that went along with AZN seemed pointless. He was far from accepting his death, however. He must delay the inevitable for a few precious months. His anger burned like a bright star in him, sustaining life, leading him onward. He had work to do before death took him.

Robert considered handcuffing the briefcase to his wrist but decided that would only flag a prospective thief. He certainly didn't have the strength to run or fight off some kid who might try to snatch it. A mugger wouldn't think much of his prize - laboratory notes, a bound leather journal, but Robert held on tight to the attaché case as though he was clutching the Holy Grail. If he lost this briefcase it would mean the loss of millions of dollars for fellow AIDS victims and his mission to Washington would be a failure.

Decrepit factories like tired old dragons spewed filth and flame from their smokestacks dulling the horizon. Robert's train made its way through the black marshes of New Jersey, dead and boring as a lunar landscape. He caught his own reflection in the dirty train window, studying it as though it were that of a stranger. The hair was thinning, cut short. He had lost weight, but hadn't yet melted into the skeletal frame that marked a terminal AIDS patient like the yellow star or pink triangle worn at Auschwitz or Buchenwald.

Tiny crows feet danced at the corners of his eyes even when he wasn't smiling. A fading charm, but he still had the face of a boy. Sometimes at the bars, an older man would approach him and instead of trying to pick him up would ask gingerly what he had on his mind. "You look like you've lost your best friend," came the cliché one night some months after Michael's death. "I have," Robert said, attempting to smile. Despite the cupid's bow, a smile that made Robert something of a local celebrity in the old days, the boy's sadness was almost tangible. Even Martin Cramer was not completely impervious to the smile.

When Robert had requested a meeting, Martin suspected the flushed cheeks and somber demeanor meant Robert was trying to get up the courage to ask for a raise, perhaps a promotion. Martin's psychological makeup was that of the chameleon and part of him had almost come to believe in the fatherly relationship he had cultivated with the Robert. All these years later, the boy still seemed so lost. Then the shy smile when Martin had agreed to the meeting.

"What's up, Robert," he had begun in his best paternal tone. "I should say before you begin how pleased I've been with your performance over these past weeks in preparation for the board meeting. I know you've really worked overtime to make the meeting a success and I won't forget about your good work in your monthly performance review next week."

"This has nothing to do with my performance," the boy shot back, his face dark with anger. "It has to do with yours."

"Well, say what you've come to say," Martin said calmly. He

was surprised and intrigued, but years of experience warned him to be cautious now, to listen quietly while he assessed his position and designed his own strategy.

"I know everything," Robert blurted out.

"I'm afraid you'll have to be more precise, Robert. I'm not with you."

"Don't give me your modulated CEO bullshit. I know you've been covering up Michael's work on the AIDS vaccine. You whitewashed his death so no one would know the truth and threaten your precious stockholders. Scientists might have cured this disease by now if you hadn't kept his work a secret. I might have had a chance to live too."

Martin regretted his earlier decision not to wear a face mask for this meeting, and moved back slightly as Robert spoke. It was too great a risk, he decided, despite the intimacy such nonchalance projected. He made a mental note to wear the mask routinely in future public meetings.

"You've glorified Michael's memory to escape your own liability. Michael made an honest mistake and he died as a result. But you are to blame for millions of deaths all over the world because of simple greed. Well, now you're going to pay, pay plenty."

Martin remained impassive despite Robert's screaming at him, but took refuge behind his desk.

"What makes you think I would keep such information from the scientific community, Robert."

Martin's impassivity only angered Robert more.

"You bastard, I saw the video memo Michael left me before he killed himself. You didn't even have the decency to let me hear the last words he spoke to me before he died. It would have all made sense, I could have understood his death. He thought he was giving me a gift. He thought his death was a gift to me and you've ruined that gift." The boy broke down.

Martin dug his nails into the palms of his hands. How could he have forgotten to purge the system of that memo? He had worked nonstop putting out fires in the horrendous weeks after Michael Riley's death. He had stemmed the tidal wave but had forgotten this little chink in the dike, which threatened to let the whole sea come crashing in.

"A memo?" Martin asked. His tried to calculate the chances that the boy had not kept or made a copy of the tape.

"Yes." Robert whispered, exhausted suddenly.

"Look Robert, I don't know what to say."

"That will be a first."

"I realize it isn't enough to tell you I was wrong, that I'm sorry. I know how you must feel. But you have to remember how it was then. The sky was falling. I had some very big decisions to make and I had to make them fast. Fair enough, I was worried about the company's responsibility for Michael's research. Can you blame me for that? Do you know how many companies have been ruined by such legal claims?

"But don't forget that Michael and I were friends too. Who do you think first brought him to Cramer and launched him in his career? I cared about his memory too. He was an elegant scientist, one of the best we ever had. Nobody could grow a cell line the way he did. He had the magic touch. I didn't want his reputation dragged through the mud, and he was so terribly sick then. I'm sure he was suffering a clinical depression at the time. There was nothing on the horizon by way of a cure for his disease. He knew he was going to die, he chose to die. What right did I have to insist on more months of sickness and torture for him, let alone the scandal he would have had to face.

"And would you have forgiven me for letting him die. Would you have accepted his decision to commit suicide? I don't think so. Was I wrong to try to protect you from the terrible knowledge of his mistake in the laboratory? Was I wrong to let him end his life with some dignity?

"I promised Michael I'd try to help you after his death. Well, I tried to look after Michael's reputation as well. Will your life be any easier now knowing what Michael did, that despite his good intentions he turned his body into a breeding laboratory for a deadly new plague."

Martin had warmed to his task and was gratified to find his eyes fill slightly with tears as he spoke, the way an actor meditates on the death of a loved one to give some emotional authority to his role.

Robert looked at Martin and regained his composure, a pallor seeping into the boy's face as though a troll had just jumped up onto the bridge with him.

"I've never believed in real evil before. But I've seen it now. And believe me you will regret all these lies before I'm through. You see, Dr. Cramer, after I found the memo you concealed from me, I began to do my own little investigation in preparation for the board meeting. It really wasn't very hard to review the latest initiatives. I wondered why the joint venture with Akan in Switzerland got such little coverage in the annual report and then I discovered the cozy financial arrangement you have set up with the account in Bern. I wondered why you should have direct access to an account which has seen no movement on a project Akan seems to think is still in the planning stages."

"Robert let's be frank. I hardly think you can call yourself an expert in international finance. The Akan account we set up is a provisional arrangement in preparation for final negotiations. I'm sorry to inform you that in the real world large corporations very often must pay significant consultation fees to corporation executives to enlist their cooperation in complex projects."

"Why don't you just call a bribe a bribe," Robert said, unsure of himself now.

"The whole world does not necessarily do business according to the moral dictates of the United States of America, Robert. In fact, this sort of special compensation is standard operating procedure in most developing nations, most industrialized nations for that matter, particularly in Japan. Do you think we could sell anything in this country, arms, or grain or airplanes or aspirins if we didn't play ball by the rules which govern the real world?

Do you have any idea what sort of losses we have sustained since the government began regulating prices on our chief vaccines and anti-hypertensive. How do you expect us to complete research and development on products that might bring us out of the red without the cooperation of wealthy partners like Akan?"

"Well, then you have just hired yourself a special marketing consultant Dr. Cramer," Robert said. "And I've designed a major new promotion that's going to bring renewed credibility to Cramer Chemical. It will be a campaign to convince all those people dying of AIDS that you are indeed a philanthropist and not the treacherous, cold-blooded bastard I know you to be. The centerpiece of this campaign will be a very large corporate contribution, five hundred million dollars to begin with let's say, to benefit People with AIDS and ACT UP and the Elizabeth Taylor Foundation, and a couple of others. Then you are going to offer all existing AIDS medications produced at Cramer to patients at cost. Then you are going to...."

"I'm afraid we're not hiring special consultants today Robert. I think, perhaps you are more ill than you realize. Perhaps it is time for you to take a leave of absence."

"We'll see what you think of my campaign once I've spoken to the Director of the Office of Research Integrity at the National Institute of Health. I'm sure Dr. Davis will be very interested in what I have to say."

"The video memo proves nothing, Robert. Such technology was determined to be inadmissible in court years ago. We can simulate anything in the virtual reality lab. In fact, we have some very interesting footage of simulations you arranged with your lover and played out in the lab, if I'm not mistaken. Not my cup of tea, but fairly erotic stuff for some people I imagine. I doubt Dr. Davis will give you any serious consideration when he's seen your work in the laboratory. And I'm sure he's run across any number of blackmailers in his time at the ORI. Some unfortunate AIDS victims become delusional quite early in the course of their illness."

Robert's pale cheeks turned apple when he thought of Martin Cramer spying on his awkward attempts to hold onto the physical love he and Michael had shared in the virtual reality lab. He was furious at the invasion of his privacy.

"You son of a bitch. You think you have everything covered, don't you. Well I don't need the video memo to prove my case. After I saw the video I went through all the boxes of Michael's things once again, and I found them. I found Michael's notebooks. He had brought them home to work on and it's all there in his own hand. How he incorporated base pairs in a secret alphabet to spell out our names and mark the DNA of the viral strain he used in his vaccine, how he inoculated himself with that vaccine, his terror that he had created the pneumonic mutation, the sequencing trials which proved the disaster. Maybe this journal entry will help you see my point."

Robert handed him a photocopy of a page from the journal in Michael's handwriting.

October 25

Wild rains this morning, bitterly cold on the river when I go to feed the swans. The cygnets almost completely white when I saw them last, all the brown and gray disappeared, big as their parents. Winter surely here now. Have they migrated? I guess I have to face the fact I won't be here next summer to see if they return.

Martin Cramer has convinced me that I am right in my decision, shown me how my death will be the best solution for everyone. Why drag out my illness for poor Robert. I don't have the energy to face the scandal or what it will do to everybody. Finally, it seems I fear life more than I fear death. And at least he won't contract the disease from me. I only pray he'll come to forgive me. Dear Robert. But he is young, strong like the cygnets that have grown so big this summer. He will heal. If only I have the courage for it.

"You could have saved Michael. You're responsible for his death and a lot many more besides. If you don't cooperate in my little charitable program you won't only be facing bankruptcy. You will rot in jail for a long time to pay for your crime. I just want to see you make a little reparation before you face a jury. I understand the contamination rate for AIDS is nearly 100% in the prisons these days. Perhaps you'll get a chance to see what the disease is like personally."

"I see," Martin said, folding the paper and putting it in his pocket. "It won't be easy to arrange such transfers of money. I've got to obtain clearances, and contact the organizations you mention. You've got to give me a few weeks to see to it."

"A week, not a day more, or I go straight to the ORI and then the FDA, the board of directors, the press, the Attorney General."

"A week. Give my secretary the names of the parties who are to receive our corporate contributions."

"I'm glad you see the wisdom of this philanthropy."

"I don't waste time trying to change something when it seems inevitable."

Robert smiled to himself again when he recalled the sick expression on Martin Cramer's face the afternoon he first confronted him. It was no compensation for dying, but seeing that bastard squirm, beating him at his own game gave Robert more pleasure than he'd had in all the years since Michael's death. His psyche wouldn't permit much pleasure, these days. The guilt he felt over Michael's last days had only grown worse if anything.

Robert could ruminate for weeks on some detail, some oversight, some minor eruption of anger or frustration, directed at Michael, that made his illness even harder. If only he had a chance to relive those final days, to do it all over again. His obsession was a cancer in his soul threatening to consume what health or pleasure remaining for him in life.

"Revenge is mine, sayeth the Lord, revenge is mine sayeth the Lord." The stupid rubric played though his mind synchronized to the clacking rhythm of the wheels beneath him as the train gathered speed heading for Washington. Some days he was able to escape the obsessive thinking, like waking up refreshed after a night of dreams. Some days he was able to simply shut off the maddening rumination as easily as turning off a faucet. The mechanism was mysterious, however, involuntary. It was like the science fiction story he'd read once where the captain is bringing back a strange creature from space to a zoo on earth and in a horrifying moment is suddenly transported into the body of the creature when he hears it say, "Hello, I exchange with you my mind."

As the train carried him on his way to Washington, Robert felt himself in control for perhaps the first time in his young life. He hadn't waited a week, of course. He wasn't naive enough to take Martin Cramer at his word. The minute he had left the office he had immediately placed a call to the Director of the Office of Research Integrity, Dr. John Davis requesting an appointment.

"I've got to be very careful with this guy," Robert had thought to himself, "and not take anything for granted."

Azrael

"I've got to be very careful with this guy," Martin Cramer thought to himself as Robert had left his office, "and not take anything for granted." Perhaps the little bastard had told someone what he had in mind. It was certainly possible. But Martin guessed Robert would savor his victory a while before he sensed any need to provide insurance for himself and trust his secret to someone else.

The clock began ticking the minute the boy walked out of the office, however. Martin could begin to see all his years of careful damage control unraveling. He had to take a chance that it wasn't too late. He had no choice.

"Jenny, tell Whitfield Bingham to meet me immediately at the gazebo at the north end of DNA park," he said to the intercom. "I've got to check something in C Building and I'll meet him in the park on the way."

"Marty, what have you got up your sleeve this time," she said, the glass doors sliding securely behind her as she breezed into his office unannounced. She stood pouting in front of his desk like a Las Vegas show girl who had just been moved to the back of the chorus. She crossed her arms, pushing her breasts into enormous mounds under her white silk blouse. Her scarlet hair cascaded all about her shoulders the same way it did when he first hired her twenty years. She had auditioned for the job right there on that very desk, and occasionally, for nostalgia's sake, he had her cancel his appointments, and turn on his voice mail so they could relive that first encounter for the rest of the afternoon.

"Why do you surround yourself with these creeps," she insisted.

If she hated anyone more than Robert Owen since he was brought into the office as Martin's executive assistant, it was Whitfield

Bingham. She didn't understand why Martin tolerated this worm, even if his mother was on the Board of Directors.

His secretary was as close as Martin would ever get to having a wife, but there were any number of things he would never confide in Jenny. Aside from the creature comforts she afforded him, and he still found her as luscious as the day they first met, hot-eyed, determined to do anything to get hold of him and keep him, Jenny had become what would normally pass for a friend in anyone less egomaniacal and more capable of friendship than Martin Cramer. Over the years he hadn't been able to resist sharing his triumphs over competitors, a particularly elegant bit of blackmail, the secret rise of his personal fortunes. He supposed he would one day have to either marry her or murder her, but for the moment she had proven to be his most fiercely loyal employee. Her friendship was a bad habit he couldn't seem to get rid of.

"Jenny, just get me goddamned Whitfield Bingham, will you? I want to go over the new employee drug policy."

"In the gazebo, in the park? Give me a break," she said, but turned and walked into the outer office, head held high in disdain.

Martin didn't relish the idea of using Whitfield Bingham once again, but this was an emergency and there wasn't much time. He decided to take Jenny's advice however, and make this the last time Bingham would be called upon to go the extra mile.

When Whitfield Bingham first came to Cramer Chemical, it seemed like the ideal position for the young pharmacy school graduate. "Nice people don't know dentists," was the standing joke told at the Bingham dinning table, but it was clear his mother was only half-joking. Certainly, nice people didn't know pharmacists, but that is precisely what her little boy had become when he failed out of medical school.

Fortunately, her position on the Cramer Board of Directors enabled her to exert a little pressure and land him a position as chief pharmacist overseeing the various in-house pharmacies that served employees at the Cramer plant. She sent him through the most expensive rehabilitation programs in the country, and he still couldn't hold a job for two months without caving into drugs once again. She thought she could buy his sobriety and never subscribed to the philosophy that change would only ever come from within. She thought she would become physically ill as he stood there in front of and a group of total strangers, sheepishly mouthing the confession proscribed by his rehabilitation program. "Mother, I am a drug addict. I have hurt a lot of people and I need your help."

Rehabilitation program. Humiliation program was more like it. These days she was grateful if he could just remain functional and didn't cause any more scandal. Presumably, the position at Cramer Chemical solved the problem of safe supply, and for three years he had actually leveled off to the point where he was fairly successful at managing his seventy employees. Then came another relapse, of course, and Martin once again had to make a delicate decision on how to handle the little prince.

Martin Cramer had no desire to publicize that his decision to help the son of a board member who was a recovering addict had been a colossal failure. He took no punitive action when Whitfield Bingham was found verging on coma in the men's toilet on the basement floor of the main administration building. Martin had simply exiled him to a plush office out of the eye of the public, facilitating his addiction, tying him even closer to the Director.

The young man was now so totally dependent on Martin's good opinion that there was virtually nothing he wouldn't do to guarantee the cool certainty, the hip detachment that flooded through him when it was time to end the pain with a needle.

"Whit, you don't seem to understand," Martin scolded him as they sat in the little gazebo among box woods and weeping cherry and plum trees. "This isn't open to debate. If he succeeds in his blackmail, Cramer Chemical is finished. And you're finished. Can you think of another employer that would overlook your use of controlled substances, let alone provide you with a limitless supply. Look at it this way, the man already is dying of AIDS. How long do you think he can live. In some ways you'll be an angel of mercy. Do you remember the Tylenol murders from the early 1980's. Those murders remain unresolved. They are extremely difficult to track despite police intelligence systems and federal regulation. There's no way to trace such tampering to your office. He gets his AZN in the free drugs program. One capsule filled with Strychnine, that's all it will take. Everyone's problem is solved."

Whitfield studied a weeping dogwood tree, a cascade of white blossoms. How many times had Martin Cramer called him into his office for some special service? This time, murder. Yes. But what did it matter? Just another blossom from the tree, floating down to sink into the muddy ground, he decided. What did anything matter?

The young man had forgotten his jacket when the secretary called to order him to meet Martin Cramer pronto. Whitfield sat in just his long sleeved shirt, which he wore winter and summer to cover his tracks. Suddenly, he was intensely aware of the spring chill cutting through the thin fabric. Winter hadn't quite dissipated from the world just yet, despite Hermes' rising naked on his crystal pedestal over Cramer Chemical, a stupid symbol of hope incarnate.

"Okay," Whitfield Bingham told his boss, anxious to satisfy a hunger he felt seeping into him that could only be appeased in the privacy of his office. "Angel of Death. Why not?"

Pool side

He had never worked with a Bulgarian before, but Abdel knew what kind of woman Major Kostov would be even before he discovered she would be in charge of the operation. He had caught her glance several times during the conference, but they hadn't met until the morning he bumped into her on the elevator. He just managed to squeeze through the elevator doors rushing to make a panel session on the revised *Biodiversity Treaty* when he found himself alone and face to face with her.

She was a big woman, but had the sort of hourglass figure Victorian ladies achieved with the help of complicated under garments. She packaged her voluptuous body in bold, tight-fitting clothes, which were cut far too short for a woman hovering somewhere at around sixty years of age. She reminded him of the American and German tourists who flocked to the beaches from Tel Aviv to Rabat in search of an exotic Arab lover, dreaming of a sheik who would carry them off against their will into some desert oasis.

Schoolboys all across North Africa spent their summers looking after the fantasy life of these ladies. Sometimes the boys could barely grow a mustache, but the women didn't seem to mind their youth. The young men wore their soccer shorts to the beach and practiced passing the ball with great dives and dramatic saves to gain the women's attention. They let the ball fall too close to some lady's beach towel retrieved it with florid apologies.

Sometimes one of them got lucky and the woman actually carried him back to Munich or Brussels, enabling him to get a European passport before the affair broke up. More often, it was just a just a two-week honeymoon on the beach with some new clothes and a little extra pocket money for his efforts. The boys compared notes, learned exactly how to use their newly emerged virility. Each side got what it wanted, no harm done. The young Casanovas ate a little better in the summer and the tourists took their memories home to keep them warm through the winter.

There was a German doctor once, he remembered, who looked just like this woman on the elevator. She had brought him to her hotel room and insisted that he handcuff her to the bed. Then she ordered him to take off his belt and whip her. He was reluctant, refused at first and then only lashed half heatedly. She had begged for more and he complied. Despite himself, he grew sexually aroused as he satisfied her demands until he couldn't hold off any longer, threw away the belt, and took his own pleasure in the game.

Remembering her, he felt the beginning tightness of an erection and made awkward small talk to distract him from the daydream.

"You have your paper, your coffee, everything you need," he said, trying to smile politely as you would when commiserating with someone in the dentist's waiting room.

"I'm a rich woman," she said, her eyes taking in his expanding problem. "Well, maybe not everything I need."

She would not let him off and pressed the question by running her hands slowly down her thighs pretending to straighten out the folds of her dress.

"The conference hall always gets so hot by the afternoon session. I go the pool at five to cool off before dinner. It looks like you could cool off too," she said as the elevator opened at the lobby. "Five o'clock?"

When she walked into the restaurant and he realized this was his comrade from the KGB, he wished he'd never spoken to her on the elevator the previous morning.

"I missed you at the spa last night," she said, seating herself at his breakfast table. "That wasn't very gallant of you to miss your appointment."

"I'm sorry, the workshop session went longer than I expected."

"Well, I like to get to know my colleagues when I'm working on a project. I'll expect to see you there this evening then?"

She patted his hand in mock retribution and Abdel realized the price was going to be a little higher than he had thought to enlist the cooperation of the KGB for their mission.

Happily, she opened her briefcase and got down to business.

"Here are your tickets. After the conference you will come to our training center at Varna. A little vacation for you on the Black Sea. Very nice. You can practice your sailing and sit around the cafes flirting with the Czech and Ukrainian tourists, after you learn how to use explosives and handle a gun.

"I know how to shoot a gun. I did my training in Jordanian refugee camps."

"You call that military experience. Do you know anything about satellite surveillance? Can you use *plastique* or create the images of fear you'll need for this mission to be successful. Have you ever taken a hostage, or killed a man?"

"I'm a hydrologist, not an assassin."

"What do you think you are playing at? In an operation this small we can't afford the luxury of separating staff functions from line functions. Do you think we're going to risk our involvement with you unless you're well trained and prepared to exterminate these people if necessary. Get it straight. You're the head of this mission, the lead assassin. If your balls are smaller than your ambition you'd better tell me right now and stop wasting my time."

She took a small cigarillo from the silver case and handed him the cigarette lighter. He flicked a light at arms length, sullen.

"Your assistants are already waiting for you in Varna. They're seasoned technicians, and highly resourceful. They managed to lift weapons from the Sikouri military base and bomb two American Air Force officers and the Prime Minister's son-in-law without a trace. They even stole a bazooka launcher from the Athens War Museum in broad daylight. Use them if you're reluctant to dirty your hands."

Cigar smoke hung about her like a blue fog. She studied him a moment trying to discern what really lay behind his desire to take these people. Money? Power? Simple hatred of the Jews? Was he really stupid enough to be risking his life for a holy Jihad?

"We have a few pieces of equipment we think you'll be pleased to have along when you leave us. Scanners to break security of responding forces, grenades, rocket launchers, a clever little system that will electrocute the hostages if your defense is compromised. Everything you'll want from masking tape to machine pistols.

We'll work out the plan in detail in Varna, but I have one private consideration for you before then. November 17 generally makes little effort to win public support, but in this case they are willing to take responsibility. So, if you run into any unexpected difficulties before you declare your demands, you are authorized to kill the Greeks. Just make sure they are identifiable. But you are not to compromise your contact in Vouliagmeni. You are not to risk exposing her under any circumstances."

Abdel was surprised that he'd be working with November 17th. The terrorist organization had bloodied Greece for decades, but it normally shunned any overtures to join forces from leftist organizations, one of the reasons for its success over the years. Even more shocking, however, was the photo Major Kostov handed him of the woman who was to ferret them out of Greece once they had secured their hostages.

He hardly needed a photograph. The child-like vulnerability of the face set against the deliciously over-ripe body of a woman draped in black lace, it was a famous image, that of a modern day Helen who had launched no small amount of trouble for men in darkened movie houses around the world.

 Greece hadn't produced an international star of this caliber since Melina Mercouri perhaps, though Fotini Theodorou was more Medea than the daughter of Apollo. Her black hair streamed out like that of a fury, her heavily-mascaraed eyes blazed in a mask of white face powder, her trademark. She rediscovered black fingernails from the 1960's which turned her long elegant hands into two elegant tarantulas. She had revitalized the image of woman as vamp from the days when the first talkies were being made. Not a girl to bring home to mother, quick to dance for the head of John the Baptist.

Abdel thought it a nice irony that this woman who had so often played Matta Hari characters in her films proved to be the real thing off the screen.

Fotini's neighbors were used to seeing men of every description come and go at her villa in Vouliagmeni. The paparazzi had her sleeping with half of the men in Greece and such speculation in the tabloids was gasoline on the fire of her career. Few heads would turn if she received a young Arab houseguest for several weeks.

Abdel looked up nervously when a late diner entered, but the waiter taking down the coffee station at the far end of the restaurant informed the latecomer that the service had closed.

"The hotel is ours, don't worry. Every table in the room in monitored. The waiter will screen out any unwanted visitors. We're as safe here as at headquarters."

She reached into a folder and handed him a new passport.

"When you leave Varna, you become Walid Rihani, a Lebanese import-export businessman who is a buyer for wine, and agricultural produce. The Athens airport is far too risky for you right now. Every security force in the world is swarming over the place since Arafat's assassination. You'll have to take the train through Macedonia. Dimitri and Panos will help you get to Vouliagmeni when you get to Athens and will disappear until it is time. Yanis and Stavros are making preparations with Ms. Theodorou now and are waiting for you. The American Ambassador is scheduling a reception for the scientists on the twenty-fifth. Our source at Cramer Chemical says their itinerary includes a week of sightseeing in Athens before they go on to meetings with Akai Chemical in Lausanne. We'll move that week.

In Varna, Abdel had finally kept his pool date with Major Kostov. She did not have the exotic tastes of the German tourist from his youth, but she was as demanding. For two weeks they met at the luxurious spa reserved for party members and after he'd completed the specialized workout she put him through, they soaked in hot mineral baths and had meals the chef catered especially for her. He'd never been happier to leave a place in his life, but it had all paid off.

Yanis and Stavros held the two hostages in the back of the truck, trussed up like mummies, stowed in a secret compartment in the floor of the van. Their ransom would establish the City of God, the state of Palestine. In a few miles they would rendezvous with the ship in which they were to make their escape. He didn't want to gag them and bind them up like sheep at Aied but he had no choice, especially after she had recognized him.

She's hasn't changed, Abdel thought to himself, remembering the first time he saw his new classmate at the university all those years ago in Beirut and his first impression then that she was the most beautiful woman he had ever seen.

Embarcation

Sometimes lovers strolled the beach in the moonlight or scruffy students hitchhiking through Europe would throw down a blanket for the night, but Fotini had selected the remote beach at Ormos for their rendezvous because generally it was deserted when the small cafe had closed up for the day and taken down the red and green umbrellas protecting the tables from the heat of the afternoon. The tiny beach lay only five kilometers around the point from the yacht club at Vouliagmeni where Fotini docked the *Ceberus*. Though it was more difficult when she was on her own, she knew these waters like the body of a lover. She spit on the water and watched the flow of the current before casting off the stern line. Then it was short work to navigate to Ormos in the dark, a white running light at the top of the mainmast to show she was under power, an emerald and a ruby fore and aft for direction.

It was always painful for Fotini to return to the beach she had visited so often with Victor before he died. She felt an terrible nostalgia if she should come across a boy and a girl swimming naked in the moonlight just as they had done. More often she and Victor just sat fishing together under a blanket of stars talking about his past, her future.

When she refused to marry the rich American Yankee, he had followed her to Greece and bought a villa in Vouliagmeni to be near her. It was a torture for him since she refused to give up other admirers who flocked around. With persistence and regular tokens of affection purchased in the gold markets in Monastiraki he established a position of preeminence among her suitors, though he was twice their age. More importantly, he had given her the greatest gift of her life when he planted in her his love of the ocean, his passion for sailing. In the last years before the cancer took him she shared that passion and devoted herself to his happiness more completely than if they had celebrated a golden wedding anniversary together.

It was like living with Clark Gable in retirement, the club smile, the slicked back hair, the ridiculous ascot. She loved the sweet smell of his tobacco, the orange glow from the pipe bowl illuminating his face as he smoked and waited patiently for the fish to bite. He hadn't really done much with his life. He readily admitted the fact with the civil resignation of the very rich who can so easily afford to be such good losers in the game of life.

Every summer right into his late teens, his mother sent him to sailing school in the Netherlands to join a classmate whose family kept a summer home in Friesland. He squeaked through Yale, married and divorced a couple of childhood sweethearts before settling into a comfortable bachelor hood. He had his clubs, followed the horses, and hadn't missed an America's Cup since 1965. He consulted with his broker and kept his hand in the family portfolio. He designed a few seasonal homes for friends in Southport or Nantucket, but never used his architect's degree with any particular fervor except when he bought a classic two-masted fishing schooner from a bankrupt Portuguese family in Stonington and created the *Ceberus*.

He restored every inch of the vessel to its original 1911 splendor, carefully camouflaging a number of concessions to modern convenience and comfort. The huge hold which formerly held sixty tons of fish, became a captain's quarters rivaling a suite at the George V with dark teak cabinets, marble counter tops and gold fixtures in the head. A small round metal housing on the mainmast and short antennae on the foremast were the only tell tail signs of the sophisticated navigational gear including Loran, Global Positioning Satellite, and the best auto pilot, radar, VHF radio and horizon depth finder money could buy.

The galley was equipped with all essential appliances but also maintained a traditional coal stove. Fotini had learned to bake a four-layer cake in the middle of a gale by propping up baking pans in the oven to accommodate the pitch of the ship. Large wooden lockers held blocks of ice to refrigerate their stores and hard fruits and vegetables hung in nets. Oil lamps cast a flickering golden light about the wooden table, which filled the galley and became the center of life on board.

Victor had the sails custom dyed in Fez to recapture the antique burgundy that sometimes appeared on the horizon like a dark omen of dried blood when tall ships ruled the seas. But twin Detroit 671 diesels converted the 80 foot ship into a motor cruiser capable of 20 knots, not exactly a racer, but a respectable voyager. They even had a black cockatoo mascot named Ganymede that Fotini had trained to spread his wings when she called, "eagle, eagle."

For the first time in her life Fotini had met someone who expected more from her than sexual favors and she welcomed the challenge. She loved the mathematics involved in plotting a course, but also the art in learning how to predict currents and counter currents to achieve the day's goal in sailing. She relished the solitude, the hard work, the independence of setting out on the open sea. She liked the stakes. Ultimately, you risked your very life if you were careless or stupid.

Victor loved his avid pupil, concocted itineraries to challenge her growing skills. Several times he had taken her to America following the historic route Columbus had taken, carried west by trade winds and east by the prevailing northern westerlies. They traveled to Asia and once round the Cape of Good Hope. The Mediterranean became familiar as their back yard. When he died, Victor had passed the *Ceberus* into her hands as though it were a child they had raised together.

"You would have made a superb argonaut, Fotini," he told her the day he died. "You could match wits with Ulysses."

"Minerva," she corrected, "Minerva would be more interesting," and she administered one of her ravishing smiles. That was the best thing about her he decided, the astonishing smile. She would be deep in thought, severe, preoccupied as though she might at any moment break into tears, and out of nowhere the astounding smile. It got him every time no matter how used to her he had become.

The security guards at Vouliagmeni's Yacht club were accustomed to Fotini's evening excursions after Victor's death. The *Ceberus* wasn't luxurious by the club's standards. She kept no crew. There was no helicopter pad. But the staff knew there wasn't an ocean on the planet she couldn't manage. Sometimes she took along friends to sail with, but occasionally she slipped out of the harbor on her own once the dock boys had helped her cast off all lines. Stavros and Yanis were hardly the sort of pretty boys she usually took on as crew and she had ordered them to remain below until they got underway. Everything would go according to plan, but she didn't want to risk their identification in any case.

For a week she had been loading the ship for a voyage and she knew the dockhands from the Yacht Club wouldn't raise any eyebrows if she set out in the middle of the night tonight alone. She had chilled the refrigerator and sent her houseboy to the dock with provisions, making sure that he had unpacked things on shore first so they wouldn't be carrying local insect populations along with them on the voyage.

The trip would take no more than three weeks, but she planned a framework of menus carefully to accommodate the crew's healthy appetite. Meats, butter, and eggs she packed in plastic boxes. Canned goods were stored in locker A, dry goods in locker B. As they sailed she would supplement the stores with tuna or grouper speared from the ocean to be cooked into thick chowders or grilled on the hibachi with lime and ginger marinade. She checked off her list item by item, everything from suntan lotion to a month's supply of the Habitrol, the nicotine gum she counted on in her incessant struggle to stop smoking. A short holiday, she explained, to the nosy servant. She needed to get to know the director of her new film more intimately before they began shooting in the spring. And everything must be perfect for him.

Fotini's fashion sense never made any concession to circumstance. She invariably wore red lace and high heels to shop for vegetables or lead an expedition of friends to the Acropolis. On the streets of Berlin or Manhattan people thought she might be a transvestite who had gone a little overboard with her costume. In Athens, her outrageous getups worked somehow. At least the paparazzi had never had any trouble spotting her.

She sat at the deck of the *Ceberus* in a white spaghetti strap gown like a swan gliding on the dark waters. The *Ceberus* lay anchored just a quarter mile off the coast, waiting for their signal. Fotini lit up a Gauloise, keeping watch. A blue phosphorescence on the water drifted by. Octopus, she thought, perhaps a shark? Sometimes they scavenged these waters for garbage the lazy waiters expected the tide to carry away.

This would be Fotini's most important assignment yet and the excitement of it was almost sexual. In times past she had served as a courier, stored weapons, made considerable financial contributions to the cause. Once she had even let some comrades hide out at her villa after they had shot off the kneecaps of a certain judge who had gone on the warpath against November 17th. But she had never dirtied her hands quite this directly before, and the danger was exhilarating. She would lose everything if she was caught, but her commitment to the organization ran deeper than mere thrill seeking.

The social elite of Athens were a relatively small band of super-rich businessmen, tired old aristocrats, and various glitterati in the arts and their patrons. Fotini knew first hand just how corrupt the politicians of Greece were, the entire spectrum from socialists to fascists. She knew a number of them intimately, visited their ranches in the United States, dawdled throughout the Mediterranean on their personal yachts the size of small battleships. Her own spectacular villa was a present from the Minister of Finance before he judiciously immigrated to Geneva, one step ahead of the new government's special prosecutor. They granted her license for her iconoclasm, a beautiful Cassandra. The more she railed against them, the more they patronized her as a charming *enfant terrible*. In retaliation, she used them as casually as they used her.

Fotini cultivated a mystery about her youth, but the facts of her childhood were far less exotic than she leaked to the tabloids through her agent. Her father was an American GI assigned to the NATO forces who never acknowledged her as his child and finally deserted her and her mother with a convenient reassignment to the States. Her hatred of Americans had been a guiding passion ever since. She despised their superficiality, their glib optimism, their naiveté. They were like spoiled children. She, on the other hand, was a European with a sense of history and the tears in things. The American dream was Mickey Mouse and Disneyland. Even her beloved Greece and its ancient culture was succumbing to the vulgarity of the Pax Americana. Expulsion of the Americans from Greece was the first principle that drew her to the November 17th organization. But she also remembered her childhood days as an ugly duckling before becoming the famous black swan of Greece. She never forgot the poverty, the squalor her American father had abandoned them to in the back alleys of Athens.

The Communist system had imperfections, but it had always taken care of the poor in society. In China it had brought health care and raised the living standard for billions of people before the AIDS epidemic took hold. China would survive because of the quarantine system the state had instituted while the rest of Asia might not. The return of Communism was the only hope for the fragmented pieces of the former Soviet empire. She had moved from ideology to militancy however, through yet another affair of the heart, the route whereby most changes came about in her life.

On several occasions she had traveled to Iraq to attend the international poetry festival in Tikrit and give dramatic readings of Greek poets to the audiences. On one visit, at the invitation of a journalist friend who took her politics seriously and knew Fotini's presence would be certain to land the interview, she found herself roaring down the back streets of Baghdad to meet the leader of the Palestinian Liberation Front, Abul Abbas. She found it difficult to approve of the attacks on the beaches of Tel Aviv or the sea-jacking of the cruise liner *Achille Lauro*, but she was intrigued by this legendary leader who had staged strikes on Israel by hang glider, rubber dinghy and even hot-air balloon.

She saw him as a modern day Sinbad, swashbuckling his way through the Mediterranean, yet he had been the youngest member of the PLO executive committee and had a highly respected organization. The PLF seemed focused, rational, not emotional, but retained an idealism she could sympathize with.

"If I as a Palestinian do not fight now," he had said when he began combing the camps in Jordan for recruits, "then I am nothing. I live only for my dream."

She had not been prepared for the soft spoken giant that greeted them in his single-story villa once the guard had frisked them and tested the tape recorder with the microphone pointed at her neck. Abbas was six foot four and broad shouldered. His thick black hair and mustache showed only a trace of gray though he had passed his fiftieth birthday some years ago. It was a handsome face, wrinkling easily into laughter, but he had trained his eyes to reveal nothing. The dim-lit office was decorated with photos of commandos setting off in speedboats to strike Israel. Turkish coffee and tea were offered while the guard kept watch at the window.

"I'm sorry for this welcome," he said, smiling at her. "This is my life, I'm afraid."

They sat for hours smoking Marlboros, discussing that life and it how it served the cause of the Palestinians.

"What about the commando who crushed the skull of a four-year-old girl with his machine gun in the attack on Nahariya," she demanded. "You were a school teacher once. How can you justify the killing of that child?"

"Accidents happen," he said, shrugging his shoulders, unrepentant. "What happens in the heat of battle isn't just killing. This is war. Israel is our enemy."

"And Klinghoffer? You shoot a man in a wheelchair in the head and push him overboard. That is an accident?"

"Klinghoffer, always I hear about this Klinghoffer," he shouted. "Nobody knows all the people who die in Palestine. But this Klinghoffer is like Jesus Christ. Let me tell you. My mother was pregnant with me when Israel stole our land and my parents fled our village near Haifa. I was born a few months later in a Syrian refugee camp and I haven't seen my family's village since. Now the traitors in the PLO have given up our land and our freedom for some kind of limited autonomy that they throw to us like a bone to a dog. But I tell you we will never give up dream of the homeland. There is an Arabic saying that revenge takes 40 years. If not my son, then the son of my son will kill you. We will have our homeland on our own terms. After that we will see about peace."

Finally, the fiery revolutionary had won her over, if only as a symbol that the PLF would not give up armed struggle, no matter what Arafat's stooges had worked out with the Jews.

She recognized her own deprived childhood when he spoke. She was attracted to a man who saw things in clear-cut terms and acted on his beliefs, when so many of the men in her life were such chameleons, instinctively changing color at the hint of a change in the psychological or political landscape. This man knew what he wanted and he went after it. And by the end of their interview it was clear that he wanted her. She had not protested when he dismissed the guard and her journalist friend and fulfilled that desire with characteristic energy and determination that same afternoon in his office.

A couple of years later, the Americans had finally tracked him down with Baghdad's complicity and he had given his life for the dream of a homeland. But the seed of his passion had been planted and had steadily grown in her despite his death. He had lived fully. That was all that mattered. In a few months Fotini would be fifty years old, about his own age when they had first met, she reflected. She had no intention of aging gracefully, would kick death in the teeth if he came courting. Helping the PLF and Islamic Rebirth on this mission was a way of paying back her lover for the gift he had given her, a way of smashing the hourglass.

On the bow of the *Ceberus*, Fotini finally detected a single beam of light announcing their arrival. She threw her cigarette into the water and returned the signal. She could not make out any figures on shore, but when she heard the small engine of the Zodiac dinghy start up, she prepared to take them aboard.

Yves sat in a stupor, but Nadia made an exhausted struggle against being loaded into the small boat. She realized the prospect of a rescue grew dimmer the further they traveled from Vouliagmeni. Before driving to the beach at Ormos, the white truck had circled a newspaper kiosk in the town several times until a radio contact came letting them know they were not being followed. Once they were on water, it would even more difficult to trace them. But Yves was still bloody from his first struggle and both had little fight left in them. Finally, they sat mute in the small craft, withered with acceptance.

The dinghy rode the gentle surf making smooth progress to the vessel lying off shore. Abdel and the short one kept guard while the kidnapper who had smashed Yves in the face manned the tiller. Without taking his eyes off them or his hand off the tiller the pilot deftly reached into the water to retrieve a line which had come undone.

When Yanis leaned back into the boat, Abdel reflected that it must have been the propeller, the way in dream we calculate dispassionately how many seconds we have before the car will crash. At first Yanis didn't say a word but only looked in white terror at the stump of his forearm which had now erupted into a fountain of blood. It was only when the elegant fin glided by them and the shark bumped gently against the thin skin of the dinghy that he began to scream.

With a smooth kick to the captain's chest, careful not to rock the boat and spill anyone else into the water, Abdel shoved him overboard and took the tiller. The trashing was brief, the creature sufficiently distracted. It was unlikely there would be anything much left of Yanis to reveal their escape. No one in the fragile dinghy was sorry to reach the *Ceberus* where from the deck above, a woman's face, powdered white as death stared down at them like the moon. Her raven hair, her black eyes were those of a fury released from hell and she studied them hard before tossing a rope ladder to come aboard.

The Breath of God

Abdel stood alone at the helm the *Ceberus* tending his watch while the mistral drove the sails and knocked the ship through the waves with drowsy regularity. Fotini had gone below to escape the sun and the crew lay snoring in a mid-day siesta after the wine and chicken and olives she had prepared. He relished the sun and the waves and a quiet moment to take stock of how far they had come. The crew deserved a rest, he decided. They had secured the hostages without mishap and hadn't slept much in three days, insomniac with the energy of fleeing Greece. The muffled crashing of the waves and the slow roller coaster ride was hypnotic. Abdel pulled from a coffee mug to ward off sleep and keep from drifting too far into daydream and stay on course.

Only a week ago, he sat on Fotini's terrace watching the wind ripple the surface of the water like a school of feeding minnows, wondering if he could really bring himself to kidnap the woman he had loved more than anything on earth all those years ago. Wind on the water, invisible and irresistible like the hand of Allah, fate. He remembered Dr. Mansur's favorite image for divine intervention in the affairs of men, beautiful and idealistic. And wrong. By the time he had finished his studies in Lebanon, it had become clear what must be done to secure a share in the bounty of God's earth for his people. He would become the spirit of God's justice made flesh by his hand, his heart. Now he had his prize safely below deck and would barter for the future of the Palestinian people or die trying.

He remembered how the bay at Vouliagmeni had come to life last Sunday morning, how the Greeks woke to their weekend pleasure as naturally as to the sun. He could just hear the calls of the children

103

at the Yacht Club as they turned over the little yellow boats lying on the dock like a bunch of bananas, and prepared for their sailing lesson. Loving parents called out encouragement as, one by one, the skiffs were strung together into a line of ducklings traipsing after the rubber motor boat towing them out to open water. A big wiry dog stood in the bow of the lead boat and added to the pandemonium by barking instructions the children paid no attention to. At the far end of the pier, boys dove among the huge rocks, sunk to pebble size in the crystal water, looking for sea urchins. Waiters began to spread white table linen and silver for the diners who would be coming to lunch in an hour or so smelling of suntan creams and perfume.

It was beautiful. Heartbreakingly so. He sensed again how his life was the life of the voyeur. He would always be standing on the other side of the window while people made love or ate their dinners by candlelight. He tried not to give into this self-pity when it came on him. Ever since he was a boy, as a cub of the stone, hurling rocks at Israeli soldiers in the *Intifadah* he had nurtured a fierce pride in his Palestinian heritage. What did it matter that he could not afford all the Western junk that filled Israeli shops. He was strong and smart. He would grow into a Fatah Hawk. Together with his friends they would build a new society in the name of Allah. God's law would rule and the spirit of Islam would flourish. He refused to be the poor urchin looking into the Israeli candy store. But sometimes it was hard not to long for the sweet things of the world, if only for the sake of those he loved. What Palestinian family could ever hope for such a day of recreation he had watched on the beach in Greece? There on the other side of the Mediterranean his people still lived in a sea of garbage and despair. The Palestinian authority couldn't even manage a sanitation department, let alone develop a future for his people. Palestinians would never live the sort of life the west took for granted as normal as long as the Israelis denied them control over their lives. The Israelis continued to steal their lands and herd them into slums at the edge of the expanding settlements, denying them the life-sustaining water which ran beneath that land so the Israelis could preserve their standard of living. For Palestinians, the cycle of poverty had continued from generation to generation even into the new millennium.

Only rarely did fate permit some lucky boy a chance to jump off this treadmill as when the Jerusalem Fund, a modest relief agency in Lebanon chose Abdel for a scholarship at the American University in Beruit. He had always been a good student, in large part to please his grandmother. She did not read herself, and when he was a boy, she watched him practice his alphabet as though he was an alchemist turning lead into gold.

"Look Baba, see how simple it is. This is *elif.* Tall and straight like a cypress tree. You try." But she only laughed and hid behind her veil, watching him trace the magic letters into his copybook. And when he was finished she would make him tea and cakes and tell him stories from the time when she was a girl.

His grandparents had been simple farmers before the government drew a red line on a map and declared their pastures to be part of the buffer zone about the new settlements. But Baba Leila revered education like most simple country people. The village Imam had been raised above other men by Allah through his study of the Koran. A doctor or teacher was likewise to be honored. His grandmother imparted a deep respect for knowledge in Abdel, whatever work Allah would finally decide for him to do in life. He studied tirelessly in the makeshift lycee which opened in Nabalus just after the first peace accord. There was little else to do in the village, and his studies were a way to escape the sense of imprisonment a teenage boy lived with in a town monitored by Israeli police.

In the end, science had captured his imagination even more profoundly than religion. For Abdel, science was like religion, the laws of the physical world as universal and irrefutable as God's law in the realm of human interaction with Divine will. The study of science was like a prayer in the physical world. Abdel would master the sciences necessary to change the world around him, particularly the study of that most crucial element for life to exist on the planet God had created, water. There could be no life without water, and his fascination with this gift from Allah was nearly as passionate as worship.

From the time he was a boy, Abdel had listened to the Israelis swagger over the miracle of their green revolution, of turning the Negev into a desert paradise. They justified the theft of his homeland with the words of Isaiah. "The parched land shall be gladdened, the desert rejoice and blossom as a rose." Scorpion Road now led to orange groves, cotton and tomato fields. Israeli computer rooms monitored systems of glass-tubed drip irrigation and from the Dead Sea. The settlers had replaced limestone chalk and dust with corporate farms exporting vegetables to all the countries of the European Community in the west and to Asia.

But there was nothing miraculous in what Israel had accomplished. With an endless supply of foreign capital from Zionist Jews around the world and the latest irrigation technology imported from the United states, they only needed to steal sufficient land to expand their commercial operations. The miracle could be duplicated if the Palestinians had their lands back again, along with reasonable capital investment, and more than anything else, life-sustaining water.

Water had been the key to Israeli growth, but there didn't seem to be enough water in the Dead Sea to accommodate their greed for territory and support the thousands of usurpers who had settled in those occupied territories. "What you have given us is not enough," Abba Ebn told the United Nations the day the West took his homeland to create the state of Israel, "We will have more." And the expansion had never abated since that day in 1948 when Palestinians were forced out of their country.

Israelis, of course, used five times as much water as any neighbor in the region, while his people had been trained from birth to regard water as precious as blood. They understood its importance to life as intuitively as a camel drinking at the river before making his way across the desert. Abdel still couldn't overcome his astonishment at seeing lemon trees, mango and jasmine growing in the private gardens about the swimming pools of Tel Aviv. He couldn't resist throwing a rock through the car's window when he came across a boy washing his father's Mercedes, the hose wide open like a severed artery pouring into the street.

When Abdel began his studies in Lebanon, he was certain that the peace process would catch up to his education, and that by the time be became a hydrologist, Palestine would be a state with its capital in Jerusalem. How could Israel continue to hold out against the Intifadah and rule an entire population as an invading army? The world must come to its senses finally. Peace must certainly come if people would only listen to each other.

His first year as a student in Beruit, however, was like living in Babel. Fundamentalists of every stripe vied for the soul of the student body. Most were bent on militant struggle to establish a theocracy based on Koranic law. A sole voice of moderation crying out in that militant wilderness was that of Dr. Hamadi Mansur.

One afternoon Abdel was studying the student union bulletin board when he happened to lift up a flyer that had been tacked over an older announcement. Dr. Mansur had come from the West Bank as part of the visiting lecturer series and was to speak on the Islamization of Knowledge. Abdel knew a little about the topic. It had been very fashionable before the *Intifadah* gained momentum and the massacre at Hebron pushed students into the arms of Hezbollah or Hamas. Hamadi Mansur remained a highly respected voice in the movement for a Palestinian state. He had been imprisoned for refusing to co-operate with Israeli forces in the continuing colonization of lands taken in 67. He had the dignity and quiet self-assurance of the old leaders like Hussein of Jordan or Hassan in Morocco, cousin to the Prophet himself.

When his daughter Nadia arrived in Beirut to begin her studies, Al Ayat and the Lebanese papers reported the news as though a beautiful princess had arrived for a state visit. Abdel was sure she would be at her father's lecture. He knew the papers did not exaggerate her beauty. He sat just three seats away from her in his organic chemistry class and was fascinated by the way her dark hair shone with red and gold light as it spilled down her beautiful neck and shoulders. Lebanon was a cosmopolitan capital, the jewel of Mediterranean before the war, and while some students wore the veil fervently as a symbol of Arab nationalism, many young women went without the veil with impunity, either as a feminist statement or merely for the sake of fashion. He didn't know her reasons, but he planned to get to know her a lot better.

It seemed as if half the student body, the male half at least, wanted to get to know her better as well. There was standing room only later that night when he entered the auditorium, and sure enough, Nadia Mansur sat close to the front surrounded by his classmates.

"We find ourselves in a world not of our own making, a world that is in conflict with our cherished traditions and values," Dr. Mansur was saying. He spoke quietly but with passion. "We have accepted the science of the West and all forms of knowledge which account for the power of the West with no reference to the values which have shaped our societies in the past. We must bring Islamic ethics to bear on all branches of knowledge from anthropology to economics to political theory. We must embrace our traditional values to bring about the very Islamization of knowledge."

His was an aristocratic face, elegant in its features with a trim, salt and pepper beard. His intelligent eyes searched the audience for those who grasped the importance of his words. Nadia's eyes shone back with a pride and love for her father. The students about her listened intently, occasionally nodding assent.

"Key ethical concepts from the Koran and the Sunna must be the analytical tools by which all intellectual disciplines are developed, our framework for looking at the world, interacting with it and shaping it. The most important of these concepts then, to review, may include God's unity (*Tawheed*), man's trusteeship (*khilafa*), and distributive knowledge (*ilm*) and justice (*adl*).

"What about *Jihad*? What about revenge for the deaths of the martyr's slaughtered by the Israeli butcher Goldstein? What about real justice."

The boy shouting from the back of the hall came rushing forward to the podium to confront the speaker. "The Israelis speak with bullets, and you babble about God's unity. They take an eye for an eye—and you answer with man's trusteeship. We are not trustees of anything, we are slaves."

Some of the students began to boo and call for the boy to sit down while others called out to let him speak and have his say. Abdel knew him, Khali Aeolus, a law student from Tunis who had organized a violent demonstration against yet another American veto of a European motion at the United Nations condemning Israel's colonization of east Jerusalem. The university had tried to expel him, but student's cry for freedom of speech had forced the dean to back down.

"Even the Pope is with us and you will not pick up a rock to fight for justice and freedom. But we will have our state even without your help. *Allah u Akbar.* "

Several students began to chant "*Allah u Akbar,*" the catchall prayer and political slogan that could be counted on to rally any Arab audience.

"God *is* greater than all," Dr. Mansur answered from the podium. "That is why we must trust Allah in our struggle with the Israelis. I fought in the war of '67. I drove a tank and killed Israeli soldiers, and saw my own comrades slain as well. But has that war brought our freedom, will another? How many generations must be sacrificed on both sides in mutual revenge before we break the cycle of death?"

"Yes, a holy war," Khali call out, "to drive them into the sea. We must unite and listen to God's law and expel this enemy. You speak of traditional values, but what kind of Islamic society have we created. Look about you. Half the women in this room sit like Western whores, heads uncovered. Your own daughter makes a mockery of Islam by refusing to wear the *chadour* and walk modestly in front of men as the prophet commands."

Abdel carefully watched him, suspecting what would come next. He had heard the same speech only last month at the anti-American demonstration before it turned violent. Kahlil took his inspiration from the vigilantes of New York and Teheran, both of whom would redress evil in the street, whether it was a woman dressed in an endangered animal fur or a mini-skirted Westerner showing off her bare legs and arms. The female students in the audience began to scream when Khali pulled out a can of red paint and like a guardian of the revolution who had spied a macerate on Avenue Motahari, began to spray those who wore nothing on their heads. When he moved toward Nadia, Abdel was on him in an instant, throwing him to the ground, pummeling him into submission. But Khali had already ruined the evening in a chaos of red paint and sobbing women and the audience filed out of the hall in disarray.

All chaos, of course, contains within itself the hope of some future moment when balance is restored and new opportunities rise phoenix-like out of the confusion, even, sometimes, laden with the weight of destiny. So, from that night, Abdel's life would be woven with Nadia's, and the first seed fate would plant in his heart would be love.

Abdel came up to Dr. Mansur as he was preparing to leave, and helped Nadia pick up his notes which had been scattered in the brawl.

"Father, this is Abdel Ayat. He is in my chemistry class." The professor called the role each morning, but he was surprised that she remembered his last name.

"How do you do sir." Abdel shook Dr. Mansur's hand.

"I must thank you for your help. There was no call to attack the women that way," Dr. Mansur said. "I guess you proved his point—sometimes a bully must be beaten. Are you hurt."

He had stopped the nosebleed earlier, but now the bleeding started up once again and large drops fell onto his shirt.

"No, I'll be okay," Abdel said. But Nadia made him sit down and tilted his head back while he applied pressure. Her hands were cool and smooth against his hot cheeks.

"I must thank you too," she said, smiling down at him. "I wouldn't like to be a redhead."

"You would be fine as a redhead," he said, swallowing the salty blood at the back of his throat.

He offered to accompany them to the hotel, just to be safe and they did not object. In the lobby he accepted Dr. Mansur's invitation of a coffee before he returned to the dormitory.

"Of course I would prefer Nadia to wear the veil voluntarily out of respect for our tradition," Dr. Mansur said as they sat at a small cafe in the hotel. "But we can not force women to do God's bidding. There is room in Islam for free will and human rights. Iran and Saudi Arabia are not the only models for what the Islamic State might one day be."

"But what about the poor women who live like chattel in those countries," Nadia protested. "The Arab world is a world of schizophrenics. We live one life at home and another life in public."

"Like it or not," her father said, "the great majority of the people in that world agree with their governments, including the women. There was a large study of this question just last week in *Le Monde Education*. It is amazing how conservative Arab societies have remained."

"If you live in a totally closed society—receiving the same message constantly how can you believe anything than what you have been told?" Nadia did not consider herself a radical feminist, but living in a more open, university environment, society had made her begin to rethink much of what she had been taught as a child. She was learning how to ask questions, the most important first step in an adult's education.

"You make a valid point," her father admitted. Dr. Mansur was not sure where it would lead, but he felt he had made the right decision in sending her to an American-style university to receive a liberal arts education. Let her test her wings. If she were going to be a leader one day, as he hoped, she would need to know how the rest of the world lived and thought.

"I heard a report on the BBC that in the U.S. universities are separating men and women for their studies the way they used to do before co-education."

"Would you like that," Nadia asked.

"No, then I wouldn't be sitting with you in chemistry class each day," he answered.

They had become friends that night and the friendship deepened over the next four years at the university. They spent hours together as study partners, drilling each other with questions in preparation for examinations, trying to piece together answers to assigned problems. Abdel was one of the best students in the class, but there was no denying that Nadia had a genuine talent for the sciences. She could balance equations in seconds leaving Abdel and his classmates stunned at the computer-like quality of her mind. It bothered him at first, but finally he accepted her brilliance and threw in the towel. Nadia was too engrossed in her studies to get involved in the sort of competitiveness that professors used as a little engine to drive student performance in the classroom. But this was a woman to whom he did not mind losing. There was a sweetness between them that made friends think of them as brother and sister. But by his sophomore year Abdel and Nadia had become lovers, the force of their affection and young sexuality overcoming all the injunctions proscribed by their religion on such intimacy. For Nadia it was just another example of the sort of double life Islam required of one in the real world. She accepted the contradictions for she had come to love him so. His dark eyes, his silences, the fire that burned in him for Palestine, his adherence to the laws of Islam in all things but his love for her.

By the time they neared graduation, however, the real world demanded choices of her that would not accommodate the double life she was living. Abdel had grown more certain than ever that armed struggle was the only answer to achieve a homeland, abandoning his studies to work in the resurgent *Intifadah*.

"What rights do we have finally, Nadia," he argued. "The right to collect garbage? The right to pick up oranges? Are we any closer to the state of Palestine than we were a decade ago? Do we have a presence in Jerusalem? They deny the right of thousands of Palestinians to return to their country. They dominate the land and the water. They flood the territory with new settlers and the minute the Israeli colonists feet threatened, their army pours in like the Red Sea."

"But we already control some the land in sector A," Nadia said. "We have made progress. Reversing a hundred years of hatred will not be easy, Abdel, especially when the first lesson means learning how to share the same living space."

"The martyrs did not sacrifice their blood so that Palestinians could live in an autonomous sector. They demanded liberation. How could Arafat have been so deceived by Rabin? How could he have hoped that the man who commanded the war that took our lands in the first place would willingly return them? And now their aggression continues in the next generation, even after Rabin's death, all in the name of security and the destiny of the Jewish state."

"We have to be patient," she said. "We have to be like the waves crashing against the shore. Things take time."

But there had not been enough time. Would never be enough time. For Hamadi Mansur, time stopped the afternoon he left his office in the West Bank and was blown apart by a car bomb planted by Mossad meant for the mayor of their village with whom he had been riding that day. For Nadia, time ended that same afternoon. Abdel begged her to stay and continue the fight in his her father's name. Now that her father was gone, Abdel would marry her and bring her to his own house. But she carried her grief with her like a husband, and would have no other. She would accept the scholarship she had been awarded to the Pasteur Institute and leave the violence and death behind her. She would take the life of science as a nun becomes the bride of Christ, to honor her father's memory and retreat from a world that no longer sang to her. And he when he could not move her, when she abandoned him and let love die, only his passion for Palestine remained like a bright garland he would have offered her. Let history take her then, and time begin anew. Her betrayal fortified him for the life he would now offer for the liberation of his people and the return of their sacred capitol of Jerusalem. .

The Ethics Czar

Robert stepped out of the silent metro car and glanced up at the concrete ceiling overhead. Traveling the N.Y. subway was like making your way through a sewer, but the system connecting suburban Maryland to the nations's capital made Robert think of a lunar space station. Geodesic domes arched high over the rails at each station, well beyond reach of graffiti artists. Discrete metal columns marked the stations along the line, and a map of the system lit up under glass in red, blue, yellow, orange and green neon lights. Well-dressed passengers spoke in muted voices or read their newspapers. Even the tourists who flooded the capital for school outings moderated their enthusiasm when they entered the subway as though they had stepped out of a bright square into a darkened church. Robert felt like a poor country cousin come to the city for Easter dinner with a rich relative.

No one had told him he needed to save his ticket to exit the metro, but he found it in his pocket finally and fed it into the turnstile, to join in the organized flow of passengers pouring out at the red line NIH station.

He glided up an escalator long enough to be taking him to heaven, which for many scientists was exactly what the NIH campus in suburban Maryland had become. Billions were spent here each year in medical research, and since the turn of the century the vast majority of these funds went to finding a cure for HIV IV. If not Mecca, the National Institute of Health had become one of the greatest world centers in the desperate search for an end to the plague. The rolling green acres of the campus were dotted with teaching hospitals, laboratories, faculty and administrative housing and even a hotel for the visiting parents of sick children. A former nunnery now used as a conference center rose on a grassy knoll surrounded by stands of oak, maple and beech trees.

Cries of "Stop the torture. Stop the torture now," blasted the flow of passengers as the escalator delivered them into the sunlight of a bright spring afternoon. It was difficult to determine who was objecting to what since demonstrators on either side of Rockville Pike were screaming the same slogan at each other, while Maryland Police and NIH security forces lined the sidewalks to keep the opposing sides from contact.

"What's going on," Robert asked a young man in a blue seer sucker suit who wore horn-rimmed glasses and carried a black medical bag.

"Oh, it's those god damned animal rights people," he said. "It's the end of the world and those crazies are wringing their hands over laboratory experiments using chimps and dogs. We ought to be using those idiots for the experiments."

"Well, who are they then," Robert asked, pointing to a line of demonstrators screaming back at them across the street. A demonstrator chose at that moment to turn a can of blood or red paint over the head of an unwitting policeman and was promptly hauled away.

"Those are the AIDS activists who think we aren't doing enough animal experiments because of the animal rights people. I wish they'd all go home and let us get on with our job. It used to be a pretty nice place to work."

The young man studied Robert a second, the sweet smile, a certain vulnerability.

"Visiting a patient," he asked.

"No, I have an appointment with Dr. Davis," Robert said, "Do you know how I can find him? He's asked me to meet him at his home. Let's see, West Cedar Lane. Is that around here?"

"You mean, John Davis? The ethics czar. ORI?"

"Yes, that's the one. His secretary wasn't clear about which NIH exit to get off at."

"Oh, administration housing is on the other side of the campus. It's a row of red brick town houses over by the hotel. Just follow this main road and turn left at the neurological center. You can't miss it. I'll walk you over if you like."

The young man looked at Robert with an intensity that went beyond his offer of assistance. It was the secret look of recognition, solicitation by which homosexuals identified each other in a hostile environment, like drawing a fish in the sand for early Christians. The religious right still blamed American faggots for the AIDS epidemic. They abandoned abortion and focused on homosexuality as the rotten core of American society. Campaigns were on to reverse the laws granting civil rights to gays that had squeaked through Congress in the early nineties. A life of duplicity, if frustrating, was still the safest course for a young professional who wanted to advance in his career and happened to be homosexual.

Robert gave him a friendly smile and offered his hand in farewell. The young man lingered in the handshake with a slight erotic pressure that changed the gesture momentarily into that of holding hands. Since Michael's death, however, Robert had grown shy about meeting new people. It happened almost every day since he reached puberty, but Robert still never really knew what to say next when it became clear someone was interested in him that way. Besides, he had business to attend to.

"No trouble. I'll find it. Thanks a lot for your help."

"Don't worry about those demonstrators," the young man said, noting how Robert clutched to his brief case. "The police keep them festering at the edge of the campus. It's safe enough to walk around here."

"Thanks," Robert said to the young man who stared after him in curiosity for a while before heading in the opposite direction.

A minute after he rang the doorbell at 42 West Cedar Lane, Robert was surprised to be greeted by a woman in her late forties who might have been a gypsy princess. New York designers had taken their inspiration from the peasants of central Europe this spring. The woman's long skirt was studded with little mirrors, she wore a black shawl over a silk paisley blouse. Her hair was obviously dyed, the most extraordinary shade of red Robert had ever seen. Scarlet, copper, henna, he just stood gawking at her until she spoke.

"I'm Ellen Davis," she said. "You must be Mr. Owen."

"Yes, that's right."

"Well, won't you come in? John's expecting you." She smiled broadly in welcome.

"Sure, thanks."

She's really beautiful, Robert thought as he stepped into the foyer. The simplest thing could trigger Michael's memory for Robert, a smell, a wild swan lifting off the river, a bowl of roses on a hallway table. Once he and Michael passed by a woman with the same beautiful color of hair walking her yellow lab in the village. "At times like this, I wish I were a lesbian," Michael had said. Robert smiled to himself again with the old joke.

"I'm afraid John's tied up on the phone with somebody on the Hill. He's been at it for hours so I hope it won't be long now. Can I offer you a cup of tea or coffee? A Coke?"

"Tea would be fine, thank you."

The room seemed to belong to two roommates rather than husband and wife Robert decided when she went away. Two very different styles of decor had been forced to coexist, not totally unsuccessfully. There was a separate living area at the far end of the room with overstuffed couches in large floral prints accented with good 19th century antiques. Robert sat near the fireplace on stark Danish furniture. The simple mantle piece was decorated with a very old microscope and an elegant water picture of a deep blue, almost purple glass. Bookcases lined either side of the fireplace with technical books in microbiology and virology on one side, and mostly art history and popular novels on the other. A long runner carpet combined colors from each room in an attempt to pull the two living rooms together.

Robert stood contemplating a single abstract painting that dominated the Spartan end of the living room, a cubist rendition of a man seated at a table writing in a book. The figure consisted of geometric forms in black, white and blue, his face, *trompe a l'oiel*, stared at the viewer and at his journal simultaneously.

"Isn't he wonderful," Ellen Davis asked, wheeling a silver tea service into the room, the cart laden with tiny sandwiches and an assortment of cookies.

"We found him on our honeymoon last spring in Spain. The painter's Swiss actually, Swiss Italian. DeLucca's his name. Do you know him by any chance?"

"I'm afraid I don't know very much about art, but I..."

"Know what you like?" she teased him. "John's the same way. This is the first piece of art we both agreed on, something of a watershed moment in our marriage. Neither one of us would give up our things when we agreed to give up the single life. So I carted down all the dear clutter from my life in New York and planted it on the other side of the Maginot line here in the living room. Now we don't have to take the train when we want to visit each other."

Robert was surprised by her breezy familiarity but was grateful for the effort she took to make him feel comfortable.

"Cream or sugar," she asked, handing him a paper-thin porcelain cup filled with fragrant tea.

In that moment the demon appeared again, of course. He always seemed to show up just when the world was offering some respite from the trials it had inflicted on him. It had been like that since the first day he settled into Robert's psyche.

Robert sat among a motley assortment of prostitutes, gay boys, junkies, and local poor at the STD Clinic listening to a dippy health care worker give the mandatory lecture on safe sex and protection from airborne infection. A silly idea, he decided, as though one could stop the spread of an airborne disease any easier than one could ultimately control people's sexual habits. He knew it was only a matter of time before he would prove to be positive for HIV, but when that day arrived it came with a very unexpected twist. All the lonely years since Michael's death he grew certain that he'd be beyond the pain, the fear of dying from AIDS. It would be a release in a way. But sitting there in front of the idiot counselor, Robert had the stunning realization that he was now a carrier, that he was poison, that the most innocent encounter with another might prove deadly. The enormity of the fact was like an evil genie suddenly released from a bottle fueling his propensity for guilt, his confessional predilections, driving his imagination to create a demon, to personalize his fetish for purity.

If he happened to sneeze in an elevator, or inadvertently drank from someone's glass, his private demon was with him for the rest of the week castigating him for spreading his disease. Nothing had helped. He even tattooed the back of his right hand with the international "IV" symbol the way AIDS patients in China and Saudi Arabia were being forced to do, a contemporary version of the leper's bell, thinking it would make things easier. But there remained unending decisions on simply how to move his body through the world each day without endangering others about him. Before Robert took the tea from Ellen Davis, he extended the back of his hand to make it clear she knew she was breaking bread with an AIDS patient.

She covered his tattooed hand with her own and smiled at him, sending the demon screaming into the shadows.

"Try the lemon drop cookies," she said. "They're my favorite."

When Robert was twelve years old he beat up a boy thirty pounds heavier than he was who was bullying his best friend in gym class, trying to extort candy bars from the weaker boy. Robert had a steely blue quality, a toughness that people underestimated throughout his life. But these days, when he was tired, a simple act of kindness like a beautiful woman taking his hand might cause him to break down on the spot. Which he was about to do when John Davis made his fortunate entrance into living room, requiring that Robert rise to another occasion.

"Don't get up, don't get up," John Davis said amiably, putting his hand on Robert's shoulder in an unsuccessful effort to keep him from standing formally. John Davis was not a big man, but he moved with an authority and energy that made him seem larger than his actual size. His intelligence was an almost physical attribute. The voracious eyes took in the entire room at a glance, assessing the psychological moment, storing information for future analysis, evaluating the newcomer with the speed of a mainframe computer. Initial readout, he liked the boy.

"I'm sorry I kept you waiting," he said placing his pipe on an ashtray to offer a firm handshake. "I see Ellen's made you comfortable."

"These are very avid bureaucrats," Ellen said, "tracking you down at home like that."

"It still hasn't sunk into my charming bride's pretty head that she is living in the heart of perhaps the biggest bureaucracy on the planet. Government servants do not put Capitol Hill on hold."

Well, is your budget being cut or is it only World War III.

"All hell's breaking loose in Senator Wagner's office."

He studied the boy's face to see if the reference produced any reaction but Robert only looked at him politely waiting for John Davis to continue. "He's been trying to have our office transferred to the Attorney General's jurisdiction for years and now he thinks he finally has the ammunition he needs."

"Uh oh. I've had Senator Wagner up to my eyeballs," Ellen Davis said. "That's my cue, Robert. Don't let him go on and on now. And make sure he comes for me when it's time to say goodbye. I'll go bake a cake or something." She gave her husband a perky little kiss and left the room.

"Before we begin, Robert, let me ask you frankly. Did you inform Senator Wagner's office that you were coming here today?"

"I didn't tell anyone. After we talked I just got a train ticket and came on down."

"You're sure you didn't talk to anyone about this meeting?"

"No one."

"And you called me from a public telephone away from your house and office?"

"Yes."

"Then we've got a problem. Someone's either bugging my office or I've got a spy working for me. You see, Senator Wagner knows all about your visit here today, and he knows the precise allegations you are making against Cramer Chemical. He intends to subpoena you before his committee and if your claims prove correct, he'll have our guts for garters, as my English grandfather used to say."

"What's your office got to do with anything? Martin Cramer is the bastard behind all this."

"We investigated Michael Riley's work when Cramer first applied for a patent on his vaccine, remember? Bayer claimed that he had used a cell line they developed and patented as the basis for his own vaccine. The charges were false, of course. We proved that Riley had developed his own cell line through independent laboratory sequencing. But the steadfast senator is anxious to prove that our office failed its mission when it overlooked Michael Riley's role in creating HIV IV. We keep original test material when a company applies for a patent. It would take a lot of work, but we do have the means of determining whether or not Michael Riley's vaccine introduced HIV IV into the population."

"Why does he want to go after Michael?"

"It's not Michael Riley. It's Martin Cramer. You see Cramer Chemical has been a very large contributor to Senator Wagner's political opponents for one thing, especially since Senator Wagner managed to get his daughter-in-law a seat on the Health Security Pricing Board. Barbara Wagner has already managed to cut Cramer's profit margins in half on a number of their star products. The drug companies can't gouge the public the way they used to now that the government is their sole customer and prices are fixed by the Health Security Administration. The big companies spend millions each year lobbying the HSA to keep the prices at a level they claim is needed to support research and development. Cramer Chemical threw a fortune at Wagner's opponent last year alone in New Mexico and the senator just narrowly kept his seat. It's not the sort of political action an incumbent appreciates or is likely to forget when he has the chance to pay back. I could barely keep him from calling a press conference this afternoon. He is very anxious to talk with you."

The thought of becoming a witness against his dead lover infuriated Robert. Events were spiraling out of his control. A press conference would ruin whatever chances he had of making Martin Cramer pay for Michael's death.

"Let him subpoena all he wants. He can't force me to say anything. They can't make me."

"Why don't you just start at the beginning Robert and tell me what you know. We'll worry about how to deal with Senator Wagner later."

They spoke for several hours, Robert carefully outlining the course of Michael's research as he understood it. Davis had spoken with hundreds of whistle blowers in his time at the ORI. On occasion, they came to him out of pure idealism—someone had cheated, fudged the results of a test, stolen someone else's work and the public health was placed at risk as a result. More often than not, however, an element of revenge surfaced - someone had been passed over for a promotion, a love affair had soured, a rival succeeded where the whistle blower had failed. Whatever the personal motivation, John Davis needed to be guided by the facts of the case. The anonymity his office afforded was the only thing that enabled such people to come forward. Davis had been sued a number of times for denying due process to those accused, they demanded that their accuser meet them face to face in court. Granting unlimited immunity to anyone wishing to bring a grievance forced him to wade through innumerable bogus claims, but it preserved the dignity of the scientific community as well.

More often than not the issue came down to sloppy science, badly kept notebooks, poor observation, in themselves a kind of malfeasance, but not exactly the same as criminal behavior. If a young researcher was stupid enough to divulge a brilliant idea over his beer at some bar that was one thing, stealing his idea from a grant proposal was quite another. Davis was able to sort things through, and quietly rebuke guilty parties without ruining careers in the glare of a public trial. If needed, he could withhold government funding for future projects as punishment without resorting to criminal proceedings.

Occasionally, the theft of intellectual property had more serious ramifications - the loss of a Nobel Prize, a fortune in patent fees. Two decades later, the controversy still raged over Gallo and Monatainger's early work in identifying the HIV virus. Davis was glad to have more sophisticated investigative support from the FBI and the Attorney General's office when the media got hold of such cases. But he much preferred to act like a university tenure committee, privately reviewing misconduct within the discrete confines of academe. Until now John Davis had managed to keep the ORI from turning into an arm of the criminal justice system. But if Senator Wagner had his way, ORI would become another giant government octopus, probing, monitoring, regulating competition, strangling free scientific inquiry. The Cramer case threatened to subvert all Davis's careful work to preserve the integrity and independence of his office. And it seemed pretty clear that Barbara Wagner, was being groomed to take control of the new agency through the patronage of her powerful Senator father.

Robert's claim that Martin Cramer had murdered his lover seemed exaggerated surely, given the evidence. The journal account of Michael Riley's tragic last days only proved that Martin Cramer had encouraged Riley to take his life. But no court would convict him of any illegality.

Suicide itself was becoming a major epidemic these days mirroring that of AIDS. Since Dr. Kavorkian's successful appeal in the Supreme Court, the Department of Health had plans for at least one obitorium for each major U.S. city, a center where desperately sick AIDS patients could end their life painlessly, and efficiently without endangering the public health. No, in the end, Michael Riley had perished by his own hand, despite any manipulation on Martin Cramer's part.

John Davis sensed there was more behind Robert Owen's accusations than revenge for the death of a lover. In years of dealing with malcontents, Davis had developed something of a sixth sense about ulterior motives. The young man was clearly doomed and didn't stand to gain much personally from any sort of blackmail he might have in mind. Why would he be so reluctant to speak to Senator Wagner? He couldn't get a more public forum if all he cared about was exposing Martin Cramer. Whatever his motives, Robert Owen had brought his case to the ORI and there was no turning back. The facts of the case were all that mattered now and they would take on a life of their own once exposed to the public.

There was no denying the importance of Michael Riley's notebooks. If gene sequencing showed that Riley had tagged his vaccine with secret markers and those markers were found to be part of HIV IV's genetic structure, it was very likely that Riley's fears were correct. His own body had served as the in vivo crucible by which the virus had mutated into its present deadly form. Such an in vitro mutation would have been virtually impossible. Riley had indeed become patient zero by injecting himself with his own vaccine.

The diary entries clearly implicated Martin Cramer in a cover-up of the disastrous accident. Robert Owen was on much stronger ground there. Researchers might have saved precious years and millions of lives if they had had the information sooner and identified the new retrovirus Michael Riley unleashed.

The prospect of breaking Michael Riley's dramatic story to the world press stimulated Senator Wagner like a shark swimming through a pool of blood. He could taste the good luck that enveloped him. At the very least, the investigation would clinch his re-election. Like a frenzied talk show host, he'd have the world in an uproar. "Human error" at Cramer Chemical had threatened human extinction. Middle Eastern terrorists had easily overcome corporate security and taken hostage the very scientists who might be able to avert the disaster. And one of the world's foremost research institutions was powerless to reproduce the work of its own missing scientists.

"It's a quite a story, Robert," John Davis said, handing him the notebooks he'd been studying. "The question now is what do we do about it? I'm not sure how much Senator Wagner has found out, but you can be sure he's not going to sit on the story very long. And if Martin Cramer has embezzled funds in Switzerland, the matter is out of our hands. It becomes a question for the FBI."

"I don't want Michael to become the scapegoat. All this is Martin Cramer's fault."

"But you're going to have to testify at some point. I can't unlearn everything you've told me today. Besides Senator Wagner's involved now and I 'm sure he feels as strongly about all this as you do. His own wife died of AIDS, did you know that Robert? From a simple operation back in the days when we were still not sure of the blood supply. Senator Wagner is sure that some anonymous homosexual blood donor killed his wife and it has become an obsession with him. His vengeance against the gay community is unjust, of course, but it is understandable. And beyond that, it has become a very powerful political issue for him. Mary Wagner was more popular than the First Lady when she died. He's focused his entire political career on this issue in the past couple of years."

"I don't know what to do. I need time to think. I need time," Robert protested. He had thought by bringing his charges and holding his evidence he could control events until Cramer paid up. But the nosy politician had his own agenda, was about to spoil everything.

"You'll be called. I can't guarantee when."

"Can you give me just a week. Can you put him off until then?"

"He's fairly rabid at this point. But I'll try. Given the importance of those notebooks, don't you think they'd be safer with me than chained to your wrist. I suspect a number of people would like to get their hands on these notebooks. I have a vault here in the house that will keep them secure, at least until we see what Senator Wagner is up to. I think you know you can trust me. I promise I'll return the material whenever you say. It belongs to you after all."

Suddenly Robert was exhausted. Even on his best days now, he rarely got by without a long rest in the afternoon. When he grew tired the fatigue became a virtual paralysis. He could barely move or think. The long ride from Connecticut, the excitement of meeting John Davis, the difficult decisions. It was too much for his frail health to accommodate in one day. Abruptly, nothing seemed to matter. Let John Davis take the evidence. Now he only wanted was the oblivion of sleep.

"I guess so," was all Robert said, handing him the briefcase.

Though the tea had gone cold hours ago, he picked up his cup and ate one of the cookies Ellen had proposed. It was delicious, the lemon sugar seemed to course directly to his blood, renewing his energy slightly. The food reminded him to take his afternoon dose of AZN. The pills always went down a little easier with a bit of food. He took one of the blue and yellow capsules from the gold box and swallowed it down with some of the tepid tea.

At first it was only a slight tickle, the sort of mild discomfort one felt with hunger pains, but the sensation built almost immediately to a roaring fire in his stomach. A part of him watched, like watching a movie as the boy clutched involuntarily at his throat, trying to stem burning lava from vomiting forth. The shock of it was stunning, like a calf struck in the forehead by a sledge hammer.

"Oh my God, my God," he heard John Davis call out. "Ellen call 911. Ellen."

He watched the boy slide onto his knees and crash into the teacart before John Davis could catch him.

"Oh, Jesus," Davis said, clearing the boy's mouth of foam with his index finger, tilting the chin back to keep the air way open.

In slight part a curious voyeur, Robert studied the *grand mal* seizure wracking his body, the trunk flexing and jerking in wild bursts of energy like an orgasm that kept building and building and would not break. The face grew red, then blue but still there was no release.

John Davis backed away from Robert's spasmodic body, wiping his fingers clean. He understood now. He would not attempt CPR. In his years as an intern, he had come across it infrequently, but he realized now that it would only be a matter of seconds before the cyanide poison completed its torture.

And as John Davis stepped back, Robert Owen looked out from his dead eyes for the last time of his young life and, mercifully, slept.

Night Breeze

Yves was on fire. When he swallowed it felt as though a razor blade had caught in his throat. He gently examined the lymph nodes under his jaw and found a nest of tender little robin's eggs. When they had first stuffed him into the false bottom of the truck floor, he thought he might suffocate from the exhaust fumes. He lay with Nadia, two spoons in a drawer, the bile rising in his throat like his own terror. The thought of drowning in his own vomit overcame him. He lost control of his bowels and made the situation twice as bad. He was so humiliated he thought he might cry with anger.

On board ship, they gave him a bucket of water and a bar of soap to wash himself, handing them at arms length as though he were a leper. For a day he sat naked, shivering in his cabin while his clothes dried. Then finally, they came for him.

He was exhilarated to be out of the stagnant cabin, to see another human being, if only his captor. Abdel took his hood off and Stavros pushed him across the deck to a companionway leading to the galley. A brilliant scattering of stars illuminated the night, pulsing in the black sky. The moon came across the water, a golden path to the horizon.

"Please, please," he said, breathing deeply of the fresh sea air. "Just for a minute."

Abdel knew that any one of those brilliant stars could in fact be an infrared surveillance satellite sophisticated enough to make out their faces from deep space. Still, they had brought him out at night and he was such a pathetic looking creature. The blood from the gash over his eye had drained into the socket swelling his eye shut. Unshaven, sweating profusely from a fever which had set in, he reeked of a sour sick-person smell.

It was a mistake, of course. Major Kostov's first rule had been never to get emotionally involved with a hostage under any circumstance. If the time came, it was hard to kill someone with whom you had just shared a cigarette. But Abdel remembered the months he'd spent in Israeli detention camps, how prisoners lay motionless, finally passive when brought back from their beatings. He couldn't deny Yves a few moments of comfort before they began their questioning.

Yves thought he might just be waking from a bad dream when they brought him into the galley. The sweet smell of cinnamon and apple filled the room from a pie baking in the coal stove oven. A cozy fire flickered in the grate and a yellow light from the oil lamps cast a warm glow across the highly polished woodwork. Benches were built in the vee of the bow around a heavy table in the middle of the dining salon. The foremast pushed up from the sole through the center of the ship, a great tree reaching for the heavens. They lashed him to it like Odysseus testing his will against the siren's song. But the only incentive they offered him for his cooperation was the chance to stay alive a little while longer.

It seemed to go on for hours. They asked questions about the BE 21 vaccine when they couldn't possibly understand his detailed answers. They grilled him on the operations of Cramer Chemical around the world about which he knew little. They reviewed every item of his itinerary since he left the United States and demanded information on dozens of people he didn't know or had only met casually.

"The Ali Center has identified David Schefflan as the CIA's second man in Athens. Who does he report to?" It could have been a scene from any one of Fotini Theodorou's films but incredibly, the woman stood there in the flesh, wearing the ridiculous black cape that had become her trademark, blowing smoke from her Galouise into his face. Her theatrical get-up would have been comical, except that, having identified her, he realized they would hardly now willingly set him free.

"I'm a scientist, not a spy. This is all a mistake. I demand..."

Fotini smacked him sharply across the face with a plastic fly swatter.

127

"You're not to demand anything," she said, striking him again to emphasize the point. "You are here to answer our questions."

Yves studied her, wondering if she enjoyed this as much as she seemed, or if she were somehow lost in a role she was playing. He imagined a movie director striding in suddenly, calling out, "Cut, cut. Miss Theodorou, would you hit him once more, with a little more authority this time. Do it flat please, the action will carry the sinister thing we want." But Yves was no stunt man and the blood flowing from the cut over his eye that her fly swatter had torn open again was real blood, his own.

"We're just two members of a scientific team," he insisted. "We can't be worth much ransom for you. And it won't be long before others reproduce our results and have the vaccine ready for production," he lied. For the hundredth time since his capture Yves cursed himself for having so scrupulously guarded the secret of the blue epitope and BE 21 vaccine. His kidnappers were luckier than they knew. But he must stick to his story and hope as much for Nadia.

"Could I have some water, please. My throat..."

"I heard the American Ambassador talking with you about November 17th at the residence. What precisely did he say to you? Every word."

Finally, when he could hardly speak anymore, they had taken him away and mercifully let him crawl into his bunk without handcuffing him to frames in his cabin. Yves woke after several hours as though he had endured a raging fire. His fever had subsided but left him faint with dehydration.

"Hello. Hello," he called weakly to the guard, but there was no answer. He tried the door to the cabin half-heartedly and was stunned to find it open. Tentatively, he stuck his head out into the passageway. No one. Were they testing him? Had they simply forgotten to lock him in? The one they called Stavros had the build of a professional wrestler and seemed to have about as much intelligence. Perhaps he figured Yves wasn't going very far on an eighty-foot schooner in the middle of the Mediterranean?

Yves crept to the companionway and stepped gingerly on the stair. He stuck his head above deck, half expecting a boot to smash into his face, but the deck was deserted. For the first time in three days his heart sang with some little hope. Nadia must certainly be on the ship somewhere. He couldn't desert her. But if he escaped, there might be some chance of getting help for her. She was a woman after all. They would treat her better than a man, he reasoned. Some of his kidnappers must certainly be Arabs. He recognized the type in the swarthy Algerians who sill infested the slums of southern France generations after the loss of the colony. These were Nadia's own people. They stuck together these Arabs. They wouldn't hurt her. Who knows, perhaps she even had a hand in all this, was somehow secretly cooperating with them. He wasn't sure of anything anymore.

He was weak, his head throbbed, but he felt the pull of survival in his soul stronger than a rip-tide cutting across the surface of the ocean. Not a mile off starboard, a small island floated on the blue water like a life raft tossed to a sailor who was about to drown.

Committee

John Wagner sat under the great seal of the U.S. Senate in the center of an oak-paneled semi circle, peering out over his reading glasses at the crowd of spectators, reporters, and lobbyists milling about in the hearing room below him. The other members of the Senate subcommittee on oversight and investigations fanning out on his right and left held informal conferences with their colleagues, microphones switched off, or gave directions to their aids while the witnesses began to file into the first rows of the auditorium accompanied by their lawyers.

His administrative assistant had done a good job drumming up press coverage for this hearing, Wagner thought. The little subway which ran under Capitol Hill and carried staff members between the House and Senate offices was abuzz all morning with rumors of indictments about to be passed on to the grand jury, and even the possibility of a secret witness who would cause a number of heads to roll. The word was out. John Wagner was mad, was putting on his red cape yet again to defend the public good, a spectacle that always guaranteed good ratings for C-Span and kept his face before voters who rarely saw the Chairman in the flesh these days except when election time came around. "Do you want a senator who works hard in Washington to get things done, or a candidate criss-crossing the state kissing babies, looking for voters at every barbecue," he demanded of his constituency. But the more he concentrated on national issues in the capitol, the less popular he seemed to grow with voters at home. John Wagner's seniority in Washington mattered less than the fact that New Mexico' education and unemployment statistics ranked worst in the nation. He desperately needed some new currency with voters, especially since his opponents were now so richly funded by Cramer Chemical.

"I'd like to begin the Committee's work here this morning ladies and gentlemen, so would you please take your seats and come to order," he said, punctuating the request with a loud thwack of his gavel.

"As we are all painfully aware, the people of the United States, indeed the people of the entire world currently find themselves in the grip of an epidemic the likes of which mankind has never known. In a few short years this plague has come to threaten our very existence as a species and while it is not the duty of this committee to monitor scientific malpractice we are charged with the responsibility of policing the policemen whose job it is to ferret out scientific misconduct and guarantee the public health and safety of our citizens.

"In the past the American scientific community has argued for a conservative, laissez-faire approach to foster the integrity of biomedical research in our country. Some have accused this committee of trying to institute a *Big Brother* control over science, of stifling its creativity. But for more than a decade now we have acquiesced to the scientific and academic insistence that it keep its own house in order based on their notion of the Final Rule. This Final Rule as outlined to our Appropriations Committee in hearings at the time when the Office of Research Integrity was first instituted defined misconduct as fabrication, falsification, plagiarism, or other practices that seriously deviate from those that are commonly accepted within the scientific community for proposing, conducting, or reporting research. The Final Rule excludes honest error or honest differences in interpretations of data. And it requires that any institution applying for or receiving Public Health Service funding for research has in place policies and procedures to deal with alleged or suspected scientific misconduct.

The question as we meet here today, however, is whether or not the Final Rule provides sufficient control of the scientific community, especially in the private sector which often has only limited ties to the academic institutions monitored by the ORI. Can it protect against the sort of accidents we have seen at Three Mile Island, Chernobyl, and the contamination that occurred only last year at the Westinghouse plant at Pusan? Can it regulate the role science plays in the industrial pollution currently threatening the planet? Can it deter the often inhumane treatment of experimental animals in private laboratories around the world outside its jurisdiction? Many such questions arise as we seek to determine if the health of the American people is sufficiently guaranteed by a philosophy based on a gentleman's code of honor without the power to punish breaches of such an honor code in a vast areas of experimentation and scientific inquiry affecting the public welfare. In short, has the ORI fulfilled its mandate.

Since we may have reached a cross roads in mankind's very existence on this fragile planet, I think it incumbent on this committee to take a long hard look at exactly how successful the Final Rule has been as a policy in guiding our scientific institutions during this past catastrophic decade and to determine what modifications may be necessary to guarantee public trust in those institutions and protect the national interest in the future.

We will be calling on a number of witnesses today, all of whom have dealt with the crisis before us in various capacities, most notably Dr. John Davis who has directed the Office of Research Integrity during most of this period. Would Dr. Davis come forth please."

"Just the facts, ma'am, just the facts," his wife Ellen had joked with him that morning before he left for his office to prepare for the senate hearing. And, in fact, she had given him the best possible advice. He had worked hard in what proved to be a very difficult position since he had taken the helm at ORI, a role that required the wisdom of Solomon as he tried to determine the truth in some very nasty cases of fraud and theft of intellectual property. He was proud of his tenure in the job and would let his record stand for itself. As he came to the witness table however, he only wished that Ellen had not insisted he leave his pipe at home during his testimony. Bad for his pubic image perhaps, but it might have eased the clamminess he felt in his palms as he took his seat in front of the microphone.

"I'd like to say what a pleasure it is to see you again, Dr. Davis. I believe the press has christened you the ethics czar in the years since you last appeared before this committee. I'm sure it hasn't been any easier for you than my role as Grand Inquisitor, as the press would have it, but perhaps you would be kind enough to give the committee some background on how the ORI has developed since its evolution from the OSI and some of the challenges your office has faced."

"Certainly Senator. Let me first say that I am equally pleased to be here today to speak on behalf of the ORI and the philosophy of scientific dialog which, despite its controversial nature has become crucial to our work. I'd like to think that because we are routinely attacked from every quarter, we must be doing something right at the ORI."

A couple of the senators chuckled appreciatively, helping him ease into his subject.

"As you point out, the ORI grew out of an earlier office established in 1989 called the Office of Scientific Integrity in a response to growing public skepticism about this country's scientific institutions. Several notorious and well-publicized cases such the Robert Gallo and David Baltimore investigations had seriously eroded public confidence in the American scientific effort. In Gallo's case, for example, the dispute over who deserved credit for discovering the HIV virus delayed important work toward a cure for AIDS while lawyers argued over patent rights for the blood test to detect HIV. Professional societies such as the Association of American Medical Colleges and the Association for the Advancement of Science worried about the divisive effect on trust among scientists. Politicians felt the public outcry for legislation to guarantee accurate information in areas such as breast implantation and cigarette smoking. The matter went far beyond the question of public funding of science in our culture. Scientists were seen as unethical, rupturing the intimate trust between doctor and patient."

"Well, were these just a couple of rotten apples in the barrel or does the problem run deeper," Wagner interrupted. "Could these case be just the tip of the iceberg?"

"It is difficult to say, Senator. But everyone agreed that it was vital to reestablish good will in the medical and scientific professions. The larger question, of course, as you correctly pointed out, was whether science could effectively govern itself to prevent such breakdowns in the public trust."

Wagner made occasional notes, and scrutinized his colleagues to see what they made of Dr. Davis's presentation.

"It is true that the scientific community has resisted any outside control, but this was not done out of mere self interest. Scientists did not wish to be governed by any agency that did not include an emphasis on the review of scientific issues in their decisions. And who else, after all, could claim the expertise to assess their achievements or failures. They wanted the objective laws of science to serve as the final standard by which they would be judged, a code of ethics essential to the very process by which science is carried out.

"One eloquent exponent of this position is Dr. Richard Feynman who sums it up best when he describes the scientific code as 'a kind of utter honesty—a leaning over backwards to provide details that could throw doubt on your interpretation.' You must do the best you can, he says, if you know anything at all wrong, or possibly wrong - to explain it. The idea is to try to give all the information to help others to judge the value of your contribution. Other experimenters will repeat your experiment and find out whether you were wrong or right. Nature's phenomena will agree or they'll disagree with your theory. And although you may gain some temporary fame and excitement, you will not gain a good reputation as a scientist if you haven't tried to be very careful in this kind of work.

"I believe the great majority of today's scientists subscribe to this philosophy, Senator, though I recognize our need to be vigilant. Everyone benefits when this philosophy is brought to bear. It is the very basis of scientific dialog that has been the guiding principle in resolving questions as they come to the ORI."

"Can you explain how this works in practical terms, Dr. Davis? What happens exactly when you discover a scientist hasn't acted in a gentlemanly fashion?"

John Davis paused a moment to consider whether he should pick up on the sarcasm in the question. He smiled and decided to push on and not take the bait.

"Well, according to the model I've been describing," Davis continued, "the ORI functions somewhat like the editor of a scientific journal. If an author makes a claim unsubstantiated by presentation of data, the editor can demand that those data be adduced or the paper will not be published. The burden of proof must always fall on the person who makes claims about his or her data. The process is one of professional challenge to examine and evaluate data rather than an accusation per se.

"An alternate model that has been advocated by the legal profession from the OSI's inception is the legal adversary model. Here the accused receives specific charges in writing, can face and cross examine witnesses, retain legal counsel and introduce evidence on his own behalf. In this model, the scientist is merely an *expert witness* and questions are resolved on the basis of civil law and not scientific evidence. This legalistic approach does not serve science nor does it offer much protection for the whistle-blower or the reputation of his accuser in such investigations.

"It is my firm belief that in de-personalizing the case and stressing the issues of science all parties are best served. The issues are often seen as more complex than those brought in the original allegation. The Office of Research Integrity becomes a scientific arbiter, responsible for identifying and framing the issues without needlessly ruining reputations or endangering the rights of the accuser. Without this balanced approach, the ORI would have been far less successful in restoring the public faith and curtailing misconduct in the sciences."

"That's a very optimistic picture you have painted for us, Dr. Davis. Very rosy. But I wonder why this honor code didn't work in the cases you brought up earlier. In fact, I wonder if there aren't in fact a lot more rotten apples in the barrel than you would have us believe."

Senator Wagner nodded to his aid on the floor, who lifted several brightly colored charts in place on the tripod before the audience.

"Just last September you'll recall that the Human Resources Subcommittee cited ten case studies of superficial and biased university handling of alleged scientific misconduct and financial conflicts of interest. And I might add these investigations resulted in significant retaliation against whistle blowers. Universities seem to get serious heartburn when it comes to actively pursuing their own faculty in such matters, and I think it's pretty clear why.

"I might remind the committee that the Patent Reform Act allows universities to retain exclusive rights to patents generated by research in their labs, even when the work has been subsidized by taxpayers. This goes beyond airing your dirty laundry in public, Dr. Davis. Some of these professors have turned into regular cash cows for university departments."

"Senator, last year we issued a report recommending that you enact legislation restricting honoraria, consultation fees, and stock holdings for grantees conducting evaluations..."

"A lot of your colleagues Dr. Davis, feel that misconduct is so rare that we're wasting our time on it," Wagner interrupted, warming to his subject. "But this recent survey by the Acadia Institute in Bar Harbor, Maine tells us that 43 percent of graduate students and 50 percent of faculty members have *direct knowledge* of some form of misconduct in their laboratories."

"That survey measures perception, Senator, and not verifiable incidence of wrongdoing. If you look at the chart..."

"A scientist who massages his data to make it appear his new drug is effective in order to land a lucrative deal with a pharmaceutical company is committing criminal conduct of the highest order and has to be treated as such, Dr. Davis. He is no gentleman and should not be judged by a system that has a tendency to protect its own. There has simply developed too great a conflict of interest for science to claim the authority to regulate its own behavior in these areas.

Perhaps you are old enough to remember the early days of atomic energy in this country Dr. Davis when the high priests of the AEC announced a limitless source of energy that would be so cheap it would not even need to be metered. This miracle of technology would make us masters of the universe. The "cleared" elite responsible for this brave new world was given absolute authority to operate under a cloak of secrecy and keep our highest officials in the dark concerning their mistakes and failures. It was only years later that we discovered how nuclear testing had turned our own citizens into guinea pigs and the risks this "clean" energy source posed for the environment. The power of the AEC in the giddy days after Hiroshima was unlimited without any Congressional oversight. Science was governing itself, all right, the same way the National Security Council and the Central

Intelligence agency ran their misguided secret operations throughout the cold war. And I'm afraid the same thing is happening today in our own Public Health Service and National Institutes of Health as they work with the private sector to develop new products, despite the honor code in place at the ORI.

"With all due respect Senator I think you are over stating the situation. The vast majority of cases brought to us involve sloppy science rather than crooked science and sloppy science in my opinion is far more dangerous because there is so much more of it. Incompetence and some misconduct remain undetected because scientists no longer have any reason to replicate the results of their colleagues. Funding is no longer given for such work by Committees such as yours and as a result we must depend on whistle blowers to bring such misconduct to light. When they come forth they are accused of being jealous or vindictive. They're taken off experiments and placed in charge of mouse husbandry for the remainder of the experiment. Who is going to take the word of a well-meaning graduate student over a Nobel Laureate on the team? This is why we must have the resources to check data and protect the honest scientists who are willing to come forth and risk all for the sake of science. Our system protects these courageous individuals."

"Then why do so many whistle blowers consider the ORI just window dressing, Dr. Davis? Why have so many had to resort to litigation to achieve vindication and some sort of restitution. "

"We do protect such scientists, Senator. The accusers name is kept absolutely confidential in our investigations."

"What about Robert Owen, Dr. Davis. The ORI was not able to protect him in its investigation. He wound up paying with his life for his efforts."

"Robert Owen's death was a tragic suicide. It is unconscionable of you Senator to accuse this office..."

"Robert Owen, for the record, was the homosexual partner of the late Dr. Michael Riley, was he not?" Wagner said, stressing the word homosexual.

"They were partners, yes."

"Isn't it true that before his death, Robert Owen came to your house to expose the fact that his 'homosexual partner' had in fact caused the HIV IV virus responsible for the world epidemic ravaging the world. And isn't it also true that early on in his work the very vaccine responsible for that virus was investigated by your offices at the complaint of a rival laboratory which claimed that he had stolen the cell line on which the vaccine was based?

"We had no way of knowing Dr. Riley would administer his own vaccine to himself causing the HIV IV mutation. There was no reason not to think he had simply contracted the disease in the course of his work. We only sequenced the vaccine after Robert Owen explained the code for the meaningless genetic segment Riley had built into the virus."

"I'm sorry, but the ORI fumbled the ball here Dr. Davis. But I don't believe you are to blame. The ORI was never constituted as an investigative agency like the FBI or the Department of Justice. If it had been, we might not have missed such crucial facts in this case. When the proper expertise is brought to bear in such investigations, however, we can avoid such tragic oversights and ineptitude. We have fortunately begun to get to the bottom of this question with the help of the FBI and I'd like to excuse you for the moment, Dr. Davis, while guards bring in a witness who should be able to shed a great deal of light on the situation."

On cue, Senator's Wagner's administrative assistant directed the rear doors of the hall to swing open where two plain clothes agents accompanied the emaciated person of Whitfield Bingham down the center aisle to the witness table. He floated into the auditorium as though it were an out of body experience, taking in the curious onlookers like a flock of sea gulls swarming about him for bits of bread thrown into the air. A lovely day, sunshine so bright, glaring in his eyes like floodlights, or the strobe flash of cameras bursting all about him to light his sallow features, expose the debauched mask of his face.

Deep-Freeze

Generally, the sentry didn't speak when spoken to unless there was something in it for him. He preferred to stand on deck, hours at a time, searching the sky, scanning the waves for the unexpected, something that would prompt a reward, a storm cloud on the horizon, a school of tuna gliding to the surface, just begging for the bow and arrow. When he got bored, he pecked neurotically at the cherry red toenails his mistress insisted painting on him when she finished weaving lanyards or cooking for the crew. He tried hanging upside down once to put her off, his red claws sunk into the wooden perch fast as death, but it only encouraged her. She thought so much of the trick she opened a can of sardines just for him.

It had been long time since anyone had come to feed him and when he noticed the man pop his head up the companionway, Ganymede began bobbing his head up and down in imitation. The cockatoo shifted his weight from foot to foot, usually a sure bet to lure one of the crew to take him up on an arm and set him on their shoulder. But the man just looked past him nervously, and crouched hiding behind the mainmast.

The bird wasn't about to give in that easily and held his peace. Instead he puffed up his downy black feathers, a gesture he knew to be irresistible, and waited for the next move in this game of hide and seek. Incredibly, the man did not come to his perch to smooth down his feathers and try to tease him into speech. More incredibly, the man carefully let his legs drop over the topside of the ship, hanging on to the rail for a while like hanging on to a perch and as they approached a tiny island floating off starboard, let himself slip silently into the sea. The bird was so shocked by this disappearance, he immediately let loose with the first thing that came to mind.

"Caw, Caw, Caw," the cockatoo cried in the rather poor imitation of a crow his mistress had once taught him as a joke. It was enough, however, to bring her on deck.

"What is it beauty," she said, stroking his feathers to calm him. "Has no one fed you yet today."

"Caw, caw," he insisted. Then finally she noticed.

"Stavros, Stavros," she cried. The guard came running immediately.

"He's making for Paximada," she said pointing to Yves, swimming awkwardly a hundred yards off into the open sea. "Go."

Stavros quickly stripped naked. It was a body Fotini knew well and despite the emergency, she enjoyed a sensual nostalgia taking in the thick torso, muscular abdomen and thighs, the classic genitalia. This boy was virtually raised in the waters of the Mediterranean and he set off to capture Yves with more power than a Barracuda. Taking his prey was more difficult, however. If he'd come willingly, like a lifeguard rescuing a swimmer who had ventured into a strong current, it would have been easy to swim back to the *Ceberus* with him. Yves did his best, but he was no match for the younger man. It was like fighting with a giant octopus in some frothy Jules Verne tale. And both men knew instinctively that one of them must drown.

Despite his exhaustion and the raging terror that kept propelling him out of the waves, from somewhere deep in his memory Yves recalled the absurd instructions. A grade-B science fiction film, a new invention, the diver would go deeper than man had ever gone, a new technology balancing ocean pressure with the fluid in your helmet, the first few minutes breathing in the fluid would be difficult, don't fight it, don't fight it, it will be all right, a natural instinct, deeper than man has ever gone.

By the time Stavros had tucked Yves' chin firmly under his arm and swam back to the ship, the rest of the crew had come on deck to haul them in. Abdel checked his pulse, tilted back his neck and locked his mouth on Yves' breathing deeply four times into the rigid chest. He continued the resuscitation for several minutes until Fotini walked over and placed her foot against Yves' neck.

"Enough of that," she said. "We still have the woman. Stavros, take him below and put him in locker A. We may have a use for him yet."

Om Kousoum

For two days Nadia listened to the steady hypnotic drip of a pipe somewhere overhead her cabin until she thought she would go mad. The only other sound was the constant brush of ocean against the ship as it made its mysterious way across the Mediterranean and occasional voices when the watches changed on deck. She struggled to make out what they were saying, but the voices were faint, distant as in dream, and her Greek was little more than that of a tourist making pleasantries.

Some hours after they were underway, the bigger of the two men in the truck came to her cabin, mercifully removed the handcuffs and hood over her head and set down a bucket for a chamber pot. Twice they came with a modest meal, bread, cheese, some fruit and water. There was no exit save through the heavy wooden door, no porthole. A single cot with built-in end table was the only furniture. A reading lamp over the cot cast a weak light in the room, barely enough to see by. She tapped quietly on the walls of the cabin trying to signal Yves without alerting her captors, but guessed from the silence that he was being held in another part of the ship. She tried to determine their direction, but it was pointless without the winds or landmarks to guide her. At a speed of nine knots they'd have covered perhaps three hundred miles she calculated. The Aegean was dotted with more than three thousand islands, they could be heading anywhere from Rhodes to Corfu. There was nothing to do but count the knots in the pine boards paneling her cabin and try to come up with some sort of plan if she ever saw the light of day again.

Nadia ruminated for hours on the incredible circumstances that ended in her captivity. Abdel Ayat, the serious boy, the dark-eyed poet she had come to love all those years ago at university, now her kidnapper. And even stranger, the ship abducting her being captained by the movie actress she had met only two days ago at the American ambassador's party. Nadia had recognized the powdered face immediately set in that famous scowl which seemed to project scorn, fear and anger all at the same time. "They will hold me for ransom," Nadia thought, fingering the blue sapphire pendant which had hung on her neck since the day Yves had placed it there. Despite their impassioned rhetoric, she knew these fundamentalists were often just simple thugs, garden variety bandits robbing banks in the name of religion. But what could Fotini Theodorou want with more money? She was said to be one of the richest women in Greece.

Nadia's secret would be worth a fortune, the kidnappers were right about that. There was no chance that anyone at Cramer Chemical could easily unravel the security codes in which they had shrouded the gene sequence of the blue epitope used to formulate the vaccine. Even if someone else discovered the blue epitope independently it would take months to test their findings while the epidemic raged over the world. Partly out of sentiment, but as an extra protection should he need to erase the computer record entirely, Yves had devised a safeguard for their discovery. Several weeks after conclusive trials on BE 21, he called Kaplan Lazare, the large New York firm that occasionally provided industrial diamonds for Cramer Chemical on special order. Yves described the high security nature of the project and they agreed to let him be the sole operator of the computer that programmed laser imprint identification numbers cut into the diamonds. Instead of a diamond, Yves purchased a three carat Ceylon Sapphire, a perfect cornflower blue. On the fine line separating top and bottom facets, the girdle of the gem, he etched the base pair sequence demarcating the boundaries of the blue epitope in characters reduced by the power of one hundred. The formula became visible when blasted with light under a microscope, or was examined by a specially modified bar code scanner, but otherwise, the formula was invisible to the naked eye.

In the right hands, the jewel she wore around her neck had a value far greater than any thief could possibly imagine. It was the physical key to all the years of work she had devoted to her discovery, both the symbol of hope and a literal record of the promise that hope inspired. But like all keys, its value depended strictly on knowing the lock it was destined to open. She considered throwing the jewel into the ocean when she got the chance, but for the moment decided the secret of the sapphire was safe. The jewel might be needed before this ordeal was over. She pulled the pendant from her neck and with great difficulty pried the four prongs holding the sapphire in its setting. She wedged the fine chain into a crevice between the pine wallboards and planted the sapphire out of sight deep in the canal of her left ear.

Why hadn't she just screamed out for help when she first saw the men burst into her room. She fantasized a hundred different scenarios for her escape. Why had she been so slow to see what was coming. Why hadn't she at least struck out at them.

On the third day of her captivity Nadia heard shouting and a commotion of voices on deck. For a while they stopped their voyage and then picked up again in the relentless pinching in and falling off as the ship cut in and out of gusts of wind. Nadia covered herself in the rough blankets and tried to sleep despite the cold wind pouring under her door and whistling about the ship. Dream like, from somewhere on the ship she heard the mournful song of *Oum Koulsoum* lamenting the nature of love and destiny from one of the cheap cassette tapes sold on every street corner of the Arab world. "Oh beloved, your eyes were like daggers in my heart. Beloved, why have you deserted me..." The Egyptian diva had given concerts from Baghdad to Rabat before her death, raising money for the Palestinian cause. Millions had crowded the streets of Cairo for her funeral. The unearthly voice gave shape to the pain and suffering of an entire people like truth incarnate for generations. She sang the single word "love" for what seemed like the eternity of love, delineating all the permutations from pain to ecstasy. The listener let go of self, sacrificed personality in the stream of emotion she created, like an old man smoking kif in the medina, lost in flow of traffic before him, or a pilgrim at Mecca bending his body in prayer with a ten thousand others, subjugating his will to the will of God. The death of a firstborn son, the treachery of a lover. What did one gain from struggling against fate? Nadia listened to the song, so familiar from her youth, and let it transport her into an exhausted sleep.

Press Conference

Martin Cramer stood behind a podium emblazoned with the stylized caduceus by which Cramer Chemical proclaimed itself to the world. A little forest of microphones had been planted in front of him and camera floodlights bathed him in a harsh, hyper-real white light. He looked out through the glare at the audience with the aid of specially tinted eyeglasses that eliminated glare without concealing his eyes. The lenses had saved him during countless press conferences, enabling him to field questions calmly and project sincerity by maintaining eye contact with reporters. He looked beyond the audience through the glass walls of the conference hall where Mercury stood exultant in a fountain of light and crystal. Martin knew he'd need all the help the wily God might offer as he called the press conference to order.

"Ladies and Gentlemen I'd like to give a brief opening statement if I might and then I'll try to answer whatever questions you might have," he said, trying to lasso in some stragglers at the periphery of the hall.

When his two star scientists were first discovered missing, the media poured over Cramer Chemical like disinfectant spilled over a contaminated laboratory work bench. Martin had to make some quick decisions on how he was going to deal with the flood of reporters converging on Connecticut from all corners of the earth.

For weeks he had carefully cultivated the world's expectation for salvation, but now the missing messiahs seemed to auger the apocalypse. Robert Owen's gruesome demise only wetted the press's appetite for sensational copy. Murder or suicide, how had the young administrative assistant died? What was he doing at the home of the ORI Director at the time? Was he tied to the recent kidnapping somehow?

Though it hadn't yet brought formal charges, Senator Wagner's Oversight committee had subpoenaed records of Michael Riley's early work on HIV IV. It was impossible to know how much Martin's assistant might have told John Davis before his death, but the millions of dollars Robert had demanded for philanthropic AIDS foundations had been safely transferred to the Akai account in Bern, an extra bonus from his decision to dispose of the little blackmailer. He was relieved to be called to Greece on behalf of his star scientists. It would be good to be out of the country, Martin thought to himself, while Robert Owen's death was investigated. Geneva was a quick flight from Athens. He could live comfortably enough in Switzerland with five hundred million dollars if things began to fall apart.

Meanwhile, Martin instinctively decided to go on the offensive while he waited for events to unfold, always the best defense. Yesterday's transmission from Athens was manna sent from heaven. Finally, he had something the swarming sharks could feed on besides Cramer Chemical.

Wonderfully, it turned out that Arab terrorists were taking responsibility for the kidnapping of his researchers. The western press had developed a very keen taste for Arab terrorism, nourished over the years by routine hijacking, bombings and political executions. Nothing galvanized public opinion better than some act of terrorism by Islamic fundamentalists. It afforded the West the luxury of looking at the world in terms of black and white, good vs. evil, GI Joe versus the swarthy assassin. The vast diversity of people, cultures, politics, and religious philosophies found in the Arab world all wore the same satanic face as Saddam Hussein, Mohamar Khadaffi, or an Iranian Ayatollah whichever villain currently held center stage in a particular confrontation with the West. Martin Cramer knew that Anti-Arabism was even more American than anti-Semitism. It would provide him with wonderful cover.

"Ladies and gentlemen, I am sorry to report that yesterday we received confirmation from the American Embassy in Athens that a group calling itself Islamic Rebirth has taken Dr. Nadia Mansur and Dr. Yves Bourret hostage and have presented a list of demands in order to secure their release.

As I am sure you are aware, Dr. Mansur and Dr. Bourret have just recently completed trials of a new AIDS vaccine here at Cramer Chemical which we feel is about to end the decades of death and suffering that have plagued the world since the appearance of this disease. Until now there has been no vaccine, no cure, and not even an indisputably effective treatment. But all these years of frustration are about to end with the new vaccine they have developed.

Initial trials have shown the BE 21 aerosol vaccine to be a safe and effective regimen in the treatment of HIV IV infection as well as the prevention of such infection and its sequelae. Their work will eradicate the most terrifying scourge of the century and they must be permitted to return to their friends and family unharmed.

It is outrageous that a group which purports to base its demands on human rights and justice would risk the lives of innocent people by denying them a life-saving vaccine. Many of these innocent people are to be found in the very refugee camps that Islamic Rebirth wants to have disbanded. We ask these terrorists to consider the fate of their own people and release the scientists who might finally put an end to the great suffering the world has endured throughout this epidemic.

Tomorrow I will leave for Athens to represent Cramer Chemical at the command post as we await negotiations for the release of Dr. Mansur and Dr. Bourret."

The conference room burst into an uproar, reporters shouting to get Martin Cramer's attention. He spotted a woman from the Post who had done a recent series on teenage pregnancy and AIDS babies. She specialized in family life and he hoped for a soft ball from her spot-lighting the female kidnap victim.

"Is that Marti Bayer," he said, pointing to her in recognition.

"The Washington Post," she said, standing. "Dr. Cramer, we are all sympathetic to the terrible ordeal these hostages must be undergoing. But regarding the larger question of the world AIDS epidemic, are you saying that the dissemination of this vaccine is somehow contingent on the physical release of these two scientists. Surely their work on this trial vaccine can be replicated."

So much for softballs.

"Marti, I'm sure you appreciate how fiercely competitive the drive to make this vaccine has been over the years. The cure for AIDS is probably the most important medical discovery for mankind that science will make. The security involved in protecting our rights has necessarily been unprecedented. I'm afraid the exact segment of the viral DNA, the blue epitope which Dr. Mansur modified and incorporated into the BE 21 vaccine has been a very closely guarded secret. At the end Dr. Bourret felt it necessary to encode the results of his work even in his own laboratory to avoid the risk of industrial espionage. So yes, for the moment, he and Dr. Mansur are the only ones who can recreate their vaccine. We will certainly begin work immediately to try to reconstruct its design from successfully immunized patients. But it's going to take some time..."

"Are we talking weeks, months," she interrupted.

"I'm afraid I just don't know that."

"But..."

"Yes, you sir, at the rear," Martin said, cutting her off..

"I am Cherif Rachid reporting for Al Ayat in London. I wish to know if Islamic Rebirth has expressed any motive other than the securement of the Palestinian State for this kidnapping. The Arab world has long regarded Dr. Mansur's father, Hamadi Mansur a martyr in the struggle for a homeland since his assassination. He was one of the earliest and most eloquent spokesmen for this cause. Some have speculated that his daughter must ultimately follow in her father's footsteps. So the question must be asked. Is there any suspicion on the part of the authorities that Dr. Mansur may not be the unwilling victim of a kidnapping. Of if, on the other hand, some vendetta is being played out by Hamas or Hezbollah against the more moderate PLO faction Hamadi Mansur represented."

"I know Nadia Mansur to be a dedicated scientist who has committed her life to ending humanity's greatest health crises. Any implication that she would pervert this work for the sake of political blackmail is absurd and reprehensible. She is a citizen of the world, her loyalties lie with mankind. That's all I can tell you. Next please..."

"Mario Paglisi, The New York Post, Dr. Cramer. Uh, what progress have the police made in the investigation of Robert Owen's death. Have they been able to confirm that his death was a suicide, or is there still any question of foul play?"

"The initial autopsy report cites respiratory failure pursuant to cyanide poisoning as the cause of Robert's death. It appears that AZN capsules he had been taking were contaminated by the cyanide. We can not say with certainty yet who is responsible. It may be the same sort of terrorism we've seen with Islamic Rebirth, but I rather think that in the end Robert will prove to be one more casualty in the onslaught of this deadly epidemic."

Martin lowered his voice and drew a little closer to the microphones. "Robert Owen was more than my assistant. When he first told me that he had contracted AIDS it was as though my own son had been given a death sentence. I immediately contacted our Corporate Medical director, Dr. James Curtis, and Robert was provided with the best care available, including psychiatric counseling. Clinical depression is often an early unfortunate complication when one is given the diagnosis of AIDS. It's an understandable psychological reaction, I think, when given the news of one's imminent demise, especially for one so young and promising.

"Robert's spirits soared when the BE 21 vaccine was first announced, but the kidnapping of Dr. Mansur and Dr. Bourret became a personal tragedy, plunging him even deeper into his depression. I can only assume that, denied hope once again, Robert, like his friend Michael Riley before him, rashly decided to take his own life. Perhaps, indirectly, Islamic Rebirth has claimed its first victim in this vicious game it has begun."

Martin paused, pleased with the effect his words seemed to have on the audience. Gradually he was beginning to manipulate the press conference in the direction he had hoped for. The questions grew more muted. A reporter from Bangkok asked if BE 21 had been tested on the strain of AWING found in Chiang Mai which preferred moist mucosal tissue for host cells and had turned the epidemic in Thailand into a disease found predominantly in heterosexuals. When he began to review the demands of Islamic Rebirth, the tone of their questions drifted into the sort of recrimination for terrorism he had hoped to elicit from the journalists. Even when things got a little closer to the bone and a reporter raised the rumor that HIV IV might somehow prove to have its origins in early work done at Cramer Chemical itself, Martin was successfully able to trot out Michael

Riley's tired old ghost in his role as heroic victim in the crusade against AIDS.

Finally, the question came that Martin had been anticipating. The one he planned to end the press conference.

"What proof do you have that Dr. Mansur and Dr. Bourret are actually in the hands of this group," Mario Paglisi asked. "How do you know they simply haven't eloped somewhere, or run their car off a mountain. How can you be sure some clever Arab commando isn't just grabbing a little free publicity until they turn up?"

"We have been advised that a video tape of Dr. Mansur will shortly be delivered in which she will report on the their condition. Meanwhile, the terrorists have provided us with solid evidence that Dr. Bourret at least is in their custody, evidence which demonstrates Islamic Rebirth's barbarity and has made us fully determined to challenge this outrage with the co-operation of international police agencies until these criminals are apprehended and brought to justice."

"So, what evidence is that exactly," Paglisi pressed.

Martin took of his glasses and read from a sheet of paper in a flat monotone.

"At 4:30 P.M. on December 25 a package was delivered to the embassy which contained the frozen index, middle and ring fingers of a human hand. Standard fingerprint analysis as well as genetic cross matching prove them to be, incontrovertibly, the severed fingers from the right hand of Dr. Yves Bourret."

Martin listened contentedly as the press conference broke up and reporters thrashed around the room, hurrying to file their stories. He imagined the boiling surface of a jungle river as a school of piranhas prepares to feed.

Sailing

When Fotini first began sailing the Aegean, long before the American cultural invasion produced establishments like the Sex Pizza Parlor and Lip Stick Disco, each of the Greek islands took its own unique character from local traditions, history and archeology. One by one the islands had been discovered, devoured and abandoned by hoards of tourists swarming in like locusts. They gave each other AIDS and syphilis and herpes throughout the season and left their legacy for the young people of Hydra. The next year, they descended on fashionable Mykonos and the dance bars blasted out the local population each night until the sun came up and the revelers wandered home through the labyrinth of tiny streets.

For many young people, contracting AIDS seemed so inevitable since the epidemic began, the only response was to abandon oneself to the pleasures of life before the grim reaper knocked on your door. Theirs were not the innocent revels of Dionysus. The islands had become a Medieval tapestry celebrating the *danse macabre*, except that death wore a pony tail and leather vest, and took you in his arms with a sweet, James Dean smile.

Fotini's chosen haven, the tiny island of Aghios Nikolaos off Crete, weathered the storm fairly well. She had bought the three-story house overlooking the harbor and little lake when the crowds moved on, and the island fell out of the limelight as a cosmopolitan resort. The Venetians built the mighty fortress of Mirabello here and now it had become her own fortress when the contemporary world enervated her with its commerce, vulgarity, and disorder. The village encircling the harbor was still said to be the most beautiful in all of Greece.

It was here that the gods were born in man's imagination, in the caves of Crete, the sun and moon were first worshiped. Before Theseus came to slay the Minotaur, Minoan colonies flourished across the Mediterranean. The wealth of this civilization, its technological development, its God-given laws became the model for the mythical Atlantis. Ten thousand windmills still turned slowly on the Lasithi plateau like the ghost acolytes mourning the death of the Vegetation God in the Idean cave as winter approached. Fotini was certain she had lived in the kingdom of Minos in another life.

In the museums of Herakleion she studied figurines of the snake goddess, the voluptuous breasts displayed in the bodice of her dress, each hand grasping a viper, her lips set in a gentle, enigmatic smile. Fotini's limbs tensed expectantly, standing before the delicious youths, boys and girls both, who cavorted across the frescoes in the sacred sport of bull-leaping. She sat in the cool shadows of the museum contemplating an image of Pasiphae in the Labyrinth. The Minotaur's young mother studied the little monster in her lap, fascinated with his every detail like any girl who had just given birth. There was the human torso in full if delicate potential, the tiny penis, and perfect little finger tips. But also the baby horns just budding above the triangular ears and brutish forehead, the large eyes like drops of currant jelly which would one day comprehend the nature of his monstrosity and develop a rage so intense that no amount of human flesh would quench his anger.

Fotini saw her own mother studying the child the American soldier had sired before abandoning her to the squalor of the labyrinth in Athens. A perfect infant, exquisite features, and unless the child lived too much in the sun or chose to concede her patrimony, the world would never know her father had been a black Marine from Washington, D.C. If her mother never spoke of him, Fotini would just develop into an olive-skinned Mediterranean beauty. Spain or Greece or Italy, what matter the country of her birth.

One day when she was a child, Fotini found her father's photograph tucked in the book her mother used to explain dreams and tell the future, and in a sentimental lapse of resolve, her mother had told Fotini everything about him. From that day on, the monster came to her daily in the mirror and Fotini grew to womanhood behind a mask of white powder, concealing the scorn she felt for the men who passed through her life. In Crete she was home, could walk barefoot among the olive trees, nurtured for centuries by the Minotaur's sacrificial blood. Without the extravagant makeup, dressed in plain black, she lived incognito, could pass for a simple widow, withered by grief and duress, lost to the category of male desire.

One useful feature Fotini had built into the little mansion on the canal in Aghios Nikolaos was a Venetian style boathouse that provided access from the water. She kept a remote control on the *Ceberus'* launch and the automatic door slid open with the touch of a button as though she were coming home to a two car garage. More than one high ranking government official had found it a convenient escape route when the tabloids got wind of a potential sex scandal and sent photographers to camp on her doorstep.

The night the *Ceberus* slipped into port and quietly dropped anchor, the fortuitous moon had clouded over, helping to conceal their arrival.

"Please, not again," Nadia begged as Stavros bridled her mouth with a towel gag. But Fotini had refused to take their hostage into the launch unless the woman was once again bound motionless, and secured out of view under a tarp like a sack of potatoes.

"What are you thinking of," she said. "Has it occurred to you that people sometimes take an interest in my coming and going here. I'm not exactly the local baker delivering fresh loaves of bread. Have you forgotten what happened to the Frenchman?"

For two days, Stavros and Yanis made trips back and forth to the ship, replenishing their stores with fresh provisions while Abdel and Nadia monitored the world media coverage of the missing scientists. CNN, Tokyo Channel 5 and the BBC all carried in-depth background stories on the hostages. The Sultan of Brunei, who had barely survived yet another AIDS related pneumonia had offered a hundred million dollars for the hostages' release, but so far, the media could do little more than speculate on the their whereabouts. Abdel was certain, however, that behind the scenes, every police agency in the world would be working overtime to track them down.

Nadia was given clean hospital surgical scrubs and locked in a soundproof room in the cellar where Fotini occasionally entertained gentlemen whose sexual tastes included controlled abuse. Weeks before they began this operation, she had installed special electronic equipment shipped from Sofia that would distort their voices beyond recognition. Fotini sometimes recorded her discipline sessions in the playroom for posterity, so cameras and lighting were already in place.

The videotape of Nadia went quite well in the end. After identifying shots of her face and body to show she was still unharmed, they filmed her from behind as she calmly read the prepared statement begging for her life, reiterating the demands of Islamic Rebirth. Fotini argued that something dramatic was needed to assure the world of their seriousness.

"We aren't butchers," Abdel insisted. "We want the world to see the justice of our cause.

"Do you think this is a holiday cruise? Do you think we can just sail across the ocean while they toy with their response? Time is our enemy. Every hour we waste the closer you are to hanging by the neck. We must show them what will happen if they do not meet our deadline. Besides, it is already a fait accompli, nothing more need be done."

"One day we will have to live with the rest of the nations of the world, not as barbarians."

But finally he had relented. At the end of the video, Fotini reiterated the threat to end Nadia's life as well as any hope for an end to the epidemic.

"Don't be mistaken," she said in the strange robot voice, looking from beneath her hood directly into the camera. "We are prepared to take action unless our demands are met."

And like Salome touting her prize at the end of her performance, she drew up the frozen head of Yves Bourret from a bucket for all the world to contemplate.

It was the first news Nadia had had of her lover since the ordeal had begun. She began screaming, and sagged into the ropes binding her to the chair. Fotini decided it couldn't have been better if she were playing the part of hostage herself.

They dispatched Stavros to Athens to deliver the videotape to the American Embassy. Two additional members of Islamic Rebirth were taken aboard for the longer voyage. Her Arab crew made her uncomfortable, but they knew the local waters at their destination and would be essential on the open sea. The remains of the French scientist she would feed into the sea, like Medea dispensing body parts of her children to retard Jason's pursuit.

There would be no King Aegeus waiting to make her his bride to thank her for her trouble, though the more she considered the prospect of Abdel's dark stubble pulling across her breasts, his strong arms pinning her to her bunk, the pleasure of losing, being taken by him, the more inclined she became to give free reign to the sexual curiosity, that sweet tension she felt building in her as they had sailed the *Ceberus*.

Abdel was an avid student on the voyage to Crete. He wanted to know everything she did, like a precocious child who has just discovered computer science or the intricacies of chess. He stood at her side at the chart table while she plotted their course from OCEAN PASSAGES FOR THE WORLD. For that time of year, it directed her 34 degrees North, 45 degrees west to avoid the shipping traffic from Cyprus to Italy. Once out of those lanes they would be westing for nearly the entire voyage. She turned on the Icom receiver, tuned in the Naval Observatory time signals and set her watch and the boat's chronometers. It had taken her a long time to feel comfortable with all the sophisticated gadgetry—she still preferred to make her way using the stars and a simple sextant when sailing for pleasure. This time out, she was glad to have the equipment do most of the work for her.

The Long Range Aid to Navigation system would take over the steering, a satellite monitoring their various positions along the way, sending heading corrections to the ship to keep them on course. If not routine, LORAN made circumnavigation of the globe an ordinary affair, even without a crew. It could pilot the ship while the captain got a few hours sleep, as long as he had trained himself to wake when the wind freshened or the sails began to soften and the ship required a change of tack. Of course, you could still have your skull crushed or be knocked into the water if the crosswinds sent you jibbing in the dark. They would have their work cut out for themselves, despite the Global Position System and other fancy equipment she had installed on the Ceberus.

"We'll head due west. If I correct for magnetic deviation, we'll be holding the compass at 270 degrees true."

"But how do you adjust the compass…"

"The compass doesn't move, the ship moves. If we want to head due north we set a course for zero degrees, due west, we follow the course at three quarters of the pie. It's different for the radar. Your own ship is always in the middle and 12:00 on the screen monitor is always straight ahead. These rings on the dial tell you how far away things are. The picture on the screen turns the opposite way the boat turns. You see."

"No, I don't exactly see." His face was very close to hers over the monitor. She was charmed to see that he was actually blushing.

"There, that bright streak at twenty miles distance. That's probably a barge with steel sides, there, to the right of our head up. If we turn to the barge, it will appear to move left on the screen. Do you see?" She rested her hand on his forearm while she instructed him.

"Yes, I understand," Abdel said. He kept his eyes fixed on the radar screen and made no effort to move away from her.

Fishing

When Nadia was a little girl she used to love to go to the small port in her village each morning as the sun rose to watch the fishermen bring in the catch from the night before. At first she was just a nuisance and they wouldn't let her near the crates filled with flopping fish. But the dark-eyed girl wouldn't go away, and finally old Mustapha who was her mother's cousin began to let her help clean the nets and sort the fish for the market. One day after a year of pleading with Mustapha and her mother, the old fisherman agreed to take her along fishing if her father accepted.

"Oh please, please Baba," she begged her father. "It must be like a seagull flying, anywhere on the ocean, to be free to sail anywhere at all. I want to see the fish come up in the nets. I want to see how they catch them, how many there are. Please let me Baba, oh please."

She was like a relentless urchin begging in the market. He would have no peace until he gave in to her.

Her mother prepared an orange, some figs and a bottle of water tied up in a filet to take along on the voyage. Nadia stood waving to her on the shore as the sun fell over the edge of the horizon and the lights of her village disappeared completely in the dark. She was a good girl and helped Mustapha and his grandson let out the nets as best she could. Then she curled up in the bow on the sheepskin he had spread out for her under a thick blanket of stars, and slept singing a poem her mother had taught her from Al-Ma'arri, "The evening/is a black bride/wearing silver necklaces."

In the middle of the night the wind rose and tossed the little boat on the sea, a sign to bring in the nets. Mustapha had set a lamp to work by as they hauled in the catch. At first the nets came in empty, snagging only a little seaweed which she would have to clean from the nets later. But then the first little red fish appeared, caught by his gills, then another and another. They came faster and faster. She thought her heart would burst. There was a phosphorescent light shimmering on the surface from their catch, as though the stars had fallen into the sea. A blowfish puffed himself up to the size of a soccer ball in defense, a small octopus escaped onto the deck and got a tentacle around her leg until Mustapha knocked it senseless and pulled it from her.

When they had finished their work, Mustapha set a coal fire in the canoun and they grilled some of the rouget for their supper. Normally, only the foreigners could afford this delicacy. She had never tasted anything so delicious in her whole life.

Nadia remembered that night from her childhood as she listened to the gentle wash of waves as the ship made its way under the stars. They were the same bright stars of her youth, but a whole lifetime had slipped away since then. How could the stars remain the same and she have changed so utterly? And how could he have so completely changed, she wondered. Didn't there have to be a human core beneath all they had become, tying their personality together over the years, a thread leading all the way back to their childhood.

Where was the gentle boy with the easy smile playing in piles of sand, who dreamed of turning Palestine into a garden? Where was the student philosopher preaching a new theocracy, a nation of Islam where citizens lived in peaceful harmony with the laws of Allah?

"What has brought you to all this Abdel," she asked him, raising her handcuffed wrists as though in prayer.

Against the captain's orders he had taken her on deck the first night after they had safely put Crete behind them and they no longer encountered other ships as they sailed. He knew it was not safe, but he regretted having to bind and gag her like an animal. The last time he had seen her, he had exactly other uses for her beautiful body. She hardly looked any different than the young woman he loved all those years ago at the university, he thought, her soft hair streaming back from the radiant face, her wide-set eyes taking him in with the enigmatic intensity of a startled child. He had first come to love her for that child-like purity before the war dispelled their youth and set them on such different roads to adulthood.

The first woman he had ever loved, the daughter of one of the holiest martyrs in the Palestinian struggle, had given herself over to a life of self-indulgence, had sacrificed her heritage to advance her career, had prostituted herself to the west for a life of luxury. She was like a thousand lost women he knew who walked the streets unveiled, in the forbidden unprotected space beyond the stronghold of Islam, all boundaries shattered, hypnotized by television images of western technology and affluence beamed down from their satellites. They used the very heavens as a weapon to destroy his people's integrity.

This was perhaps the saddest legacy of three generations of occupation, the loss of so many Islamic women who had simply lost heart, women who had lost their soul in the struggle merely to survive. He felt sorry for her, for them all, like a brother whose sister has been raped. But he felt anger as well, the Arab righteousness of a father who blames the victim for her defilement.

Nadia stared at him in a transparent effort to prove she was not afraid. The aim of the terrorist was to inflict terror. She knew that, and she was determined to deny him such power over her.

Abdel remembered the disbelief in her face, her screams when they lifted the Frenchman's severed head if front of her. He regretted they had gone that far. It raised a number of questions he hadn't counted on. What had the man meant to her really? Was it simply hysteria? Did she really love him? But instead, he asked her, "Brought me to what," taking a key from his hip pocket to unlock her handcuffs.

"This violence, this cruelty," she said, massaging the red bracelets which the cuffs had etched into her wrists. "You were always the man of peace. You used to talk of reconstructing Islamic civilization, integrating the split personality of the Muslim, infusing modern disciplines with Islamic ethics. Instead you have become just another gangster spouting fundamentalist rhetoric."

"And what about you, what have you become in the West, there, where the sun sinks at the black edge of the earth. In the Gharb, you have engulfed your soul in darkness. You've been blinded by wealth and privilege, your elaborate laboratory, your life as a celebrity."

"I am a scientist, not a celebrity. I have been struggling to preserve life, not destroy it."

"This is God's domain. 'He hath power over all things.'"

"Our DNA research will shape the future of life itself. We can insert natural or synthetic genes into the host cells and study genetic functions. We can even produce living systems we've never known before. At last we have some real hope to direct mankind's future course and correct all the horrors of the 20th century."

"You steal the sacred gift Allah has given and exploit it in the name of science. Have you ever thought of what you ought to be doing before you begin doing it. If you leave the ethical questions for the end, you leave no place for ethics at all.

"We always review the ethical implications of any experiment we undertake."

"Will you plant perfect Aryan children in artificial wombs for them? Will you grow monsters for the sake of your own scientific curiosity? Who will decide exactly what will constitute human nature in the future Paradise you are designing. The board of directors for your Cramer Chemical? That is very reassuring."

"The ethics committee at Cramer Chemical..."

"I tell you, you will be expelled like Eve with a flaming sword turning in all directions to keep the way of the tree of life, and man shall return to dust from which he came. Listen to the Prophet. 'Is there a creator other than God, who nourisheth you with the gifts of heaven and earth? There is no God but He! How then are ye turned aside from Him?'"

There were millions like him, she thought, in millions of mosques across the world from Jakarta to Dubai. Dark eyed young men in black beards aping the misguided passion of dark eyed old mullahs in white beards, starting the cycle all over again. Would the serpent never spit out its tail and break the circle of ignorance?

"Don't speak of the Koran to me. You use it to enslave women, eliminate free inquiry, justify your barbarity against those with whom you disagree. It has taken me my whole life to see the world objectively, to overcome all the religious rhetoric that poisoned my youth."

"Jihad is a way of seeing the future, Nadia, a process for achieving the nation of Palestine. It is not just religious rhetoric. Don't you see that? We're aren't going to survive by assimilating western values, living cheap imitations of a culture that has nothing to do with us. We have to create the world anew according to the principles God has given us through the prophet. These principles are timeless, they will unify our people and bring us to the glory Allah intends for us.

And we aren't going to achieve the nation of God by throwing stones at Israeli armored personnel carriers. The settlers in Hebron are not using imaginary bullets to kills us while they desecrated the grave of Abraham. Now we must fight back with real bombs, real bullets or they will destroy us. They will destroy us the way their temple has entombed the sacred rock of the prophet on Haram as Sharif, the same way they were destroyed in their own holocaust.

"Do you think generations of revenge killing will ever bring about peace," she asked. "What good did it do to set the children of Afula on fire like torches in retaliation for Hebron. If you were only as good at politics as you were at killing the innocent there might be some hope. Why did you have to kill Yves? You butcher a man like an animal in the name of Islam? What of God the merciful, the compassionate?"

"What of the innocence of your own people? There is nothing accidental about their genocide. You've buried yourself in your laboratory so many years you've become blind to the blood of your own people running in the gutter. Did your own father's death mean so little to you? Wasn't he innocent enough? Is this how a daughter honors her father's memory. You become the enemy's whore? Is this a daughter's love?"

He didn't mean to say that. Why did he?

Her father's face came to her again with Abdel's words. She was beginning to forget him as the years wore on, one of the great sadness of her adult life. Now he came to her again, his gentle face filled with pride, the way he looked the morning she brought back three little red fishes from her night on the sea and grandly presented one to each of her parents. Hardly a meal, her father had pretended it was a great banquet that night at supper. "God bless this meal and the fisher girl who has brought us this bounty," he had prayed.

"Yes, he was innocent enough," she said, remembering his sweet face on another occasion, set in a deep peace, when she had been called to identify his remains. She took comfort imagining that he never knew what killed him, suffered no pain. There was so little left of him to identify.

"But he was butchered by your religious fanaticism as surely as the Mossad explosives that demolished his car and took him from me. Mysticism, revelation. What does it ever come to. The inquisition? The holocaust? The genocide of Muslims in Bosnia and Kosovo? The massacre at Hebron. All in the name of the God in defense of his chosen people. If I could find a cure for all the madness religion has brought into the world, I would do more for mankind than any scientist ever born. You needn't worry about science creating monsters. Religion will spawn enough monsters like you to take us to the end of history."

It was an unthinking gesture, a physical expletive one might use to emphasize a point or fend off a friend in play. She thrust out her arms, striking Abdel's chest with an unintended, unexpected force that knocked Abdel off balance teetering backwards against the handrail. In a second he would have fallen into the sea beyond any hope of rescue except that a second burst of energy sent her flying into his arms, throwing them to the deck at the last possible moment. Later she would attribute the rescue to mere animal instinct, the way a cat will knock a ball of yarn to the edge of the stair and stop it dead in mid air as it is about to tumble over the edge for sheer skill, play.

She lay in his arms, shocked by this sudden intimacy, memory flooding through her.

The Red Villa

"**I'm** getting sloppy," Martin Cramer thought, adjusting the volume and settling down in front of the T.V. on the glassed in terrace overlooking the lake. "How could I have neglected to kill that little cockroach before I left town," he said, indulging his anger by hurling the remote control to the terra cotta floor in a shower of batteries and electronics parts. Martin's secretary had tracked him down at the villa in Geneva just minutes after Whitfield Bingham began to give his testimony.

"It's on CNN live right now," she cried. "He's telling everything. He says you knew about Michael Riley's vaccine from the beginning, that you lied to the NIH and covered it up..."

"Okay, okay Jenny. I'll call you back when it's over. Don't worry, everything's going to be all right. I'll call you back later."

On the screen, Senator Wagner banged his gavel trying to restore order to the hall. CNN hadn't had such a live scoop since their cameras caught O.J. Simpson speeding down the L.A. freeways after murdering his wife, loyal sports fans cheering him on his way.

"And you personally added the cyanide to Robert Owen's medication before dispensing the capsules to him," Senator Wagner asked, staring down ferociously at the witness from the bench.

"Yeah, that's right."

"And what made you follow Martin Cramer's order to murder Robert Owen this way? Why did you agree to such a hideous act."

"Smack."

"What are you saying? Smack?"

"Smack, Senator. Horse. Hair o whine. Hair of the dog. I've been self-medicating, shall we say, ever since I left medical school and

Martin Cramer has provided me with very special employee health benefits in this regard. He's been very sympathetic, a regular Florence Nightingale."

No one would believe Bingham, Martin thought, at least at first. The witness droned on and on with his accusations, obsessively twisting a lock of long greasy hair, erupting into manic fits of giggling at odd points in the interrogation. But the facts were all there, and only needed to be corroborated by the pit bull Senator from New Mexico.

Cramer Chemical had spent millions trying to unseat John Wagner and dislodge his sanctimonious daughter from the Drug Pricing Board. The Senator could barely conceal the pleasure he took as he settled the score. He milked every lurid detail in Bingham's confession and carefully outlined the incriminating evidence found in Michael Riley's notebooks like a trial lawyer painting a pattern of evil in a prosecutions's opening statement.

Martin congratulated himself once again on his "select staff," the special consultants sprinkled in various offices on Capitol Hill who were paid generously when they provided him with particularly useful information. Margaret Alverez, the secretary to John Wagner's administrative assistant was an especially important "microphone." She had first alerted him to the wire tap Senator Wagner had arranged for the Office of Research Integrity. She couldn't give him all the details, but she had given him enough advance warning of Wagner's hearings to re-route his return from Athens through Switzerland, just to be on the safe side.

Somewhat premature, but Martin could take his "retirement" a year or so early. Jenny and one or two others on his special services payroll could tie up loose ends for him in the states. Switzerland was the ideal country to let his golden parachute spank open.

He'd had the foresight to purchase the Red Villa, one of the spectacular mansions lining the shores of Lake Geneva facing Mont Blanc when he first set up the Akai account. Though it served as the official Cramer hospitality and conference center, he had managed, with a few judicious contributions to the local bureaucracy beyond the necessary taxes and tariffs in order to register the deed in his own name.

The villa was just down the way from the Gatt headquarters, the Palais Wilson and the UN Headquarters for Europe, a perfect, low-keyed diplomatic neighborhood where people tended to mind their own business.

The Chateau Rouge was named for the deep red bricks of its turrets that rose mysteriously over the trees and gardens protecting it from the tourists cameras. The castle had been owned by a mid-east potentate who used it to house his harem when he was traveling in Europe, but some unfortunate gambling debts had caused a run on the Emir's cash reserves and Martin had purchased the palace for a fraction of its worth.

No one asked many questions in Switzerland when there was sufficient money to assure one's privacy. There was very little money could not buy, from citizenship to anonymity. Like family physicians, Swiss bankers considered a customer's confidentiality the highest ethical consideration of their profession. They would look after his economic health and see to it that he did not face extradition to the U.S. It would be a life of exile, but he would make himself very comfortable in the Red Villa. There were any number of "expatriate businessmen" of his rank and stature from all over the world living in the mansions along the lake front. If he were careful, he might even risk slipping in and out of the country on occasion if things got too claustrophobic. And Jenny would fit right into the polite cafe society that entertained each other so pleasantly while carefully averting any real familiarity. There were plenty of corporate mistresses and professional companions to keep her company on shopping trips, and more than enough haute couture salons and designer shops along the Rue des Eaux-Vives to assuage even her voracious appetite for clothes and jewelry. He could already see her, top down, long red hair streaming as she cruised the boulevards in her cream-colored Rolls, slowing down for any attentive pedestrian eye.

She claimed to love him, but Martin was wise enough not to trust this emotion to carry the day. Over the years he had carefully secured her loyalty with a fortune in baubles. "Money," he thought wearily. "How the world turns on money. And the affairs of the heart." It was a reassuring truism.

Twilight settled over Lac Leman and the lights of Geneva blinked on like fireflies on the opposite shore. Martin sat in the gathering darkness with only the flickering blue light of the television to illuminate the terrace. You didn't have to be clairvoyant, he thought to see how much the two men on the screen hated each other. Senator Wagner and David Schefflan sat at the edge of their chairs, like two cocks about to be released into the blood theater of the ring.

Martin Cramer had also taken an immediate dislike to David Schefflan when they first met in Athens. So aggressive, so sure of himself, he was far too young to be placed in charge of the hostage negotiations at the Embassy. Schefflan had sent Martin packing within two days when Martin protested as much to the Ambassador.

"Mr. Schefflan, it doesn't seem that your negotiating team has made much progress with these terrorists. Perhaps if we you had accommodated some of their more moderate demands in the beginning at least, we'd be further along in the resolution of this crisis. I don't need to remind you what's in store for us all if we don't retrieve these scientists."

He hasn't changed a bit, Schefflan thought, the same patronizing old bastard who had dressed him down in Santa Fe all those years ago and changed the direction of his life. David struggled to control the tone of his response. Keep it neutral, professional, he thought. But he could hear an edge sharpen in his voice as he spoke, despite himself.

"Accommodation is not the answer with terrorists, Senator. You only put hostages in even greater danger. Neville Chamberlain taught us the first great lesson of appeasement. Sacrificing Poland did nothing to stave off Hitler or World War Two."

"Don't you presume to lecture me on history or conflict resolution. I've been negotiating of the laws of the land in this chamber all of my adult life. And let me tell you son, communication is the key to any successful negotiation. The American people have a right to know what they are dealing with here. Why don't you just tell us where we stand with these people."

"Senator, Islamic Rebirth is a good example of what has been called 'free lance' terrorism, a kind of ad hoc, religiously inspired violence," David said in a level voice. "This is not the traditional tightly organized, centrally directed, state financed network of highly trained terrorists. Or if they are financed by a state, we can't be sure they are controlled or directed by anyone in particular. This lack of structure makes them more difficult to predict and penetrate. We are always looking for a central headquarters, but the new terrorists are more religious, more ecumenical, less organized, less structured. It is far more difficult when there is no serpent's head to cut off.

"We have received a C-3, however, that makes us believe Islamic Rebirth is working with a Greek terrorist organization called November 17th, one of the oldest and bloodiest in Europe."

"A 3-c Mr. Schefflan?"

"All of our information must be evaluated and transformed into a usable form, Senator. Information is ranked in terms of its reliability and accuracy. A C-3 piece of information means it came from a fairly reliable source and is possibly true."

"Well, has your computerized information taken into account the human dimension of this ordeal? Why haven't you at least communicated the conditions these kidnappers have set, the way they have insisted?"

"It is our belief Senator that publication of terrorist demands provides a forum to incite further political action among fundamentalist cells that…"

"I'd like to introduce into the record at this time a document we have just received from the National Security Council which was first delivered by this so-called Islamic Rebirth organization to our embassy in Athens on December 9th of this year."

"Senator Wagner, you can't disclose this communiqué to the public now. It will…"

"Don't you tell me what I can and can not do, sir. The release of this document has already been cleared with Director Nunn at CIA and the President himself, Mr. Schefflan. The American people are begging us to get to the bottom of this disaster."

He listened helpless as the Senator began to read the demands of Islamic Rebirth, knowing he'd been hung out to dry for sheer political expediency. The people wanted action and John Wagner's constituents would watch him take the bull by the horns.

David sat silently at the witness table, seething. Islamic Rebirth had commandeered the nation's most august body, the floor of the

United States Senate, to proclaim their message to the world. He listened, helpless, as the senior Senator from New Mexico entered their lies and distortions into the public record for all the world to contemplate.

"In the name of God, the merciful, the compassionate," the text began, "No voice can rise above the voice of the Palestinian people, the spirit of the martyrs who have entered Paradise, knowing the peace of God's embrace and the certain future of their people on earth—et cetera, et cetera. Let's see now, the demands begin here on page three," Senator Wagner interrupted himself. "We reveal to you that on December first, Islamic Rebirth has taken custody of the two scientists most proclaimed by the western press for discovering a cure of the world AIDS epidemic, Dr. Yves Bourret and Dr. Nadia Mansur. They are unharmed but will be kept from completing their work and held hostage until the plight of our people is addressed by Western governments and their hirelings in the United Nations. Unless our legitimate demands are met, this plague will continue to ravage the world the way Zionism and fascism have ravaged us for three generations ever since the United Nations first created the illegal state of Israel.

We are prepared to hold them as many years as it takes for the world to recognize the injustice we have suffered and begin to make amends. We will share your fate with this epidemic until you acquiesce to our requirements. Death and deprivation are not new to our people."

Senator Wagner adjusted the tortoise shell glasses perched on the end of his thin nose. "Let's see. Here we are." He continued reading from the folder in front of him. "The following provisions must be met in their entirety and are not subject to compromise: 1. The withdrawal of Israel from all the Palestinian and Arab territories it occupied in 1967, including most especially the sacred city of Jerusalem. 2. The annulment of all measures of annexation and appropriations and the removal of settlements established by Israel in the Palestinian and Arab territories since 1967. 3. Formation of a fact finding commission through the Arab League to expose the continuous subjugation of the Palestinian people during this phase of so called autonomy, to prove how oppression, starvation, killing, detention, terrorism, deportation, and psychological warfare continue to be waged by the Zionist enemy with the co-operation of their PLO puppets in Jericho.

"Number four. Let 's see. Ah, here we are," he said, shuffling through the papers. "4. Establishment of a permanent fund to channel financial support from Arab nations, the World Bank and western governments to help the Palestinian people to replace the inept and corrupt financial institutions governed by the illegitimate ruling council of the Palestinian Authority.

"Well, now here is something that I believe we could reasonably consider a basis for negotiations. We've certainly heard enough reports of the corruption and mismanagement taking place in the interim council. What is to be lost by at least investigating the possibility of such a fund. Might this not be a place where we could show some good will and maybe make a little progress with these people?"

"Good will," Schefflan asked incredulously, "Senator, you don't have any idea what sort of animals we are dealing with here. Since the original communication from Islamic Rebirth, we have received additional evidence of their resolve and brutality. For one of the hostages it already appears to be too late.

"What are you talking about. What information do you have?"

"This week we received a video tape that we believe to be authentic in which these *negotiators* force Doctor Mansur to beg for her life to meet their demands. The tape ends with one of terrorists parading the decapitated head of Dr. Yves Bourret for the camera to prove their point. These are butchers, not some misguided fundamentalist partisans."

The committee room burst into an uproar as Schefflan revealed the new information.

"Why wasn't I informed of this development," Senator Wagner shouted, banging his gavel impotently, trying to regain order. He was furious when upstaged by a witness in front of his own committee.

"I can assure you and the American people, however, that we are making progress. Islamic Rebirth has called for a meeting with a representative from the American Government, which is to take place soon at a location that must remain a secret. I'm sure you can appreciate the need for such secrecy. We can not jeopardize the safety of Dr.

Mansur or other hostages by revealing sensitive elements of this investigation."

"What other hostages? Have they taken additional hostages," Senator Wagner sputtered, confused.

"Since December first, the time of the abduction, a Greek national of some celebrity has been missing from her home in Athens. We suspect foul play in this disappearance and believe that Fotini Theodorou may have been taken hostage by Islamic Rebirth at the same time as Dr. Bourret and Mansur. We ask that anyone who knows anything about Ms. Theodorou's whereabouts after that date come forward immediately."

Martin watched the pandemonium on the television screen and got out of his chair to adjust the volume. He couldn't have been more surprised if Schefflan had announced that Mother Theresa had just shot the President, and he didn't like it. Such surprises made him nervous. He had enough to contend with in his own chaotic life at the moment without having to factor in this bizarre development in the hostage crisis.

Events were spiraling out of control since Robert Owen's death, Martin decided. He sat in the flickering blue light of the television set lost in thought like a suicide musing on life's trials for the thousandth time before accepting the inevitable, drawn to the bridge railing like an apple snapped from its stem, heeding gravity's resolute call to earth.

He could not remember a time when he wasn't scurrying just one step ahead of some reporter, preparing for a board committee meeting or NIH investigation in an effort to save Cramer Chemical's reputation and the empire his grandfather had built. And for what finally, he mused. The honor of presenting the Cramer Cup to some snotty-nosed tennis genius fanning himself out like a peacock for all his pea-chicken fans? What did he get from serving on Memorial Hospital's board of directors, the Historical Society's Diamond Circle, or the Mayor's commission to restore the State Opera House? People recognized him immediately on the society page, he had a room full of trophies and plaques collecting dust which honored his sense of civic duty, but it all came down to the fortune of charitable contributions his family had pumped into community organizations.

He remembered how hard grandfather Cramer had struggled to find acceptance with the Yankee blue bloods among whom he had pitched his tent. When the Captain's Club of Stonington invited him to join their ranks, Franz Cramer achieved a pinnacle of personal satisfaction that transcended even his achievements as a businessman and patriarch. He could rest in peace, comfortably installed in the most fashionable cemetery in Connecticut.

Martin's father worked just as tirelessly at dynasty building so his son could play with the Kennedy's or the Cabots. By the time Martin was invited to his first charity ball, there wasn't a brighter catch to be found among young bachelors from relatively old money swimming through the social season of Palm Beach like a school of neon fish in the reef off shore at the Breakers Hotel where they held forth. Martin was, finally, an official *notable*. Like Donald Trump or Stephen Spielberg, he could light from his limousine certain to enjoy the deferential treatment afforded stars that had achieved the national ideal of super wealth.

Martin's father worked too hard to enjoy the fruits of his labor except vicariously through his children, and while still in his 60's he had crashed spectacularly into death with a massive heart attack sitting at his desk barking orders into the phone. "Time is money," he liked to say, but "money is not time," as the local sage would have it.

What would he really lose, Martin asked himself again, if he just gave up the struggle at this point. He knew from the inside what barracuda the rich really were. None of his society friends would shed a tear if he went down in flames. It would only fuel their sense of superiority and liven up the cocktail circuit for a night or two.

He still had a few good years left and Jenny was a far superior companion to the impeccably-coifed, discretely-jeweled mannequins at the club with faces frozen into polite wonder from too many surgical alterations. He wouldn't wind up splayed across his desk, defending the family's honor like his father. The great fatigue he felt was a kind of catharsis, like a man ten years younger mired down in mid-life crisis who vowed to seize the day and change the direction of his life.

Years ago when he first discovered Michael Riley's part in the AIDS epidemic and the threat to Cramer Chemical, Martin had conceived of an insurance plan, a doomsday scenario as it were, should the walls ever begin to fall in around him and he needed to cut his losses. He knew from experience that a really professional arsonist could make any fire look like an industrial accident. Martin had retained the services of the very best in the business once, when a competitor threatened to beat them to the market with a product Cramer Chemical was in the process of developing.

Such an explosion would destroy any evidence of his role in the whole Riley affair, and at least temporarily cover his money's tracks to its new home Switzerland. Jenny could provide needed access to the Cramer compound before joining him in their new life in Geneva. He was sad to think of the years he spent building and defending his inheritance, but the world had changed since this epidemic and he was very tired of the fight.

Martin turned off the television with the same sense of relief the jumper feels when he has given up the debate and resolved to put an end to his pain. The elation was a kind of fever in him as he began to punch in the numbers of his secure telephone line to Jenny in Connecticut. His silk shirt stuck to his clammy chest, and he took a handkerchief to wipe his brow. He felt his heart beat with the sweet excitement a gambler feels as he watches the roulette ball click into the numbered slot, red or black on which he has waged a fortune.

And then suddenly, with the sort of revulsion the same gambler feels when, inconceivably, the ball drops into the single, green, double zero slot on the wheel, Martin's heart began to race. In the vision, he remembered the sweating face of Robert Owen, dying of AIDS, just inches in front of his own, shouting at him with rage. He remembered his foolishness at not wearing a face-mask to their interview. And his epiphany turned to terror when he realized that in looking into the dying face of Robert Owen, Martin Cramer was looking into a mirror.

Radiance

She struggled when Abdel first kissed her. Remembering how her kidnappers had abused her over the past days, Nadia's immediate instinct was to strike back when she found herself so close to him. She felt his weight as he took each of her hands in his own, but she bit hard into his lip and he tasted the salty blood as it began to flow.

Abdel pulled back, looking into her face as if a scorpion had just stung him. Her mouth was a beautiful scarlet, his own blood nourishing her like a pelican with its chick. Despite her anger, the doctor in her tried to reach up to stem the flow of blood from the gash she had created. He studied her carefully, letting her minister to him. She was so beautiful, lying flushed in his arms, the way she had in his youth. He felt the painful straining of his erection. He gently took her finger and traced his lips with his own blood. He pushed his body against hers, questioning, but insistent. He kissed her finger, took it in his mouth as his hand carefully undid her blouse and caressed her breast. Her breath quickened, her body still tense with resistance. He covered her breast with his triumphant mouth, the passionate hunger a grown man remembers from his infancy. She cried softly, her body eased in affirmation, inflaming his desire. She was his, she would not stop him. Yes, she would let him. She was his again. He would go where he wished, place his hands where he wished. He could caress her nakedness, explore the shadows of her body and kiss her as he wished, deeply time and again until she more than acquiesced to his demands. Until she returned the kiss, taking him further into his passion—their mutual passion as she accepted, took him into her with that velvet pain which begs for release. Yes, he would be so deep into her that he must escape his own body in the effort to go further, until his very being released now. Yes lost in her exactly at the moment when she is lost in him, like ghosts walking through each other in one exuberant moment of light and coincidence to overcome the predictability, the routine certainty of the long gray afternoon we call death.

The labyrinth leading to this light was for Nadia a more tortured course. It was with a kind of animal relish that she had first bitten into his flesh, pain from pain, kicking at the lion's jaws at your heels, instinctive as a mother's cries at birth. It was a gesture of rage for one's defenselessness, primal fear, the eloquence of dumb blood. But the sight of his torn lip, brought her to, like the first fall of autumn leaves for Eve in the garden.

She studied his ruined smile with curiosity and then with a tender remorse that left her suddenly exhausted. Everything, everything came to that ruin ultimately. When she was a young medical student she thought she could at least stem the tide of that ruin. She came to the hospital each morning, bright as the sun itself, that much hope, that much energy. But by the time the sun set on her youth she had watched the blood wash upon the shore too long, mesmerized by the pull of ocean, while the ubiquitous vultures stood preening themselves for the children on the arid bank.

Then remarkably, as they sometimes did, the vultures lifted in a black cloud to a far thorn tree as he covered her mouth with his own bleeding smile, becoming now a kiss, seeking her permission, inviting her to do as she wished with him. Love blossomed in her again like the breast swelling beneath his hand, yes. Taking his sweet hungry head to her breast. Yes. His black head ranging over her body where he wished, where she wished. Her hair was undone cascading now on his own bare chest. Her hands explored his body like the lover now and not the doctor, flesh so young and supple.

She was free with him. Un-self-conscious free with him, barely able to tell his body from her own. Deep inside him, or he her, she could not tell. And her mother was not weeping in the corner, and her father's face did not float like a flower on the horizon. It was a freedom she had never felt with Yves.

She had never believed in that mystical death of self that poets sometimes sang of in lovemaking, the reconciliation of opposites, being and non-being coincidental at a point in time and space, light and dark, pain and pleasure brought into harmony and transcendent wholeness. But incredibly, somewhere outside her body, she and Abdel watched the two beautiful creatures making love, a moment that would always carry it's own eternity, but which was dragged back into time and space more abruptly than either of them would ever have expected.

Ganymede might have sounded the alarm. It had nothing to do with any sort of loyalty he felt toward his mistress. It simply all happened so quickly, the cockatoo could only bob on his perch with excitement with barely a squawk, before Fotini flew at them. Nadia and Abdel were so taken up in their lovemaking they didn't noticed her come on deck. They never saw the dark storm which blew up in her face, or the rage that drove her to pick up the first thing that came to hand—a two by four Stavros had left wedged in the aft hatch to keep it from sliding across the companionway. Swinging it with a batter's precision to the back of Nadia's head, she delivered the young lover from her vision of Paradise just at its most incandescent.

"Sleeping with the enemy," Fotini said scornfully, as they lay Nadia's body on the deck. Another desertion, just when she thought she might have found a man to love again. "Have you forgotten this is your hostage?"

"I think you've killed her," Abdel said, blowing deep into her lungs, trying to restore consciousness.

"She seemed to be out of control," was all Fotini said, leaving him to his work.

Athens

"**Martha,** bring in some coffee, will you please," David Schefflan asked, stopping, arms full, in front of his secretary's desk.

"How was your flight," she asked, rising unthinking to the task. She was career state, old enough to be his mother, and as dedicated. Thirty-five years of service overseas left her behind the times. She didn't insist on the title of executive assistant, was content merely to be a superlative secretary.

It was archaic, but also a great relief sometimes to be treated like a son. He was so comfortable with her, and it showed in their work.

"Oh man, I didn't sleep a minute," he said. "I just sat there for hours with my headphones on trying to block out some screaming baby. I couldn't stop thinking about that goddamned Senator Wagner. The baby seemed to be doing all the screaming for me."

"He was a real shit," Martha said with her disarming talent for the occasional four-letter word. "We stayed up late and watched it all. You'd have thought we were the terrorists. Whose side is that guy on anyway?"

"That's what I tried to tell the Ambassador this morning."

"You mean you came straight to the embassy from the airport? Your brains must be oatmeal. Why don't you go home and get some sleep?"

"No rest for the wicked," he said. "I've got lots to catch up on after this morning's meeting."

"I'll make it espresso," she said.

Someone had to placate the rabid senator and David was the press officer after all, but he hated being called to Washington for the stupid window dressing that interrupted his real work. And to be undercut by his own Ambassador only added insult to injury.

"Why wasn't I told he had their communiqué," David fumed at the command post meeting that morning. "Wagner made these bastards sound like the Arabian knights. The papers are filled with articles on Islamic Rebirth. They couldn't have dreamed of such a publicity bonanza. The United Nations is actually considering a resolution to address their demands now."

"The order from the Secretary to go public came just before you were called into the committee," Ambassador Lehfeldt said. "They short sheeted us David. There was nothing we could do, I'm sorry," He administered one of his diplomatic smiles and placed his hand on the young man's shoulder. "I know you were upset. But you handled yourself very well in front of Senator Wagner. Perhaps it was better that you didn't know."

"If I'm going to be part of this team, sir, I can't be kept in the dark. I want to be useful, I want to help rescue Dr. Mansur, to retrieve this vaccine. But I won't just be a flak man sent out to rationalize our mistakes. I want to be part of the decisions that are made, to take responsibility."

Fatigue pushed him out of line. He'd never spoken to his boss this directly. He felt his eyes smart from anger, exhaustion, and the humiliation John Wagner had put him through.

"Don't worry David. There will be plenty of opportunity to demonstrate your heroism. It seems you've become a celebrity yourself since your trip to Washington. You've even caught the attention of these born-again Muslims. They are demanding that you be the envoy to carry out further negotiations for the release of Nadia Mansur."

The Ambassador studied his reaction, watching to see if David flinched at idea of this dangerous assignment.

"Normally, we would expect a trained agent to take this mission," he continued. "We can't force you, of course, but we seem to have no choice in the matter. You realize..."

"I accept," David had interrupted, without a second thought. The prospect of getting close to these criminals produced a kind of animal joy in him, like a bloodhound picking up the scent. And Ambassador Lehfeldt had no idea what a highly trained agent he would in fact be sending into whatever swamp the terrorists had taken as refuge. It had been an easy decision for both of them.

David sat at his desk pouring through the photographs taken at Fotini Theodorou's villa on Crete. The soundproof dungeon they discovered in the cellar of the villa was modeled on the melodramatic stage set from *Blue Desire*, an early film in her career based on the exploits of the Marquise de Sade. Manacles chained to the brick walls, whips and various instruments of torture, this exotic playpen might just have been a harmless den to act out her eccentric fantasy life, save for the genuine blood they discovered soaked into the wooden floor boards and sawdust. DNA analysis confirmed that blood to be the same found in the remains of Yves Bourret the terrorists had sent with Nadia Mansur's video taped message. They found no evidence of any other blood fortunately, which might mean she was still useful to them as a hostage and remained unharmed for the moment.

David studied Nadia Mansur's exquisite face in the video freeze frames. The dark eyes were those of a gazelle, paralyzed in that deadly moment just before the lion springs. She was nearly a different person than the lovely creature with whom he had traded life stories only a month ago on a terrace overlooking Athens. The professional in him tried to assess how close she was to breaking, how much more she could take. He detected the Stockholm syndrome in her, that child-like subservience and identification with her captors. But that was a normal enough self-defense mechanism as time wore on.

He'd seen what grisly performances November 17th was capable of, however, and the Arabs were just as savage. David remembered Saul Lebowitz, a tank sergeant who became his friend the summer he lived in Israel. Hezbollah had nabbed him at a bus stop and taken him prisoner. The soles of the young soldier's feet had been whipped to a bloody pulp, an Arab speciality, and he was begging for death when they found him dumped like a side of beef along the road to Kibbutz Gallel.

"Get in touch with John Burns, Martha," he said as Martha set the cup of coffee on his desk. "Tell him to meet me at one this afternoon at Lehfeldt's office. Top priority."

The memory of his Israeli friend renewed a fury in David and set him to action. John Burns was an experienced pilot as well as the military attaché at the American Embassy. The skies over the Mediterranean were as familiar to him as his own smell. If anyone could get David into Tunis safely and undetected for his meeting with Islamic Rebirth, Burns was the man.

Why Tunis though, David wondered. Conventional wisdom had it that all the snakes had slithered back to Gaza and the West Bank along with Arafat when he made his ludicrous "triumphant" return. But it looked as though he'd left a few eggs in the nest before he left town.

Lifeguard

For two days the *Ceberus* floated motionless on the quiet sea, the faint breeze useless, despite a ghoster jib Fotini had raised to coax air, a big light sail with a Kevlar luff sheeted to the afterdeck. She checked the radar obsessively, but nothing seemed promising on the horizon. A watched pot...

She would have welcomed a gale at this point, anything but this deadly calm which fixed them on the glass surface of the water like a tiny boat anchored to the mirror of a music box. They were as defenseless as a mouse caught in the shadow of a sparrow hawk. It was only a question of time before the CIA or NATO intelligence would track them down, sitting out in the open this way. Just yesterday she had tuned into *Radio Monte Carlo* when an hysterical D.J. interrupted the *Hard Rock Hour* with a sensational bulletin: Fotini Theodorou missing. Film Star wanted in connection with the abduction of American scientists. He was breathless with his good luck.

Fotini's name filled the airwaves and the implications were not lost on her. She ruminated by the hour, eyes fixed on the horizon of how her life must change, forever change now that she had been discovered. Her career in film, her houses, her lovers. She seemed to be condemned to live the rest of her life among the sort of cretins they had taken aboard before setting sail for Tunisia.

She was utterly bored with the crew's constant turning to Mecca for prayer, the somber, deferential way they took orders, the ugly guttural conversations in Arabic, their body odor from days at sea.

Nadia Mansur lay in a comma, and Fotini couldn't pry Abdel from her side as he tended to her. Even Ganymede had deserted her, his head buried in his black shoulder feathers as he stood sleeping in the shade of the mainsail. The cockatoo seemed a bad omen, like a shiny raven that had lighted on the boom. The infernal sun made things even worse. She hated the sun, every year she fled Greece in the summer months, and now she found the burning noonday heat intolerable.

A thin trickle of current flowed under the keel of the *Ceberus*, virtually imperceptible. She played out a sheet to trail behind the ship as a safety line and placed a towel and bar of saltwater soap on the afterdeck. What did the crew matter, a swim might even liven things up.

Fotini stripped out of her sundress and sandals, and made a perfect art deco swan dive into the aquamarine water below. The sea engulfed her nakedness—a delicious, cool refreshment. She burst into the air finally like a silver dolphin and swam to the ship's ladder. She soaped down her silky body and drifted away from the Ceberus on her back letting the water play over her like a lover.

The sky was so blue, the great white clouds such perfect puzzles. There was an elephant, a mushroom cloud, Ganymede in flight. Such peace, she might have slept as she floated.

"Fotini, Fotini," Abdel shouted from the deck.

She turned to see the *Ceberus*, sails freshening, the jib carrying her forward, the safety line trailing fifty yards ahead. Fotini had been lulled into carelessness as the breeze came up and she drifted from the ship.

She was strong swimmer and set off frantically to catch up, but the line was gaining on her as she swam. She suddenly remembered the sharks off Vouliagmeni and swarm harder. Would Abdel be able to bring the ship about if it got too far ahead of her?

When he first saw Fotini in the water, Abdel immediately slackened sail, but the ship seemed to be caught in a strong current now and he didn't know what more to do to help her. When it was clear she was losing the contest, he stripped his clothes, grabbed a coil of line lying on the deck and jumped into the water.

He reached the end of the safety line and attached the rope he carried to the end, swimming toward her, dividing the distance between them. She was exhausted when he reached her, but at last she was firmly tethered to the ship, and slowly, hand over hand, they made their way against the current back to the *Ceberus*. With difficulty, she pushed her way up the ladder and lay naked and panting on the deck.

"Well, where did this wind come from," she asked half-choking, half-laughing. "But isn't it wonderful. You are my hero," she said. "You saved me, darling. According to tradition, my life belongs to you now."

Her right hand lay tucked between her thighs like modest Venus rising on the shell. With her other hand she brought his head to hers and rewarded him with a kiss. The warm breeze played over his own nakedness lying beside her in the sun. Then both her arms were about his neck, proud Venus, glistening with sea water, no longer shy in her desire. Her skin was satin against his body, her mouth a silky mystery drawing him in. But he resisted her play, like a wary humming bird that hovers at the rim before sipping the blossom of a morning glory.

Half the men of the Western world had dreamed of being in his exact position at that moment. Despite his reservations he felt himself stirring against the dark island between her legs. He ought to lash himself against the mast like Ulysses and fill his ears with wax against the sweet siren call. The sails were luffing in the fresh breeze, the ship should be set on course anew. They must push on to Africa. But Fotini's hands glided over his body like velvet, complicating the situation.

Then Abdel remembered how readily she plunged those same hands into the bloody bucket to fish up the head of Yves Bourret. Kiss of the scorpion, he thought. Didn't the female kill its partner after mating? She was as obstinate as a scorpion as she made for what she wanted. In his village, boys sometimes set a scorpion in a ring of fire and watched the creature sting itself to death with a diamond barb before relenting to the flames. He'd better be a little careful here. Was it only two days ago that she had nearly killed their hostage in this very spot, refusing to lift even a hand since then to save her life.

Fotini's long delicate fingers traced little circles all over his body. She was irresistible. He was caught in the delicious embrace of a sweet octopus. Now she had taken him in hand and would lead him where her passion willed.

"Abdel, Abdel," Youssef screamed from the companionway below and followed with a little storm of Arabic she did not understand.

"It's Nadia," Abdel explained, bobbing on the deck as he stumbled back into his blue jeans and with difficulty, zipped up his fly. "She's awake. She has come awake."

Fotini lay staring at the sky, alone on the deck, as her passion ebbed. Her mother always said that revenge is a dish that is best savored cold and as the breeze came up and Fotini put on her clothes, she took a small consolation in planning exactly how she would kill Nadia Mansur when the time came.

Lausanne

The villas perched along the lakefront in Lausanne were as functional and non-descript as the bank buildings of Geneva, but it was to these private clinics hidden along the coastal road that the super rich of the world made pilgrimage like Ponce de Leon in search of immortality. A presidential assassin could come to have his face and fingerprints erased, an aging actress, disappear and re-emerge the ingenue. Medical treatments that had not yet been approved for use in humans were available upon request. A rock star who had killed his liver with alcohol and drugs didn't have to put his name on a waiting list for a transplant. There was always a supply of organs when the people in demand were willing to pay the price. Every day private planes routinely delivered emergency ice chests from Brazil or the Philippines with the needed body parts, donated, prematurely if necessary, from a healthy if impoverished peasant.

When Jenny landed from New York and found Martin nearly incoherent with fever and pneumonia, she had immediately checked him into the best and most discrete of the lot, the Clinique Beau Sejour. She wasn't about to lose him to AIDS now that Martin had finally proposed marriage.

"I guess I really have loved you all these years," he had said to her over the phone. "I never knew how much I depended on you, and now I need you more than ever, Jenny." He sounded so far away, so lost. "John Wagner isn't going to let up on us, now that he has Whitfield Bingham squealing like a stuck pig. Remember the plan we discussed if things ever really got bad? I've been thinking all night about this, Jenny. I guess maybe that time has come and I'm going to need your help to execute the plan. I'm tired, baby. I don't feel well. You've got to come be with me and get me on my feet again."

She vowed she would save him. But the elegant Moroccan physician who directed the clinic, Dr. Malouf was cautious as he outlined the situation. He played the beautiful red head like an expert angler who keeps the line taut against the salmon's aching need to spit out the hook.

"We are dealing with frank disease here," Dr. Malouf had said. "There is no telling when toxoplasmosis, cytomegalovirus, pneumonia or some other opportunistic infection may occur. His CD-4 count is all ready well below two hundred."

"There's got to be something, some way to help him get better," Jenny cried, denying the inevitable like any loved one when the death sentence is first pronounced.

She really is exquisite, Dr. Malouf thought. The great milky white breasts brimming over, her scarlet hair like the hennaed hair his mother and sisters affected to imitate the voluptuous wives of the royal harem. When this was over, and certainly Martin Cramer would die, Dr. Malouf might try to pick up the spoils of the rich American's death. But for the moment, the clinic director was in the business of selling hope.

"Dr. Lefrere in Paris has shown slowed progression of the disease with repeated injections of plasma from otherwise healthy HIV-infected patients," he said. "And the Chinese have developed an experimental herbal treatment which seems to interrupt viral replication at least temporarily. Finding the necessary supply may be difficult," he said, certain now that he had landed a new client.

"Anything," she said. ""I'll pay anything. Martin can't die." It was the first time she had spoken of his death out loud, giving the prospect an added reality that set her sobbing. Dr. Malouf rose from his desk and took her in his arms like a child who had just wakened from a nightmare, rubbing her back ever so slightly to comfort her.

She relaxed and let him take her in. Normally she was shy about her body, stood slightly stoop-shouldered to conceal her enormous breasts. She wanted to have them reduced surgically, but Martin had forbidden it. Riding her great breasts was one of the things he liked most about their lovemaking. Now a different passion filled her and she yielded to the safe harbor of Dr. Malouf's.

For a while his miracle cures had worked. Pentamidine made short order of the Martin's pneumocystosis pneumonia and gradually

CD-4 count began to rise. Dr. Malouf had Martin moved to the larger suite usually reserved for heads of state or other celebrities requiring absolute anonymity. Jenny could be near him during the recuperation.

"I'll have to go on a diet," she said one afternoon as they sat on his terrace in the brilliant spring sunshine finishing up a gourmet lunch. She speared a ripe strawberry and dipped it into the chocolate fondue pot steaming in front of them, but Martin couldn't be tempted. It was growing harder and harder to deny the portent of his wasted figure. The flesh had melted from his cheeks and a bony skull now haunted the vestiges of his handsome face.

The night CAN broadcast a special segment on the bombing of Cramer Chemical, Martin and Jenny ordered a bottle of Dom Perignon '76 to celebrate their victory. Martin stared at the screen transfixed, however, and the champagne sat unopened in the ice bucket.

Hundreds of Cramer workers had been caught in the main explosion that shattered the glass dome over their dining hall during the second lunch shift. The room was drenched in blood and glass, bodies lay shredded as though harvested by a large farm machine. Martin recognized some of the workers despite their condition. A toxic cloud from chemical fires hung over Long Island Sound forcing the evacuation of communities in a fifty-mile radius. Remarkably, Mercury stood in tact on his pedestal at the main entrance of the building though the caduceus he held had snapped, taking off his arm at the wrist.

The perky blond news anchor announced that the chemical company's CEO, Martin Cramer may have been among the victims, though the process of identifying bodies was ongoing. The program traced the history of the corporate giant through three generations of Cramers using boilerplates Martin had himself developed to promote the company's reputation. She speculated with her co-anchor on the economic impact such a loss would have on Southeastern Connecticut, but the greatest fear, fueled by ominous meteorological reports on wind conditions on the east coast was that the toxic fumes might drift south over Manhattan before blowing out to sea.

"We have to get out, we have to leave," Martin cried to Jenny. "The toxic fumes."

"No, honey. We're safe here. We're in Switzerland. They can't hurt us here." She stood behind his wheel chair and took his head to her breast trying to soothe him.

Martin slipped in and out of reality more and more lately as though a toxic cloud of his own bathed his poor brain. The encephalopathy was progressive, Dr. Malouf explained. They would help him any time she chose to give her consent. It was a staple of hospice care. Increasing doses of morphine would end his pain and end his life in the process, once the inevitable dementia set in.

After the broadcast, Martin refused to eat. He screamed that Dr. Malouf was poisoning him when food was brought to his room. Jenny became hysterical the morning she came into his room and found him bound in padded mittens strapped to his bedside, a catheter strung into the large vein in his neck for nutrients.

"No, Robert, No. Help me, Jenny. I didn't poison him, Jenny. Don't let them poison me Jenny. I didn't kill Robert. Help me."

That night Jenny gave her consent to begin a morphine drip and for the first time in weeks Martin seemed to sleep soundly. Close to midnight, however, he threw himself against his restraints as though struggling against an unseen assailant.

"I didn't, I didn't" he screamed, drifting back into his pillows, shriveled by death and whatever torment lay beyond.

Jenny kept Martin's ashes in an alabaster urn on the large mantle in the main foyer of the Red Villa. She would talk to him every day as she repaired her makeup or readied herself to go shopping. She had loved Martin passionately, had given him the best years of his life, but she was still an attractive woman. Martin wouldn't want her to dry up like an old prune and waste the rest of her years grieving. Dr. Malouf was right about that. He even offered to introduce her to some of the right people in Lausanne society to help ease her loneliness.

One afternoon Jenny came home to find the maid in a fit of tears. Nothing would console the simple country girl who was certain she was to be fired. Finally, Jenny coaxed the news out of the poor girl.

Madeline had been dusting and had inadvertently tipped the urn with Martin's remains onto the marble floor of the foyer smashing it into a great heap of alabaster shards, pieces of bone and ashes.

"It's all right. It's all right Madeline," she said, embracing her like a sister to reassure her. "I'm sure it was only an accident. Anyone can have an accident. Just put the stuff in the trash now, and stop your crying, you hear. Dr. Malouf will be here soon for dinner and we can't have you all hysterical when he comes, now can we?"

Falcon

In all the years he had been flying, no matter the size of the plane or the sophistication of the ground crew, John Burns never forgot his instructor's first rule that a pilot always took personal responsibility for inspection of his aircraft before takeoff. The F4B was perfect for this mission, he decided, as he reviewed the plane's maintenance records and performed a counter clockwise inspection of the landing gear, wing structure, and fuselage.

The F4B was well known in Europe, an old Marine precursor of the F14, and it would cause little attention when they left the NATO air base outside Athens on what he hoped would look like a routine training mission. Islamic Rebirth had demanded a secret meeting and David Schefflan wasn't going to have much luck if the world press was waiting for him on the beaches when he arrived at his destination.

In spite of its age, the plane had a good range and plenty of moxie if they should get into any trouble on the flight. And as it was a straight shot over the Mediterranean to Tunisia, they didn't need to request any unnecessary fly-over corridors or mach noise permissions. With an air speed of 1100 knots, they could get to Tunis in less than an hour and still fly as low as a hundred feet to foil the ARSR surveillance radar. He would lose all depth perception and would have to keep his eyes fixed carefully on the horizon at that altitude, but John Burns always preferred visual flying anyhow. Computers had taken a lot of the fun out of being a pilot as far as he was concerned.

"Uh, John, what's with the black forehead." David asked his friend as he joined him on the runway. "You doing your own oil changes these days, or what?"

"Ash Wednesday, man. Remember thou art dust and unto dust thou SHALL return. My mother would kill me if I didn't get my ashes on Ash Wednesday."

"Great John. Just what I need as I enter the lion's den."

David liked hanging out with the cocky young pilot. You never knew what he was going to do next. He wished he could take him along in his suitcase.

"You all set, Red Baron," John Burns called as he crawled into the front seat. "Fasten your seatbelt, buddy."

"Roger, Batman," David said, as the canopy set hydraulically over them, sealing the glass cocoon of the cockpit.

David tried to pretend his friend had invited him along on another island reconnaissance flight, one of those weekend excursions that was really just an excuse to have a good time and break the boredom of diplomatic life in Athens. A little hop down to Mykonos for some grilled herring and retsina, the fish far too expensive in Athens. This time, however, he was not just out for a lark. He speculated on the chances that Nadia Mansur was still alive. The whole world was depending on him to get her back. David felt a queasiness in his stomach that had nothing to do with the roar of the jet engine anxious to explode behind him.

"Frank 4 Barbara, 4-5-9-0 Charlie, you are cleared for take off," the tower announced on a standard UHF military frequency. "Have a good flight Colonel." From this point on they would have no further contact with command until the F4B returned to base.

John Burns released the brake, eased back on the control stick between his legs and ignited the rocket blasting white-hot at his tail, catapulting them into the purple dome overhead. When he first started flying jets, John Burns couldn't manage a take off without having an erection, and he still couldn't get over the power and pleasure it gave him to blast off this way.

David Schefflan sat lost in the blue silence like one of the majestic falcons he had trained in Israel. A German immigrant in the kibbutz who had lived in Saudi Arabia, taught them the art of falconry and he had excelled in the ancient desert sport. He loved the exquisite creatures with their keen eyes, and beauty. Despite their independence, they always returned with their prey. Corny, but he had asked the intelligence team to use falcon as his code name for this mission.

The centimeter incision at the back of his arm had all ready healed over where Mossad had implanted a tiny homing device. Agents in Tunis would be able to follow his movements without difficulty, but Islamic Rebirth still controlled the hostages. And there was always the risk they would take him for a hostage instead of negotiating. Terry Anderson had gone in with a white flag and wound up spending years in a Lebanese rat hole. David couldn't forget the grotesque image of Yves Bourret's head hanging over the bloody bucket. And David was a Jew after all, a detail that would not go unnoticed by the terrorists.

"Hey man, lighten up," John Burns said, pulling the controls hard right and flipping the plane upside down. They flew along staring up at the ocean a hundred feet above them.

"Do you mind not killing me, even before the Arabs get their hands on me," David said.

"This is a training mission, David. We need a little verisimilitude if anyone has us on visual," he said, but he righted the plane. "Air speed 1050 knots. Don't worry, we'll have you on the ground in no time. INS says we've got 13 minutes," he said, checking the black box that fed out their running record.

"Unidentified air craft, heading 230 degrees, this is Tunis Central, correct to flight level 270 and identify immediately. We have no flight progress strip on ARS Radar, over."

"Roger, Tunis Central, this is Frank 4 Barbara 4-5-9-0- Charlie, destination Base Arrienne FRA. Request terminate flight following, over."

"Roger. Squawk VFR code 398. Radar Service terminated. Frequency change approved. Cleared to Base Arrienne, 34 approach. Beinvenue, Colonel. Over."

John Burns was well known to the young controllers running the tower. By the end of the year, Tunis would have a state-of-the-art ATC to monitor traffic over the Mediterranean that would rival even the sophisticated system the United States had built for the Royal Moroccan Air Force. Now that the PLO had been ejected from Tunisia, the U.S. rewarded the tiny Arab country with massive foreign aid projects. Consultants invaded the ministries with development schemes to increase poultry production, expand harbor whereabouts capacity, catalog tribal tattoo patterns among Berber women in the south. No project was too big or too small. Colonel Burns had spent several months on loan from the embassy to develop ATC procedures and help train controllers in IFR communication. He was more popular than a soccer hero among the young country boys training to control the skies over Tunisia.

John Burns over flew the runway and received the flashing green light gun signal letting him know all was well, that he could return and circle for landing. The Presidential palace sat glimmering beside the ruins of Carthage on the coast. The little orange car commuter train connected the elegant residential villages, brilliant white villas cresting on the cliffs like white caps on the ocean.

He rolled the control stick right and pushed forward feeling the increased drag on the stick as the landing gear dropped. He adjusted the flaps to 25 degrees and engaged the spoilers to save his brakes. It was a perfect landing.

"Welcome to Africa, Bwana," he said as the plane came to a stop on the scorching runway. The air was stifling, unlike the dry heat of Athens. It even smelled like a different continent. Orange blossom and freshly tilled soil permeated the humid air from a farm just beyond the airport security fence.

It had been decided that John Burns would turn around immediately for Greece once he had delivered his passenger. The two friends stood on the tarmac, awkward at the farewell.

"Well, good luck, *mon* General," John said, bussing David's cheeks as though he were presenting the Legion of Honor. David embraced his friend and slapped John's back in a farewell, pulling back with a mock salute.

"Don't take any wooden *dinars*."

From the terminal, David watched as John Burns fired his engines and hurtled down the runway. The plane banked east then streaked low over the runway one more time, tipping its wings like a tightrope walker in farewell before disappearing into the clouds above the Mediterranean.

A line of red and white toy taxicabs queued up outside the air base waiting to carry civilian personnel to and from work. Even the lowest paid ex-pat working on the ATC project could live like a prince in Tunisia with servants taking care of every need. The taxi drivers fed on their business like piranha. Those who chose to brave the traffic and find their way through the labyrinth of the city in their own vehicle, hired full-time car keepers, who guarded and dusted them throughout the day. Less conspicuous to take a taxi, David explained, turning down Colonel Kabaj's offer of a limousine, and one particularly aggressive driver grabbed his suitcase and had it in the tiny Renault the minute he stepped outside the gate of the air base.

"*Ween Meshi, Ya sidi*," the cabbie asked him. "Where you are going?" Tiny Christmas tree lights blinked about the edge of the window. The Arabic letters for Allah were sewn in gold into the black velvet slipcases covering the sun visors. The scent of gardenia wafted from a bejewelled plastic crown concealing the car deodorizer.

"*La Marsa, min fudlik*," David said.

"*Brubi*," the cabbie cried, "*Titkellim bil Tunsi*," surprised that the American could speak the local dialect.

"Villa Akhdar," David instructed.

"Dr. Hershey's villa. Very beautiful villa," pleased to show off his English.

"*Esh ismik?*" David asked.

The response, of course, "Mohammed."

The hospital ship *HOPE* had come to Tunisia years ago to teach the latest medical techniques to hospital interns at Mohamed V Hospital. The American Embassy's guest house would forever take the name of the American physician who had become a legend among the local population for his kindness and skill.

David chatted with the driver as they made their way out the coastal road to the furthest and most elegant of the resort villages on the outskirts of Tunis. In self-defense against the garrulous driver, David asked Mohammed about his family, a question sure to keep him occupied. As the driver began an account of the treachery against his third son at the hands of the agricultural cooperative manager in Sfax, Mohammed reached into the glove box and pulled out a plastic bag. He took a piece of crystallized resin from the bag and in several minutes was producing loud irritating popping noises as he chewed.

In the back of his mind, David half-registered the odd fact. The only country where he had ever seen *mustika*, the natural chewing gum peasants collected from pine boughs, was in Greece.

Omen

Her first instinct was to get up from the cot, but when she tried to raise her head from the pillow, pain knifed down Nadia's spine as though a chef were extracting the vein of a live shrimp. She rested, her body clammy from the effort she'd made. As her mind began to clear she studied herself like an emergency room physician examining a patient. She could move her feet, had sensation in her limbs. A bullet had not severed the spinal cord. She could lift her shoulders with great difficulty. But the pain was focused in the cervical vertebrae. C2 through C4 had been severely traumatized she calculated, perhaps an occipital fracture accounted for the excruciating throbbing at the base of her skull. The force of the blow must have been terrific.

She tried to remember what could have caused it. He had taken her, she was enraptured, beyond pleasure beyond her senses. The ethereal, out-of body sensation held at the edge of her consciousness. And as she strained to pull herself from the memory, to make sense of the pain she now felt, suddenly he was there again, dreamlike, standing over her with a steaming mug in his hand.

"What happened? Why...?" She gasped with the effort it took even to speak.

"Don't try to talk," he said, lifting her head with great care so that she might drink from the cup. "You need nourishment."

"Oh," she murmured. A simple beef bouillon, but she had never tasted anything so delicious in her life. She could almost sense it flowing through her, restoring her strength.

"Food tastes better at sea." he said.

"How long have I..."

"You've been out for two days. I was beginning to think we lost you." He placed her cheek in the palm of his hand.

"Lost your hostage," she said, remembering he was the enemy. She winced from the pain it took to push his hand away.

"Fotini became overzealous. But I'm going to take care of you now."

"To barter for the heroic liberation of Palestine?" Her head hurt so, she was utterly exhausted. Her eyes filled with tears.

"No, because I love you Nadia."

She studied him, the concern and longing. Expectation played across his face like clouds racing over the ocean before a storm. Her eyes mirrored his emotions until her smile broke through like the sun dispersing all confusion.

He bent over and kissed her gingerly. When he looked at her again, she had already slipped back into sleep.

"Rest now. Get strong and come back to me. I promise that nothing will happen to you. I'm never going to lose you now that I have found you again.

As Abdel came on deck a blue nosed dolphin broke the surface of the water with an elegant arc at the bow of the *Ceberus*. The sailor's sign of good luck, Fotini had explained to him off Crete when another such creature had burst into the air unexpectedly. But the dark look Fotini gave him, standing fixed to the wheel like Ahab, her back turned to the wind, seemed to portend anything but good luck.

Sheep

For three days David kept the low profile of an American visitor taking a quiet break at the Villa Akhdar. The mansion sat on a bluff over the Mediterranean, the great green doors for which it was named turned away from the spectacular view of water. It had been built long before independence by an eccentric French colonel who had been raised as an Arab and had assimilated the local people's fear of the sea. It was said that something evil came out of the waves to defile a man's daughters and contaminate his lungs. Before tourists re-colonized North Africa, the sea was only a place to throw the garbage.

The beach at Villa Akhdar had long since been turned into a swimmer's paradise, however. Every morning David rose with the sun, long before anyone else in the team, and threaded his way down the stairs carved into the face of the cliff to the little beach and cafe along the coastal road below. His instructions were to wait for contact outside the La Mansa train station, but he couldn't resist an early morning swim in the exquisite aquamarine water before making his way to the station each day. That early in the morning there was no other bathers or customers at the cafe and he had the ocean all to himself. He could strip off his blue tank suit and swim free, far out into the water. He might have been a youth from antiquity in search of sponges, making his way out to the rocky island a mile off shore. The water was pure glass, bracing, not yet warmed by the summer sun. The swim was invigorating, his body and mind came alive as he took stock of their situation.

They had begun to worry that they'd been spotted. The terrorists had insisted that David come to the station alone and wait in public view beside the newspaper kiosk. Arabia and Moncef, the Tunisian agents on the team, were as good as they came, could disappear in a crowd better than a chameleon in a rain forest. Tunisia was a world crossroads long before Aeneas first showed his face on its shores, and there were enough westerners in this metropolitan capitol for Jerry and Sandy to pass unnoticed in the busy train station.

But it had been three days now and still no one had made a move. It was logical that the kidnappers would wait a while, of course, to see if David was following their commands and foil any ambush. Maybe today he wouldn't have to stand in the sun all day, scrutinizing every pedestrian who walked by, looking for recognition. Maybe today the rats would feel secure enough to crawl out of their nest. Still, he hated coming ashore to climb back up the cliff and begin his cat and mouse game with them again.

David strode out of the water naked and breathless, unaware that Arabia had him firmly fixed in the sights of her binoculars from the terrace at the villa. Her job was surveillance, after all, but this was one moment in the day, unknown to David, when she did her job particularly well.

The water glistened on his back as he finished his morning exercises with a set of pushups. He was extremely well-developed for an embassy press officer, in all areas, she decided, as David toweled himself off and stepped back into his bathing suit.

When the little red taxicab parked in front of the cafe pulled slowly up to David, Arabia turned on the long range microphone and aimed it at the two men.

"*May selish, Mohammed.* I don't need a cab today. I'm walking back to the villa. Thanks anyhow," he said. David seemed to know the cabbie, and she relaxed a bit. But she kept the microphone pointed at him anyway.

"Yes, the cab," the driver insisted.

"No really, it's not far. The exercise is good for me," slapping his mid-section.

"Get in the taxi. Now. Or the Western doctor dies."

Of course they would be following him, had tracked him from the very beginning. He was furious that he hadn't paid enough attention to his instincts about Mohammed when the cabbie first picked him up at the air base.

"I have no clothes. Let me go up to the villa first and get dressed." He tried to stall, to alert the team that he was moving. Mossad at least would be able to track him. He imagined the homing device glowing like an emerald, blinking green just below his skin.

"*May selish*. No matter about clothes. Get in now."

David slipped in the rear seat and slammed the flimsy door of the little tin Renault as Mohammed pulled onto the coastal road.

"Mobile units, come in. All units," Arabia spoke calmly into the radio before sounding the villa's alarm. They had been lax in letting him have his private swim each morning, but at least they had twenty-four hour backup units covering all approaches to the villa.

"Our falcon has flown. Traveling east along coastal road toward airport. Red mini-cab. License, SD-428. Monitor only. Do not apprehend."

She had a response in four minutes.

"Roger base. Falcon in view. Trailing."

A mini-van, and a boy and girl on a motorcycle passed an old Peugeot truck filled with sheep and fell into line at some distance behind the taxi. Things were under control. She wouldn't need to risk tipping their hand with helicopter surveillance. The hook was baited and now all they had to do was to keep sight of the line until they had landed the terrorists.

"They've entered the port access road," the girl on the motorcycle said into the radio backpack the driver wore. "They're heading for the industrial park B where houses. We'll take up position beyond the port. Mustapha and Salim are going in."

When the taxi came to the last where house along the water, the huge corrugated door slid open granting them access. The little car drove down an aisle between rows of sea vans and came to a stop in front of one that had been turned into an office for the shipping foreman. They got out of the car and Mohammed handed David a towel. He tied it about his waist.

"Your head," Mohammed commanded.

"I can't discuss Dr. Mansur's release with a towel over my head."

"Put it on."

David didn't like the implications of being blindfolded, but for the moment he had to do what he was told. He had no choice if he wanted to get to their leader. Looking down from beneath his towel he saw the hands of men on either side of him as they led him to the back of the building. One pair was delicate and pale, could even have been the hands of a girl. On his right, the hands were strong, callused from some sort of hard physical labor.

He heard a door open to the wharf behind the building, sunlight filtering through the hood of his towel. The cool of the warehouse and breeze off the ocean made his skin rise with goose bumps. When the guards pulled his hands behind his back and the metal handcuffs locked his wrists into place, he realized they had no intention of negotiating anything with him, that he had simply taken Yves Bourret place as a hostage. David felt unable to breathe suddenly, straining against his handcuffs as claustrophobia began to take him over.

"No," he yowled, throwing back his head like an animal with its foot caught in a metal trap. The towel fell and he was just able to catch a glimpse of the stocky, ape-like guard before the butt of a Kalashnikov smashed into his face. Darkness.

By nightfall, the team from Villa Akhdar had settled into their posts waiting for any sign of activity from the building. Infrared binoculars turned night into day. The taxi couldn't possibly escape undetected. They prepared for a long wait. A good agent had a talent for waiting. Patience paid even bigger dividends than courage sometimes.

The Peugeot truck had long since pulled along side the port road and unloaded its sheep to graze. In the cab of the truck, a young shepherd studied the green radar monitor beneath the dash as the steady blip on the screen moved now beyond the confines of the port warehouse.

"Shimon," he called to the shepherd leaning against the cork tree, glasses trained on the building where the cab had disappeared. "Let's go. Let's go."

"What?" the startled boy said as he jumped into the truck.

"They're on the water. They're taking him by ship. Call headquarters. Get a boat out there before we lose him," he said, leaving the sheep to graze contentedly along with the American intelligence agents assigned to protect David Schefflan from harm.

Land of the Lotus Eaters

When Ofek-3 was launched in the late 1990's, *Jane's Defense Weekly* in London described it as a photographic reconnaissance vehicle with real-time down link that could transmit accurate video in almost any weather. Angered at Washington's refusal to share all its satellite pictures on Iraq during the Gulf War, Israel had set out on an ambitious spy satellite program of its own. By the turn of the century, Mossad technicians could brag of video signals sharp enough to make out license plates in Baghdad. The latest model, Ofek-6, could fix its orbit over a designated target to provide non-stop, twenty-four hour surveillance anywhere on the planet. But Ofek-6 had far more important work in the weeks following David Schefflan's disappearance than spying on the enemy in Baghdad or Damascus.

It had trained its sleepless eye on the coast of Tunisia, scanning each grid of Mediterranean section by section, like a mother whale singing across the ocean for a lost child. Finally, the satellite had locked onto the invisible signal emanating from the homing device planted beneath the skin of David Schefflan's triceps. Now Ofek-6 sat in the heavens like cyclops, its monocular attention riveted on the tiny desert island of Djerba, floating just of the southern coast off Tunisia.

In myth, the island of Djerba was said to be so fair, the inhabitants so seductively beautiful, the food so intoxicating that Ulysses and his men were powerless to leave. They passed their days in an ecstasy of pleasure, a drugged forgetfulness of their own homeland from the lotus fruit that grew abundantly in the garden paradise.

The Djerba Ofek-6 scanned night and day, was now a barren wasteland. Exactly three date palms were all that remained of the luxurious groves flourishing about the small oasis at the center of the island. The olive trees had long since withered or were sacrificed to the kilns. The tiny village of Galella, once famous throughout the country for its unique, brick-red pottery was virtually deserted since the blue death had come to visit the island. The tourists no longer fished its waters for rouget and grouper, no students camped on its beaches, playing at Robinson Crusoe. The epidemic had devastated more than just the health of the villagers.

When the boys keeping watch sent out the alarm, the old men still working in the village loaded up what pottery they had produced and pulled their stubborn donkeys through the scrub brush to the port. The government kept the ferry running sporadically and these occasional visits were the only chance they had to trade for oil and flower, sugar and tea. When the ferry stopped, the village would die.

The sole anomaly in the desolate landscape was the large stucco farmhouse hidden behind walls that fenced off the northern third of the island. It was built in the classic Arab fashion, four walls connecting into a fortress like structure about a courtyard. The mud ramparts in desert villages baked like cement and could soar many stories high. The underground beehives called *gorphas* buried under the sands along the coast tunneled just as deeply.

In the center of the farmhouse courtyard, a circular fountain decorated in triangular blue and white tiles completed the geometric harmony of the house. This was the center of life in every Arab home or Mosque. Here one could escape the hellish heart of mid-day heat, drink Allah's precious gift of water; cleanse oneself before prayer.

Ofek-6 focused on several of the out buildings that would have housed animals, grain and farming equipment for the French family that built the house. It might only have been a rustic memory from the colonial past, except for the yacht that lay off shore, and the radar antennae on the roof that Affix-6 projected on the monitors in Jerusalem. When the satellite had first panned in on the ornate script for *Ceberus* carved into the stern of the ship, the Mossad agents analyzing the photographic data gave a shout of triumph. At last they had discovered the secret haven where Islamic Rebirth kept David Schefflan and Nadia Mansur prisoner. Now they were left with an even bigger problem, what to do with the information.

Mitzvah

The only light penetrating the darkness rose from a crack beneath the heavy wooden door to David's cell. He lay on a filthy straw mattress, drained of all energy. For two days he hadn't eaten the food they pushed under the door. Yesterday, his captors tried tempting him with a *bric a l'oeuf,* but he left the Tunisian specialty of egg and paper thin crepe untouched on his plate. He watched impassively as a field rat came upon the lucky hoard and began to eat furiously, the creature's hunger temporarily overcoming its fear of the man studying him in the shadows. But David was far too weak to pick up a stone and only stared back listlessly into the rat's beady eyes.

When they had first transported him from the boat to this prison, David was consumed with trying to find an escape route. The building must have been some sort of root cellar or storage silo, he decided. The earthen floor was dug out several feet below the stone foundation but without ventilation the dark room was stiflingly hot. The roof was sound and several meters above his reach, an unlikely way out.

Every morning the guard banged on the door calling "*Hammam,*" and David was marched off, towel over his head to the primitive outhouse. He couldn't always relieve himself on this sort of schedule, but he was glad to know that they hadn't forgotten him. He considered a plan to overpower the guard as he came into the cell, but David's head throbbed, and he could feel himself weaken by the hour as the infection set in. He was certain he was going to pass out yesterday from the stench and heat of the filthy toilet. Only a rush of adrenaline revived him when a scorpion scurried across the dirt floor and into a crevice at the base of the wall. They carried him back to his cell and simply let him drop to his bed.

Once when David was a teenager, his doctor had ordered an MRI after a swimming accident and David never recovered from the claustrophobia that test had triggered. As his body slid into the coffin-like tube and the machine's loud banging began, a man in the adjacent room went into cardiac arrest, sending all the technicians flying. He tried to remain calm as the paramedics shouted to each other trying to resuscitate the patient in the room next door, but a half an hour later they found David stuck half way out of the tube, hysterical as he tried to escape the machine. He had trusted his body to them, and they had abandoned him. After that he couldn't stand to be in a confined space. And the problem only worsened as he grew older. It took two orderlies to restrain him the following summer when they tried to administer general anesthesia for an appendectomy. In a recurrent dream, he would bang on the window of Pan Am 103 trying to warn his parents of the impending explosion and the nightmare was always the same as his father smiled and waved from the other side of the glass. With the guile of a clever alcoholic, he managed to hide his phobia from Mossad the year he spent as a young recruit leaning basic trade craft—codes, use of handguns, self-defense, surveillance work. They never detected his obsession with fire exits, or noticed how he avoided elevators and airplanes.

David's captors had no idea what a successful torture they had devised by this darkened cell. The isolation devastated for him. He would have preferred electrodes attached to his genitals to life in this black hole straining at the door throughout the day to hear the sound of a human voice.

His first night in the darkened cell, he thought he heard a woman singing faintly, like a dream, somewhere in the building. He tried banging against the wall, but the stones were too solid. When he called out to that voice his guards stormed in and beat him about the head. Then they left a transistor radio at full volume tuned into static hanging outside his door through the night. The white noise was an agony. It burned into his brain, robbing him of sleep. He tried to shut it out by plugging his ears with bits of straw and wrapping himself in the dirty mattress, but the high-pitched screech was relentless. In several days, what began as a nuisance grew to the point where he thought he would go insane. The only relief from the noise came when he went to the foul toilet.

After several days he began to feel an irritation in his ear canals where he had packed them with straw. They grew swollen and painful.

His fury overcame his exhaustion and he began to kick at the door begging them to turn off the radio. His guards finally relented, but the relief came too late. David woke the next night with an excruciating pain in his inner ears that brought tears to his eyes, and even worse, the horrifying realization that he could no longer hear.

"You must help me, you must get a doctor," he called out to the guards, his voice registering only a faint bussing pressure in his head. The image of living the handicapped life of a deaf person electrified him, unable to interact normally with others, a world of silence, without music or a lover's voice.

"I can't hear you, I can't hear you," he shouted when the guards came into his cell. "You must get tell your leader I need help." But the guards just left him to his rumination.

He was certain this was more than a childhood earache. He studied the individual shapes of the stones, like so many skulls decorating the walls of the dimly lit cell, trying to sidestep the excruciating pain, the fever. Children did sometimes get meningitis from an earache. He tried to remember the name of the king, was it Hamlet's father, murdered by a poison poured into his ear as he slept beneath a tree? The irony made David furious and panicky. He had spent his entire life listening intently for anything, any information that might help Israel survive, the way he himself had survived all the dangers of secret service to Mossad. Now it seemed a couple of imbecile guards would end his life with a transistor radio.

His parents followed his life in Mossad somehow from beyond the grave, David was certain of that. They took pride the way he sought out vengeance for their death, all the dangerous missions he had accomplished. To die at the hands of these Arab cretins, the indignity of such a death, filled David with shame and grief. He knew that he would be defeated if he fell into self-pity and let go of his reason, but the pain and loneliness began to overwhelm him.

"David, dear, don't you worry," his mother said, the sweet flesh of her face blooming amid the skulls floating on the wall before him. David couldn't resist the hallucination. Her smile was a delicious refreshment. "I'm going to send you a *mitzvah*, David. You'll be fine, dear. A wonderful miracle."

With her words, the room burst into light, blinding him. Two angels stood at the door of his cell in the brilliance. They moved to him and floated down to his mattress.

"We've got to get him out of this heat, we've got to cool him down Aznia," she said. "He's burning up."

"We have orders," Aznia said, her Kalishnikov aimed at David on the mattress. "Abdel said…"

"He wants this man kept alive. We can't leave him here to suffocate. Don't worry. He's not strong enough to get up, let alone escape."

"It is on your head," she said, motioning the guards into the room. Together they lifted David Schefflan out of the building and brought him to the fountain in the center of the courtyard."

"A miracle," he said, when in broad day light, the angel transformed herself into the form of Nadia Mansur and soaked a towel in the fountain to lay on his brow.

The Patriarch

Once a week, in a medium sized, non-descript building on Jaffa street in the business district of Tel-Aviv, the fate of Israel is decided over coffee. At about eight o'clock, middle-aged men, dressed casually in short-sleeved shirts and khakis arrive in modest sedans and assemble at a conference room on the tenth floor. The conference room can only be entered by way of a private, locked elevator starting from the underground parking lot. There are no windows in this conference room and special security precautions guarantee privacy against unwanted electronic spy ships that might be drifting on the Mediterranean along the coast. These are no bland bureaucrats, however, or price-fixing corporate moguls in disguise. Each week at "coffee morning," the chiefs of Israeli intelligence gather to address emergencies and plan projects. Their membership included: the director of Shin Beth, the inspector general of police, the senior man from the foreign affairs ministry—with his head of research and political planning, the head of the Aman military intelligence; and at the top of the pyramid, the Patriarch himself, the supreme boss of Mossad. These officers lived the simple style of the kibbutzim, would stand out as oddities in the splendor of CIA headquarters in Langley, or the gentlemen's clubs preferred by senior men from the British M16. Yet they direct an intelligence agency that is the envy of the world.

Any man on the busy streets of Tel Aviv would tell you why. Though forbidden by international law, all countries conduct such espionage activity. But only Israel, they would explain, can justify intelligence gathering, living as it does, a little blue star-shaped island in a sea of Arab hate and vengeance. Without this crucial service, the Arabs would drown Israel out like the Red Sea crashing over the heads of Pharaoh's soldiers. Mossad is an organ of self-defense in a war of survival, they would tell you. Mossad recruited only tough, intellectual Zionists who saw their service as a patriotic duty, and even at that, fewer than half such recruits make the final grade. Who else would protect Israel against it's enemies in the U.N.? Who else would look after Jewish minorities in the diaspora, or bring international villains such as Eichmann to justice? And unlike other such agencies, Israeli citizens knew that Mossad was guided by the highest moral considerations. Every member of the Wrath of God received dossiers proving the guilt of their targets when the butchers of Munich were assassinated. Such acts of war had to be sanctioned by the agents themselves and not just their intelligence chiefs.

The Mossad legend, however, like all public relations coups managed to cloak a slightly different reality. The man in the street was not likely to mention the number of Arabs incarcerated in Israeli prisons without due process. Nor the massacres at Sabra and Chatila; or the pre-emptive strikes against terrorist camps in neighboring countries and political assassinations. Or the use of mercenaries like Jonathan Pollard to spy on Israel's own allies. And the man in the street was likely to overlook the occasional use of secret intelligence to bolster government policy.

"Gentlemen we've got a problem," Chaim Be'eri announced at that morning's coffee conference. At sixty, he was one of the older men in the group, sought out because of his particular expertise as a political analyst. Mossad agents usually retired by age fifty-two. More than anyone else, he was responsible for Likud's triumphant victory in the last round of elections and had helped manage world opinion from the earliest days of the disastrous peace initiative after Helsinki.

"Last night's poll is conclusive. Prime Minister Barak cannot win May's election without a dramatic shift in the electorate. His approval rating has slipped to twenty-four percent and he has very high negatives. Fencing off Gaza simply hasn't worked. The *Issedin el Qassem* are training openly in the Golan Heights. None of the settlements are any more secure than they were twenty years ago.

People are exhausted by the bombings, the destruction. They want to give Likud another chance to bring peace."

"Let's sweep Gaza City again, and really clean it out this time," the Inspector General of Police said. "We still have a mandate to protect our people in the territories."

"We've got to do something spectacular to show the voters we intend victory," said the head of Aman. "Let's invade the Golan Heights and destroy all those Hamas villages."

"The Hell with the Golan. I say we hit Damascus and take on Assad once and for all. Why do we pretend we will ever have peace with Syria?" the director of Shin Beth said. "A new military action will certainly unite the people behind the Prime Minister and prove we mean business."

"What about this David Schefflan," the foreign ministry representative asked? "Didn't you say he had been positively identified by satellite in Tunisia? Who would blame us for trying to rescue our own agent in a hostile country? And if we manage to bring back the woman scientist they are holding and end this epidemic, the Prime Minister will be the world's hero. Look what the rescue at Entebbe did for Rabin's government in '76."

"We can't risk exposing Schefflan," the assistant to the Patriarch explained. "Jewish populations all over the world suffer when it becomes clear we have used local Jews in espionage work. It raises the specter of anti-Semitism everywhere. Do I need to remind you of the importance of the American Jewish community to our survival? And if David Schefflan is identified as a Mossad agent, it is certain to bring down the Likud government."

"What if he were to die in the process of being rescued," the director of Aman asked. "The despicable terrorists create one more martyr and give us a justification for trying to rescue Dr. Mansur in the first place."

"We can't kill one of our own agents. The Prime Minister would never approve of such an action, even if Schefflan isn't an Israeli."

"The American knew the risk he was taking. He compromised himself when he got himself captured. If Islamic Rebirth finds out that he's a Mossad agent you can be damn sure they will broadcast that to the world. Think of how it would compromise our operations."

"The Prime Minister doesn't have to know how David Schefflan dies," the Patriarch said finally, putting an end to further discussion. "In fact, I'm sure the Prime Minister would prefer not to know the details. If challenged later, he can truthfully deny all knowledge of the operation. It's our responsibility to provide plausible deniability. But let me warn you. None of us will survive if this mission fails."

The Patriarch leaned over the table and poured a cup of thick black coffee from the thermos. Despite the hour, the coffee was still hot, steam rising from the tiny cup. He had acquired his taste for Turkish coffee years ago when he served in Egypt. He was one of the old guard who spoke Arabic fluently despite his Hebrew nationalism. These days parents wouldn't risk having their children absorb enemy culture by studying Arabic and Mossad was gradually losing its linguistic advantage in the game of espionage.

The Patriarch sipped his coffee and did not wait for the black sediment to filter to the bottom of the cup. There was much to do, now that he had made his decision to rescue David Schefflan.

Fatima

Youssef had ordered her to keep the female hostage in her cell, but Fatima was selective about what orders she would obey from the camp commander. Life in the camp mirrored the segregation between the sexes in the outside world, and among the women, Fatima was the final authority.

She had fought for years with the women of south Lebanon during the Israeli invasion and had earned her position as a leader. It began when she was just a girl carrying grenades beneath her skirts to blow up army trucks patrolling her village. On one raid she tripped as she tried to escape the fiery blast and the shrapnel buried in her legs left her with a heavy limp. But she could still run faster than any girl in camp if she had to. She didn't need a man to tell her how to handle prisoners. She had managed plenty of prisoners in her day, men and women both. In the new Palestine women would stand beside men as equals. The women of south Lebanon had bought that equality with their own blood. She wasn't about to let Youssef chain her to the wash tub once again when they had won this war.

Not all the men were as hard headed as Youssef, fortunately. Abdel was more lenient on their hostage. Where could she flee to on the island, after all, he reasoned with Youssef - and no one could get away from Fatima once she was assigned guard duty. Besides, Nadia's medical training might be useful if she were brought into the life of the camp. She might even begin to see her duty to Allah and help them in their struggle.

Fatima watched the way he looked at Nadia. The woman doctor was more than just a hostage to him. That was clear. Fatima caught them kissing once on the beach and fired her machine gun into the air to douse their passion and flush out the little love birds. It was always the same with men. He followed her around like a dog. And the Greek one, all painted up like a whore, followed him around like a bitch in heat. They were worse than those romance picture-books all her friends in the village wasted their money on when she was a girl. Women were sometimes even more stupid then men, she decided.

In the evenings after they had served supper to the camp and washed up the clay pots and put out the kanoun, she sometimes took Nadia outside the villa to share their meal sitting in the courtyard. Fatima had turned her prisoner into a kitchen helper and they both welcomed the evening breeze after cooking hot plates of *cous cous* or *tahini*.

Helping Fatima prepare the food, Nadia remembered all the years she had worked with her mother in the kitchen when she was young. Islam dictated separate lives for men and women, at the mosque, at social events, and daily family life. There were no females to be found even among the ranks of the angels according to the Koran. Before she went to the university, Nadia had spent her entire life in the company of other women, though it was difficult to explain the segregated life of the harem to her western friends, the way it permeated Arab thinking.

"How can you stand to wear that thing," her friend Cindy asked once as Nadia adjusted the scarf about her head in the ladies room mirror, making sure all her hair was covered."

"I'm going to JFK to meet my uncle," she said. "He's arriving from Jordan this afternoon."

"Nadia, this is the United States of America, remember? You are not living in a medieval harem," she said, adjusting her garters to keep her stockings from creeping below the hem of her mini-skirt. She had a rich arsenal of outfits like this one, was a high-ranking field officer in the battle of the sexes. She had her sights set on Martin Cramer himself, and was planning to initiate her campaign that very evening at Bravo Bravo's happy hour where he had been spotted of late on Friday evenings.

"A lot of young, well-educated women prefer to wear the veil, to show pride in their heritage, to stand with Arab nationalism. The harem isn't always what you make it out to be in the west, Cindy."

"So what is so hard to understand about life in a prison? You're given prison issue, your veil there. You're locked away from society out of the sight of men, forbidden to drive a car, kept like an animal in a barn for breeding and domestic purposes. No thank you. I don't see why Arab women didn't rise up centuries ago." She applied black liner to the margins of her crimson lips like a jeweler engraving a precious cup.

"Arabs consider the harem an asylum for women, Cindy. Protection, not a prison. There is no security in a world without boundaries, symbolic boundaries or the actual stone-built Casbahs that protect against one's enemies. A woman without the veil is seen as defenseless and out of bounds, like a house without security. It is *awra*, or naked, like a prostitute parading in the streets tempting men to adultery and the Koran tells us "man was created weak."

"So much the better, I say. And forget the Koran. Every girl knows that fact by the time she's twelve. But what do you think? Do you like dressing up like a nun every time you have to meet a man from your hometown?"

"It's a sign of respect. A difference in cultures, that's all. You'd be surprised just how much women really run an Arab household, Cindy. And I'll tell you, the friendships among women in the harem are very deep."

"I guess so without any men around."

"Sometimes the friendship is physical, yes. Holding hands, a kiss, even sexual love. But so much of life is shared by women in our world, the boredom, the joys, everyday life. A kind of sorority grows that feminists here couldn't begin to understand. Arab women help each other raise their children, they work together and entertain each other, they care for each other in ways a man can't."

"Men really are bastards, aren't they," she said, making a final survey of herself in the mirror. "But what are you going to do? I for one can't live without them. I think you're protesting a little too much, sweetie. I certainly wouldn't kick Yves Bourret out of bed for the warm fuzzies of the harem if I were in your nightie."

And true to her word, Cindy had gone on to prove her point by successfully seducing Dr. Bourret into a short-lived affair before moving on to bigger game. It was nothing personal really, she explained to Nadia after the affair was over, she simply couldn't resist the challenge. All's fair...

Yves returned to Nadia like a penitent child but for weeks she had wished him dead until time healed her pain and the web of love and habit ensnared her once again.

It all seemed like a dream, Nadia thought, as the evening stars began to pierce the evening sky over Djerba. It was as though she'd never really known Yves Bourret. Now he really was dead and it was all she could do to keep his image alive as she fell into the routine duties of life among the women in the camp. How could she let him slip so easily into memory. His death should call her to some sort of terrible vengeance, but her growing love for Abdel only intensified her complicity and guilt. Though she had been taken hostage against her will, Abdel's compassion for his people, his sense of the world's injustice against Palestine, and his willingness to fight the whole world despite the odds of winning broke her heart. He was like every poor Arab boy on any dirt soccer field in the Mideast, angry, hurt, making a great show of bravado against the West. When what they wanted most deep in their hearts was not to be hated just for being an Arab, to have a share of the wealth, a future. They dreamed of living like Omar Sharif, a Pharaoh among all the blond beauties of Hollywood, or Gamudi, streaking to victory and the Olympic gold medal, when the best life would offer them was daydreams in a dirt soccer field.

Nadia could not deny the comfort she had begun to feel living among her own people again. She almost wondered if it were genetic, the sense of ease she felt, like a little duckling waddling after its mother, impressed in its earliest youth with the need to follow her own kind.

She continued to demand her release and that of the American, but she kept her growing sympathy for Abdel's cause to herself. When ordered to do something she considered useful, however, she agreed to help. To their amazement she had nursed the American back to health. Fatima watched hypnotized, as Nadia deftly lanced his eardrums and drained the pus that had collected there. They found only an outdated supply of penicillin in the first aid stores, but the drug worked, along with heat compresses, rest, and nutritious meals Fatima prepared for him.

Nadia spent hours each day, working to exhaustion with villagers who came to the compound to beg for food or just to die. There was little she could do against the Blue Death that raged on, even here in this remote desert island. But she ministered to villagers with the very mercy of the Prophet. She showed such love and concern for her patients, eventually, Fatima put down her Kalashnikov and worked beside Nadia as a nurse.

She had never known such a doctor. Doctors were men who sat behind desks and wrote prescriptions for pills after you told them your symptoms. When they carried her to the hospital, legs riddled with metal shards, the Israeli doctor guessed soon enough how she had injured herself and did little more than patch her up. Once when he got to the scene of a terrorist attack in the Diamond district of Tel Aviv, he found the severed arm of a girl still spinning on the floor of the bus. He no longer felt any moral obligation to keep the enemy alive for another ambush.

But Dr. Nadia accepted anyone to the makeshift clinic Abdel had let her set up in the barn, even the poorest from the village. She was not afraid to touch her patients and did not dismiss their suffering. Once she sat with a child in her arms through the night because there was nothing more she could do until the sun came and the baby stopped crying forever. Fatima and Nadia had spent many such nights together and Fatima watched over her more like a devoted body guard than a jailer.

"How can you work this way, help these sick people, and not believe in Allah," Fatima asked her one evening as they sat at the fountain. She rolled bits of bread between her fingers and dropped them into the water for the little red fish gliding over the green tiles at the bottom of the water.

"I didn't say I don't believe in God. I just don't see his work as you do, Fatima. I believe in science. God has made us the stewards of the world he created. He works through our stewardship."

"A Muslim is he who believes and obeys," Fatima said. "Religion is obedience. An obeying Muslim is religious."

"You can't have science without freedom of thought, Fatima. You have to be able to question and find the truth. Science has been our great universal heritage, science in the service of humanity. While

Europe was perfecting the extinction of witches, Islamic astronomers were mapping the stars."

"He who gives priority to his own opinion is a modernizing innovator and a creator." She was never taught to read or write, but could repeat great sections of the Koran from memory as well as an Imam's sermon. "Creation is the province of Allah. This egoism weakens the power of the community."

Their arguments went on for days and always left Nadia frustrated and saddened. It was impossible to penetrate the medieval superstition and fundamentalist conditioning that had poisoned the soul of this proud and courageous woman. It was like trying to talk to someone trapped under ice. While Nadia attended medical lectures and worked her way up the medical hierarchy, Fatima had been attacking Israeli tanks with home made bombs to drive the enemy out of her homeland. She and her friends walked right up to the barbed wires surrounding the Israeli prisons and demanded that their sons and brothers be released. Day after day they stood at the fence screaming abuse and throwing rocks at the guards risking their lives until conditions were improved. Once Fatima had been imprisoned herself and been beaten badly. A tear at the corner of her mouth left her with a permanently crooked smile that she wore like a badge of honor and vowed to repay someday.

"The killing will never stop Fatima unless we give up the creed of vengeance. How many generations will it take? How will we break the cycle? If every act of violence is met with more violence we sacrifice the next generation, and the next. We have to look each other in the eyes and see each other's humanity, we have to see that when we kill our neighbor we are killing ourselves. It's simple logic. One side or the other must simply stop seeking revenge and end it once and for all."

"Not our side," Fatima said, a somber child, her spoiled smile set in a firm if tortured line of determination.

"You're more stubborn than a donkey on his way to market," Nadia said.

"You're a stubborn donkey. My *bahimi.*"

And the two women might give up on each other for the day and walk to the beach, arm-in-arm, to cool off in the aquamarine water on which the island floated.

Revenge

Fotini grieved for her lost life as though it were a dead child. There was nothing to do on this wretched island and even the shade offered no respite from the heat. It was impossible to keep dry, to keep her makeup fresh, to dress as she wished. The heat seemed to make her very flesh burn.

She had always loved the isolation of an island. Her home in Crete was a place to escape all the people who were constantly after her for something. In the real world she was the center of attention wherever she went. But now no one seemed to want or need her. The men in the camp eyed her as though she were a tarantula. They made no attempt to touch her as they would have in the streets of Rome or Athens. They were as tame as a flock of dung-caked sheep grazing in a field.

She had served her purpose in transporting them all to this God forsaken place and now she was just extra baggage. The one man who could have made a difference was lost to her. Abdel never left Nadia Mansur's side as though he were her prisoner. It was clear that he loved her. Everyone in the camp seemed to have fallen under the doctor's spell, even the American hostage who she treated in her clinic. Fotini's hatred for this woman burned stronger than the atomic star that stared down on them with an unrelenting glare throughout the long day.

They hadn't achieved a single thing with this hostage taking. None of the demands made by Islamic Rebirth had been met. She had sacrificed her life and career for nothing; not even their gratitude.

"You're no better than us," the fat one they called Fatima shouted at her one night. "You do nothing to help. You walk around like a queen, powdering your face and painting you lips, and swinging your

216

hips. What good does that do anybody?" All the men laughed when Fatima performed a rough pantomime of the film star parading seductively in front of them.

Fotini decided that night that she must kill them both. She would find a way, then radio the authorities for help. Somehow she would make the police believe she had been forced to co-operate in this kidnaping. In her head she began to write and rehearse the script that might save her life, the most important role she would ever play.

She saw her chance one blistering afternoon as Nadia and Fatima walked together along the path heading toward the beach. Fotini hid in the scrub at the edge of the beach watching them undress. Fatima wrapped her Kalishnikov in the black *jellaba* she wore and hid the gun behind a rock. Nadia was shy and Fatima tugged playfully at her dress until they were both naked. Nadia dove into the water and swam off shore. Fatima waded into the water more carefully and was up to her pendulous breasts when Fotini shot out from hiding and ran to the beach. She was sure neither of the bathers would beat her to machine gun, certainly not the gimpy old Arab guard who lumbered about the camp giving directions. Fotini didn't know how often Fatima had saved her life by running away from a bomb about to explode any minute from beneath an Israeli truck. She didn't know the acute sixth sense Fatima had developed for danger that seemed to extend her peripheral vision three hundred and sixty degrees. She couldn't have imagined how quickly Fatima dragged herself from the suck of ocean or the brute strength of her hands as they closed like a vice about Fotini's throat when they fell together wrestling on the sand. She couldn't have guessed the animal fury and survival intelligence that kept Fatima locked on her prey like a pit bull, despite Nadia's attempt to unlock her death grip. The shocked surprise was still frozen on her face long after Fatima crushed Fotini's larynx and pulled back from the purple, wide-eyed surprise that would be the last face Fotini's Theodorou would ever show to the world.

"This was a rotten woman, who needed death," was all Fatima said, when Nadia finally gave up trying to resuscitate her. Fatima didn't like the idea, "grieve not for the wicked, nor their devisings," she quoted from the Koran, but finally she agreed to bury the body - after a fashion.

Later that day when the sun was about to set and it grew a little cooler, Fatima hauled the corpse onto the back of her donkey and led it to the south end of the island. The village well had dried up years ago and was now half filled with broken shards of pottery and garbage. Fatima dumped the remains of Fotini Theodorou into the well and limped her tired way back to the camp singing a song about uncle Jaha to her donkey as she went.

Surgery

"We've got to do something about this," Nadia said to David Schefflan, but he pulled back as she tried to examine his upper right arm, swollen now to the size of a football. She had convinced Youssef that the hostage would die if they kept David confined to the inferno of his cell and they had agreed to move him to a storage shed in the barn where she had set up her clinic. But this new injury looked to be even more life threatening than the first.

The guards had beaten him badly when they first came to the island but that didn't necessarily account for the angry infection spreading through his body. And she was baffled by his refusal to let her do anything about it.

"You've got to let me examine this arm. Those red striations up your neck are serious David. If you develop encephalitis, or gangrene you will die here. There will be nothing I can do for you."

He had recovered his hearing under her care, but the fever had never really abated despite the antibiotics she gave him. He began to look emaciated from his weight loss. She helped him sponge his body off when she got to see him, but Youssef refused to let him bathe, or even cool off in the ocean. Her patient began to smell rancid from his illness. Unshaven, and unkempt she wondered if his combativeness was the beginning of delirium.

"I can have the guards restrain you David. Please don't make me do that. They want you kept alive. And so do I - so we can escape from this place together. I must get back to my laboratory and the vaccine. The whole world is dying while we wait here. You have to stay alive." She took his hand in both of hers. "You have to trust me David. Please, I want to help you."

He had seen her treating patients with Abdel. Why did their jailer let her come and go as she willed? Could she have begun to cooperate with their kidnappers? He wasn't sure of anything anymore. The pain from his arm extended deep into his chest, his hand had grown numb and discolored.

"All right," he said, using his good arm to lift the dead weight from the sling he devised.

She helped him out of his shirt and sat on a stool in front of him for a closer examination. The cellulitis was massive, his flesh was burning to the touch. There seemed to be no puncture wound or focal point for an insect or scorpion sting. When she lifted his arm gingerly to palpate the axillary nodes she noticed a thin white scar running vertically along the length of the triceps muscle.

"What's this," she said probing gently, and, "I'm sorry," when David began to groan with pain.

"There's some sort of calcification or tumor here. Almost like a stone or some sort of foreign body."

"Electronics," David said. "It's a high frequency transmitter."

"What?"

"The CIA doctors implanted it there before I came to Tunis," he said. "They can track my movements. It's just a question of time before they find us."

"Unless the thing has been damaged, David. You sustained some pretty forceful blows in this region. The injured tissue is infected, probably an anaerobic organism, and the body's defense mechanism is trying to reject the intruder. You're flesh is being poisoned from within, David. The device has got to come out."

"If you tell them about this, they will kill me for a spy. I'm sure of it. Look how they murdered Fotini Theodorou. My life is in your hands, Nadia."

"We are going to get out of this together David. I promise you. Do you remember the yellow rose I left for you in Athens? I knew you would come for me. You risked your life to negotiate for hostages. I would never sacrifice the gift you gave me." She placed her hand tenderly on his cheek.

"You are more than just a hostage. You mean far more to me than that," he said taking her hand and kissing it gently.

"It's going to be a primitive surgery," she said, pulling back from his intimacy. She felt so sorry for him, would take him in her arms and hold him until the pain went away if she could. But she was all ready in such emotional confusion with Abdel she couldn't risk indulging her feelings for David. It would make a difficult matter more complicated and so she retreated into her role as healer.

"I don't even have any suturing material. But I think the wound will heal better by secondary intention anyway. We've got to let the incision drain."

She focused on the work at hand, doing her best to provide a sterile field for the operation. She had no anesthetic to offer him, not even a glass of alcohol. And for a scalpel, she used an old double-edged razor Fatima gave her secretly when she told her nurse what must be done.

"You will not cut my throat in the middle of the night," she asked Nadia. "Youssef sees this and you will have to feed me to the fishes."

Exhaustion or pain, she couldn't tell which, but she was grateful when he finally lost consciousness and she was able to manipulate the arm as she wished. The vile discharge and bleeding had been profuse, but she was finally able to apply sufficient pressure to slow it to an oozing. She inspected the inch long catheter in the palm of her hand. She did not need to be an electronics wizard to see it had been smashed irreparably against the humerus in David's Schefflan's right arm. She cleaned the wound the best she could and helped the guards lay David on a straw mattress before they locked the door to his cell.

She felt exhausted herself now, had lately felt so drained of energy, she could barely move to her own bed by the end of the day. Depression began to seep in, staining her spirit. Day after day as a hostage, the physician in her knew she was at high risk for depression. She prescribed long hours of hard work for herself to keep the mind distracted. A part of her was beginning to lose hope, but the fatigue that flowed through her was more than the psyche's defense against desperation. She put her head down on the wooden table as though invited by the executioner to rest on a chopping block, and fell into a deep sleep.

Kelev Hayam

The six men sat huddled together shoulder to shoulder like attentive sea lions scanning the waves for killer whales. They stared straight ahead from behind their diving masks without saying a word. There was no need to speak at this point. They had rehearsed this mission until they began to dream about the extraction in their sleep. They memorized every detail, every alleyway and entry point from an exact replica modeled on satellite reconnaissance photos of the compound. They checked and double checked their equipment with the Jaeger commandos brought in from Norway to train them. Inflatable, munitions, radio back pack units, all in order. They spent hours in the kill house practicing close quarters combat. Finally, it was time to move. They sat like so many raccoons, faces streaked with black to camouflage them in the night, listening to the hounds bay under the moon.

"Lock out chamber clear," the ensign called out, turning the wheel full speed. "Valves opened to the max."

Each man bit into the scuba regulator as the water began to fill the chamber. Each monitored pressure gauges on the double tank set up of the man beside him, and adjusted the horse collar buoyancy compensator that would maintain flotation should they need to swim to shore. When the water had totally engulfed them and the cabin pressure stabilized, the ensign released the hatch and one by one the men were expelled into the black water like baby sharks slipping from their mother at birth.

The men worked fast, with a single flashlight to unleash the inflatable from the submarine's hull and fill it with pressurized gas. Their Barracuda SS 440 floated below the surface at periscope level and in just a minute the small rubber craft popped to the surface of the water. The frogmen swam to the little boat and pulled themselves on board. They unzipped watertight duffel bags and outfitted themselves with machine guns and radio gear.

"All check audio," their leader said softly into the micro speaker extending from his headset.

"Number two, check."

"Number three, check."

Each man joined the web by which they would communicate when they reached the shore, invisible six miles out into the darkness. They had chosen a moonless night, but with infrared binoculars, Number one could just make out their target, pale-green and ghostly on the horizon.

Nightmare

Nadia's friend Emily has invited her to the restaurant at the top of the World Trade Center to see the commission Emily has just completed. The mural is a masterpiece. Emily has paid exquisite attention to detail and you can barely tell where the real clouds begin and the painted clouds leave off. Sitting at the bar is like sitting in the cockpit of a glider, floating over a peaceful white world below. Nadia tilts her head back to inspect the blue dome of heaven above her where Emily has turned the ceiling spots into pinpoints of star light. Nadia's head floats on it's stalk as easily as a sunflower tracing the movement of the sun. No pain radiates down her neck, she does not guard against the knife thrust at the base of her skull when she moves her head from side to side. Emily smiles at her friend over the ruby Campari and soda in her hand.

"You have to decide Nadia," she says, "But, David sounds pretty dreamy to me."

A blond-haired man lifts his glass to toast them from the far end of the bar. Yves Bourret is motioning them to join him for a drink. She notices now that the lab coat she is wearing is stained with carnage. The evening clouds have turned brilliant red with the sunset in the window behind him. Nadia studies the clouds and watches them turn into the same caldrons of boiling flesh she used to dream of when she was in medical school after a day of autopsies. She has been thrown into the lowest rung of Dante's hell, and somehow Nadia knows she is responsible for all this rancid flesh, stinking of formaldehyde and putrefaction. She hears the great engines processing bones like a rendering plant, the sky filling with clouds of black ash like the sky over Dachau. In one cloud she sees a blue face emerge. It begins to groan. The cloud dissipates and black ashes, oily to the touch, rain down. She is filled with revulsion for the gore that continues beyond death. She intuits the process of decay and human decomposition like an animal, with her very being. She can not get the smell out of her clothes, her skin, her lungs. It is a dream and not a dream, breathing deeply at the bottom of a lake.

"Nadia, Nadia," Abdel says, calling to her from beyond the grotesque. She cannot overcome the weight in her chest.

"Nadia," he calls again. She sees him now, standing just outside the window, his arms open wide to her from the other side of the glass. His head fills up the sun, a brilliant corona lights up his face like a halo. Nadia runs to him and they are falling through the sky together, secure in each other's embrace.

And

"**You** are having a nightmare, Nadia," Abdel said finally, shaking her into semi-consciousness.

"Oh, so awful," she cried, her arms about his neck, still struggling to forget the smell of that horrible landscape.

He pulled away from her embrace.

"Here," he said, pouring out a glass of tea, thick as syrup, that they kept boiling on the canoun throughout the day.

"You're burning up, Nadia," he said. "What's wrong?" He looked intently into her face and wiped her brow which was soaked from the fever.

She felt an aching in her back when she coughed as though she had broken a rib. Her respiration was shallow and painful. Her sputum was tacky and rust colored. She knew she was very sick. There were enough signs to make a clinical diagnosis. She didn't need a white cell count. She didn't need a stethoscope to detect the ominous rales and wheezing as she struggled to breathe.

It was possible she had contracted the infection from one of her patients without any dysfunction in her own immune system. But she knew that was unlikely given the exposure she had undergone treating the villagers in her clinic. A culture and sensitivity might reveal the offending organism, P. carinii, histoplasmosis, microsporidium. But even if AIDS hadn't compromised her health, she wouldn't be able to obtain the atovaquone or trimetrexate necessary to control any of the virulent new strains that had proliferated since the beginning of the AIDS epidemic. For some drug-resistant organisms there were no medications available anyway. She would die like all the other patients she had tried to save since she came to this island, drowning in her own body fluids. She thought of the vaccine that might have saved her, the outrageous prospect of dying from AIDS before she could share her discovery with the world.

"I have pneumonia," was all she said to Abdel.

He had seen enough of the blue death to know what her words meant, the torture that lay in store for her.

"I will go to Tunis. I will get medicine, a doctor for you."

"The whole world is looking for you Abdel. You will certainly be captured. Besides, it is too late." She spoke of her own prognosis, but remembered too David's words about a rescue attempt. To speak of the transmitter she had removed from his arm might mean David Schefflan's death; not to speak of it, would endanger Abdel and Fatima. But she had given David her word, he was still her patient.

"You are young and strong Nadia. You will survive this." He took her arms in his hands as though he could lift her up into health with physical force and his own will power. "My life will mean nothing without you."

Abdel held her close and kissed her. He didn't care if she carried the epidemic. On the Ceberus he had decided he would share the remainder of his life with this woman. If she were to die, he would share her death as well. All of his work, all his philosophy and political theory came down to this, finally. One person loving another. It was all he had, all he was certain of now. He had given his life to Islam and the Palestinian people and he was no closer to the City of God now than when he first began his work and faith burned like a brilliant star in his young heart.

When he trained for this mission in Bulgaria, Major Kostov had helped Abdel develop a part of himself which always sat on his shoulder, observant, a subconscious warning system that never slept. The genie caught his attention, despite the love flowing in his heart, as somewhere in the camp Sirius barked ferociously for a few moments, then stopped. The old women in his village always began to pray when a dog began to howl near a house, for it was said a dog could distinguish the awful form of Azrael himself.

"Sleep, darling," he said, easing Nadia back onto her pillow. "I'll be back in just a minute." He took the automatic handgun from its holster, checked the ammunition clip, and released the safety before walking out into the moonless night.

Sirius

A dog was a rare pet in most Arab households, for the Prophet has said, "When a dog drinks in a vessel, it must be washed seven times." But a watch dog was another story, more useful and less costly than camera surveillance, heat sensors or electronic warning systems.

The men in the camp at first had kicked the mongrel away when he came begging for scraps, but after some few months he had proven his worth to even the slowest of them. And he was an old dog, which went for something among them - had lost two toes and an ear somehow in his past, but could still bark ferociously to defend his territory.

Abdel called him Sirius for the Dog Star, but the others just called him *kalb*, or dog, and let him wonder the compound freely now as he made his rounds. He could still drag his old body up on top of the walls, stepping carefully through the shards of glass sewn against intruders without cutting his paws. He knew every corner of the compound, the coolest spots of earth on which to collapse when they forgot to give him water and the sun burned the ground to clay.

His eyes weren't what they used to be. At first he thought the dark shape playing over the compound wall might just be a shadow. But then he smelled the man and began barking. The man dropped to the ground and put out his hand for the dog to try in friendship. In the seconds it took the old dog to smell the man, Number One tore him to pieces with a quiet tap tap tap from his silenced MP-5. The intruder crouched low, scanning the area with a Noctron-V night sighting device.

"I'm in black," he whispered, holding his weapon high to let the Seals know he was undetected. "Two, take the northeast corner of the wall and cover."

Fatima heard a sharp crack in her thigh as the femur smashed to pieces. The bullet came from nowhere. These devils were invisible and could see in the dark. She lay on the ground stuffing her skirts into the bullet hole in her leg, trying to stop the bleeding.

Abdel's hope was to carry Nadia to the sea, to hide her there and take her out of harm's way. But when he lifted her into his arms, a spray of automatic fire filled the room like swarming hornets, as three, burst through the door. Abdel felt the bullet pierce his heart - cold, sharp - and sank with Nadia still in his arms, as gently as he could, in the generous seconds that remained before death claimed him.

Gift

"**Shalom,**" number three said when they finally located David's cell and gave the code letting him know he was among friends, "Jerusalem eternal."

"Where is Nadia Mansur?"

"We're doing the best we can. We found one of them lying on top of her. Looks like she took his bullet, maybe a perforated lung. But I think she'll make it. We've started a line of Ringers Lactate. Helicopter's on route."

When they took him to her, Nadia lay on the same table she had used for surgery when she removed the transmitter from his arm. They had stripped her of the blood soaked blouse and one of the commandos was applying a pressure bandage above her left breast.

"Let me do that," he said, sending the medic out of the room. She had lost a lot of blood, her skin was pale, almost translucent. If anything, her ordeal had made her even more beautiful. She was so peaceful. She reminded David of one of those Italian Madonnas waiting patiently for God to announce himself.

She stirred under his hand and began to cough with the spasm. A wave of pain played across her face, and she looked up at him.

"Abdel?" she asked.

"He's dead," David said. It angered him that she loved him still. He was not unhappy to give the news.

"They killed him." Her face took him in, questioning.

"Don't talk. Just rest, Nadia. Help will come."

"It's too late," she said. "This pneumonia is the first sign. Even your CIA can't save me now, David." She smiled up.

He hated lying to her. She would have to know the truth at some point, certainly when they got her back to Israel.

"We are Mossad," he said. "The Israeli government would not be blackmailed by these terrorists. You must get well, for my sake, the sake of the whole world."

Nadia closed her eyes. The pain was subsiding as the narcotic coursed through her intravenous line and into her veins. What did it matter finally who had the vaccine, as long as it saved lives. She remembered the first day at Cramer Chemical when she had discovered the blue epitope, her elation. It was spring and the oak trees were just beginning to send out delicate leaves that hung in clusters like tiny pink and green bats throughout the village. As she drove through Stonington on her way back from the laboratory, she noticed they had finally taken down the purple robe that hung on a wooden cross all through Lent outside the Catholic church in the town square. Easter. Redemption. Renewal. The whole world coming alive again.

"I love you, Lord of life. Thank you for this gift," she had prayed, her eyes filling with tears of gratitude. She was a scientist, had given her whole life to science, body and soul. She had no idea what part of her the prayer, the tears had come from.

She would return the gift of life God had given her. Perhaps it would achieve a measure of reconciliation. The Israelis might offer her people life through this vaccine.

"The vaccine," she said, attempting to raise herself. "David, under the drawer. I've hidden it. My pen. Please."

He searched the kitchen and finally found the hidden pen fastened to the underside of a heavy drawer of cooking utensils. He unscrewed the barrel of the pen as she directed and into his palm fell a brilliant blue jewel.

"Give it to your scientists. The gene sequence is etched into the sapphire where the facets meet. Laser light, the scientists will know what to do. Reconstruct the vaccine."

She closed her eyes again and rested. She felt a rocking sensation, the gentle to and fro of the ocean, lulling her into sleep. She looked up in amazement to see her father, pulling in the net, with her mother in the bow of the little boat, helping him. Their net was filled with fat red fish. One escaped from the net and flopped wildly on the bottom of the wooden boat.

"Catch it Nadia, and we will have a fine supper," her mother laughed." The sky was blue with great white clouds floating by. Light shone from her mother's eyes. Her father smiled and took her up in his arms.

"What a pretty little girl I have," he said. "What a pretty little girl."

Song

It is the moment just before the orange blade of sun cuts through the purple sky of morning. Gray light begins to illuminate the dead faces of fourteen bodies lined up in the courtyard. An order and formality have been imposed on death. It is peaceful.

Fatima sits beside the last body, caressing Nadia's gray face, swaying gently as she sings a Lebanese song, "The earth in the south was molded in a special way, fertile it bears its grain, and so too a woman tender and sweet, gifted by nature, and inspired from above."

In the distance, David Schefflan can hear the muffled sound of helicopter blades cutting through the night. He holds a blue jewel up to the sky. Chameleon-like, it disappears a moment, before becoming a star against the sapphire dawn, brilliant as hope.

www.vivisphere.com